THE

BANANA

WARS

THE

BANANA

WARS

A NOVEL

ALAN GROSTEPHAN

DZANC
BOOKS

DZANC
BOOKS

2580 Craig Rd.
Ann Arbor, MI 48103
www.dzancbooks.org

Library of Congress Cataloging-in-Publication Data Available on Request

ISBN 9781950539949
First edition: May 2024
Cover design by Steven Seighman
Interior design by Michelle Dotter

Printed in the United States of America

10   9   8   7   6   5   4   3   2   1

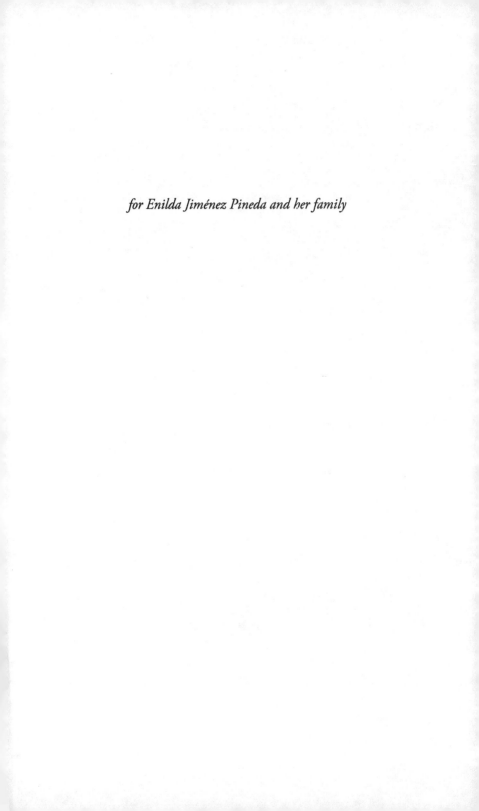

for Enilda Jiménez Pineda and her family

for Enilda Jiménez Pineda and her family

Y ahora dice que todavía sangra, pero que en el pueblo, desde los tiempos de la masacre, no hay ni puesto de salud ni médico permanente. Yo la miro en silencio, cierro mi libreta de notas, me despido de ella y me alejo, procurando pisar con cuidado para no patinar en la bajada de la cuesta. Veo las calles barrosas, veo un perro sarnoso, veo una casucha con agujeros de bala en las paredes. Y me digo que los paramilitares y guerrilleros, pese a que son un par de manadas de asesinos, no son los únicos que han atropellado a esta pobre gente.

El pueblo que sobrevivió a una masacre amenizada con gaitas

And now she says that she is still bleeding, but in the village, since the time of the massacre, there's no permanent clinic or doctor. I watch her in silence, I close my notebook, I say goodbye to her and I move away, trying to walk carefully and not slip on the steep hill. I see muddy streets, I see a mangy dog, I see a shack with bullet holes in the wall. And I tell myself that the paramilitaries and guerrillas, despite being a pack of killers, are not the only ones that have trampled these poor people.

"The Town That Survived a Massacre to the Sound of Flutes"
Alberto Salcedo Ramos

THE STRIKE
1990

1.

THEY CAME DOWN FROM THE MOUNTAINS and across the fields on horses and motorcycles and trucks and on foot. They blocked the road to the ocean and blew apart the bridge over el Río Currulao that connected plantations to the port in Turbo and the canal in Nueva Colonia.

Before dawn, they invaded the fields of the first banana plantation, Finca la Bella, and cut the head-high cables for transporting banana stems, then attacked the empty office, dousing with gasoline its desks and shelves and ledgers that contained salary numbers and an inventory of how many bananas planted and how many boxes shipped and with what exporter. They tossed gasoline across wall maps with little red pins to mark the fumigations and blue pins to mark the next rows due for harvest and shipment. A terrified security guard, an old man with a rusty Winchester double-chambered shotgun, emerged from the bathroom, and they handcuffed him, slid a blindfold over his eyes, and later dropped him on the outskirts of Apartadó, where he was lost for a day. They doused the packing area, the high stacks of flattened banana boxes, the rubber conveyor belt, the steel tubs, the thatched roof of the cafeteria, and the little store that sold drinks and sandwiches. Next to the giant steel tubs, they cut all nine cables that united in the packing area and spread out on a grid across the fields. They poured a trail of gasoline out to the road, and the leader, Samuel Yuletis a.k.a. Orejas, dropped the match, as he dreamt of doing as a child. The grass and gravel lit up blue and orange, and as fast as he could blink, the whole conglomeration of buildings and awnings were on fire and in a state of their greatest beauty and vitality, like the open eyes of a man right before death. The heads of nails Orejas had pounded into the wood glowed brightly in the fire. He still had little white scars on his hands from when he used to sweat in these fields for Mr. Morris, and his comandante had allowed him this pleasure, to burn down the thing he had helped build. Though he wanted to stay and admire it, there was no time. It was dawn, the sun already pushing over the sierra to the east, and there were more plantations to burn.

Simultaneously, Gerardo Reyes, his manager at Finca la Bella, was dragged from the doorway of his house in Apartadó, and a guerrilla in plainclothes with a red bandana over his face shot him twice in the side of the head so that his skull fell apart on the pavement while his wife and children hid under the bed.

Five other managers were murdered in their beds or doorways while their plantations burned, and word traveled fast among the workers—the grunts, the dirty ones, the slaves, the illiterates, the strong-wristed, the ones with two machetes strapped to their waists, the ones who inhaled pesticides from the planes, who killed snakes in the drainages, who broke their backs dragging the stems on cables—that today was not just an insurrection against the planters but a general strike across the country.

The guerrillas set fire to the gravel runways and the airplane hangars. In Apartadó, they burned down the banana corporation office with its computers, typewriters, fax machines, file cabinets, telephones, maps, inventories, and little family photos taped to the sides of desks. They surrounded the factory that made the blue plastic bags for the banana stems and the other one that made the cardboard banana boxes. Here they shot Armando Benavides, a security guard who raised his shotgun, not realizing that the factory was surrounded by men with better guns and a plan. The cardboard and raw paper and chemicals made it all burn fast. The aluminum siding of the factory melted and collapsed, a gaping hole forming where flames curled out in search of fuel. The expensive machines all burned, and this was a pleasure for the guerrillas. The more money the planters lost, the more they would feel the shame of their position.

Here and there they exchanged fire with soldiers who were caught off guard, despite their informers, and found themselves trapped at the base of the 17th Brigade in Carepa, receiving reports that the guerrillas had also cut cables and set fire to Finca San Jorge, Finca María del Rosario Güaro 1 and 2, and Finca Villa Alicia. How many guerrillas were out there? More than anyone had anticipated.

The fire was either fascinating or horrible, depending on who was looking at it, the thick black smoke rising from the fields, the cement walls painted with the acronyms of their groups. For some, the smoke tasted like progress, a better salary, and justice against the planters for killing workers and union leaders. For others, for some of those who worked on those same plantations, for the wives of the dead managers, for the pilots of the fumigation planes, it smelled like the end of everything—the tenuous order that held them together over the last couple years. It smelled like war.

While a few trees near the packing areas caught fire and burned, the wet fertile soil around the bananas, mounted on humps of soft earth along the drainages, did not burn. But the bananas that were supposed to be shipped that day began to ripen on their stems. The rhythm of the operation, measured down to the hour and minute, was interrupted. It would not resume for forty-five days. Every field from Chigorodó to the ocean would have to be cleared, the stems and leaves and roots, all of it chopped down and hacked into fertilizer.

Not far up the road from Finca la Bellas was Finca los Bongos, where guerrillas set fire to the four buildings in the packing area, including the old encampment where the workers used to live with no privacy, shat in holes, and cooked over fires. Now it was a place to store equipment, and there was also a tractor-trailer with a couple pickup trucks. Into their gas tanks Orejas shoved fuses. Someone said they should siphon the gas first and sell it at the port in Turbo. But Orejas—nicknamed for his big ears and knowledge of so much hearsay; a sea-like memory with the names of people who had crossed him in his twenty years since birth, his mother's ex-boyfriends, his brothers' enemies, the names and origins of every prostitute at la Picardía, so you had to be careful what you said around him—said the more gas, the louder the boom, and he wanted to hear it. His younger brother had worked here when it belonged to the German, and after Mr. Morris had fired Orejas, he had begged for work at this same office. Orejas unraveled the waxy fuse to join the others, told everyone to move past the gate to the road, and he lit a match.

The boom was exquisite. The guerrillas flinched and a couple ducked behind a tree, but kept their eyes open. The cab of the tractor-trailer levitated for a moment over a spring of blue flames and smashed through the roof of the packing area. Orejas was mesmerized—it woke him up even more, and he knew the planters, safe in Medellín, would see it in photos and know he was more trouble to them than la vacuna they should be paying and the workers they should stop killing. It was payback for the massacres at Finca Honduras, La Negra, and Punta Coquitos. It was power in its purest light. You could burn down all the temples and cathedrals and all the scriptures and all the statues of saints and even the equestrian statues of the liberators and conquerors who thought themselves gods but were just opportunists. You could burn the rich in their cars. You could drag Mario Zuluaga Espinel, the owner of Finca San Jorge, and rub his face in the ashes for the murder of twenty workers. You could sink the gringo ships over the water. You could dynamite the policemen trapped within their sandbag bunkers.

While most towns in Colombia were built with a main plaza and a cathedral, a bell in a tower to be rung for mass, the towns in Urabá had no design, no sacred places. They were all ramshackle, one street dug into another, one neighborhood spilling out the back side of a banana field. Orejas believed they were meant to be burned.

*

A few hours later, when Orejas knocked on his mother's door in Turbo, he heard a faucet running and a knife chopping. Maybe a fish. He had buried his camouflage in a field and wore jeans and a white T-shirt. He had not been home in a year. He knocked louder, a guerrilla knock, and said, "Mamá, mami, soy yo, Samuel," and it felt wrong to pronounce his real name. A little girl with dirty hair all out of sorts, her face spotted with mosquito bites, opened the door. She smiled at him, and behind her appeared his mother who seemed bigger than before, her face old with a missing front tooth, her arms lumped with muscle and her long legs arching out from her polyester shorts. He expected an embrace, but she slapped him. It was like being hit by a falling tree, it knocked him back into the street. She stepped aside, grabbing the girl who was probably his niece. He followed them to a two-burner stove set upon a cornered triangle of wood in the kitchen that was also a living room.

"I don't know if you can stay," his mother said.

She pinched his chin, and he thought she was going to slap him again. If she did, he would grab her arm and yank it to the floor, mother or no mother. He needed somewhere to sleep. She had brought him into the world and put him in Turbo, a place he never would have chosen on his own, and he had taught himself to survive in it. It was her obligation to feed him a piece of that fish and find him at least a sheet to sleep on. But she only pinched his chin with fingers that stunk of garlic and tilted his head up so he would have to look into her huge black eyes.

"Are you going to work or steal?" she asked.

"Work."

"I don't have a fan for you. You can sleep where you fall."

She certainly knew he was lying. After dark, a truck would pick him up, and he would unearth his camouflage and follow orders. Maybe they would attack the police station in Chigorodó or he would be summoned into the mountains, where he would be forced to sleep in the rain and tax the villagers.

His brothers arrived with a bottle of rum. They were both banana workers at Finca la Gloria, drunk already and happy about the strike. One's hands were bleached from chemicals. The other had a giant hump behind his neck and a shoulder that fell out of joint.

"¿Entonces qué?" they said to him. "¿Cómo va la revolución?"

The fish was meager for so many. Once his mother added water to the soup it was all potato and yucca. She oversalted it and squeezed in two limes for some flavor. His brothers poured the last of the rum and asked him for stories. His heart wasn't in it, but he bragged about stealing land for the campesinos, slicing wire fences, walking up behind ranchers in Bajirá with a machete and watching their eyes roll in their heads. He said the guerrillas were on the verge of seizing every municipality in Urabá. He saw his mother holding her breath not to speak, her lips pursed like dirty water was spraying from his mouth.

As he spoke, he felt the waxy fuse unraveling in his fingers. He saw gasoline before it became fire, and he looked through their faces and felt short of breath as if he had been running all night, the gasoline poured, the gasoline lit, the wood and cardboard ripe for it the way a body was ripe, and all this while he spooned watery broth into his mouth and picked a bone from his teeth. Fire lit in the grease of the cables and smoke rose off his mother's stove. He spun around from the remembered fire to the quiet heat of the table, past to present, so that everyone began to seem in slow motion, the house itself a hallucination, and he could not understand their speech. He leaned off his stool and found a flattened cardboard box against the wall, the flies buzzing, his brothers laughing at something. He lay by their feet and dreamed he was swimming in the gulf, his father nearby in a fishing boat, dragging in a net full of garbage and asking, "What now? We caught nothing."

*

Orejas's mother felt hungry after the meal, like she was pregnant again. At any moment her son would stand up and sleepwalk around the house. He might jump onto her back or grab her legs with both arms. Of all her children, Orejas was the one she feared, the one who did not believe in anything, who, raised in poverty, was a picky eater, who loved sugar and had stolen it once from the corner store, crouched in a vacant lot with another girl just as crazed as him, scooping sugar into her mouth and into his, and that's when she knew. The look. When he started at the plantations with his father, they had to drag him from bed by his ankles, force-feed him breakfast, and push him down the street to the bus stop. There were rumors he slept in the fields. Not because he was tired. He did not believe in the work.

She sat in the front door and stretched her legs, removed her rubber flip-flops and spread her toes apart. She never felt full, and maybe here was where her son was right. Her sister had witnessed the Punta Coquitos massacre and showed up with only her clothes. Her house raided by paramilitaries who set it on fire as an afterthought. The whole village rounded up to watch the killings. Maybe the one they all knew as Orejas would fill this house with better fish and potatoes and mangoes and heavy cream and sacks of sugar. The one you least expected was the one who loved you most. Her neighbors glared from their doors. Oh, fuck you, she thought. Malparidos. There was something hot in her blood, maybe magic, but she doubted it. When her son awoke, she would caress his face and tell him he could stay as long as he wished.

2.

IN MEDELLÍN, SERVANTS TIPTOED into dark master bedrooms, trespassing like the guerrillas in the banana fields, whispering their employers' names. The planters reached out in the dark as if to shield themselves. Their wives woke up too, but their husbands told them to sleep, that nothing was happening.

"¿Qué pasa?" Rafael said, seeing his maid in her baggy white nightgown looming over him.

"Forgive me, señor, it's that they are calling you urgently."

"Speak well."

"The phone, señor."

My plantations are burning, Rafael thought, tying up his flannel bathrobe, because he had a worst-case scenario frame of mind. He did not turn on his reading lamp, so he became briefly lost in the room, entering his closet, reaching his hands into his dead wife's clothes on hangers, and for a second he could be anywhere, in some dark lagoon or drainage hiding from the men who were coming to kill him.

At the phone in the living room, he heard the voice of Ernesto Echevarría, his old friend, the colossus of the banana empire—the Fascist, his wife used to call him—but Rafael felt Ernesto was one of the few people in Colombia who actually said things as they were. Ernesto apologized for calling at such an early hour, cleared spit from his throat, and said that both Rafael's plantations, Finca la Bella and Finca los Bongos, had been burned down completely, his cables cut, and one of his managers murdered. That much he knew. Rafael ceased to have a body for a second. He floated above the sofa. A now-familiar prickly feeling covered his face and neck, his vision blurry in a hot flash that made him fear he would just black out. He wrenched open the front of the bathrobe to let the cool air hit his chest and stomach. His bare, hairless knees pressed against the hardwood of his desk. He looked down at the curly black hairs on his hands. He felt the heat swirl through his body, and he flexed his feet against the carpet to feel them.

"¿Estás ahí?" Ernesto said.

"I am ruined," Rafael said.

"We're all in trouble. This has happened before, and we'll figure it out."

"No, not you. I am in a deep hole, hermano."

"Tranquilo," Ernesto said. "We'll support you."

When the strike ended, Ernesto said, he would help Rafael get his bananas packed, and the other planters would collaborate. The damage was ugly. Dead policemen. Blown bridges. The cardboard factory and the corporate office looted and burned to the ground. The strike was general throughout the country, so they were not alone. Oil was spilling from the pipelines and mines were caved in. The board was set to meet ASAP, as soon as he could get to the office.

Rafael hung up and went to the balcony. He found these late hours when the night lingered to be bad ones. The hours when people left discotecas and were not right in the head and got kidnapped. His wife had been killed at night, and whenever he was out after dark, he saw her killers in all the teenagers on motorcycles, the taxi drivers, the corner peddlers selling empanadas. He saw his picture in the business section of *El Mundo*, bankrupt, the old name and the old face with his aristocratic nose and trimmed beard. Overextended, he thought. "Esto ha excedido los límites. Estoy quebrado."

He sat down at his desk and looked at his accounts. He had paid his vacuna to the guerrillas, but like all the others, he had paid to kill certain union leaders and blacklisted workers. He unfolded the intercepted memo from the guerrillas that he had first seen in July. It outlined their plan to study the routines of the banana planters, to kidnap them and organize long strikes until the planters sold off their land and left Urabá. And then? You could bulldoze the whole industry. He might sell his land to Ernesto Echevarría, who would screw him and shake his head and say he was giving him a high price out of friendship and shared memories of the old Medellín, before the vulgarians took over and became their neighbors and invaded their favorite restaurants and night clubs and tried to fuck their daughters and run for office and make sure everyone was continuously on edge and ready to die.

He imagined the fields, the green banana plants swaying in the wind, a light rain falling. He saw thousands of workers in their houses, their machetes hanging by the doors, the clock ticking on the bananas that would be yellow in a week. All of it garbage. The white ships in Turbo rocking in the waves, the fines accumulating for all the canceled shipments. He looked around his living room, a single lamp beside a reading chair, his maid in the doorway to the kitchen, changed out of her nightgown into her blue working smock. He looked around for untidiness in the room and wanted to reprimand her for something.

"¿Está bien, Don Rafael?" she asked.

"Mal. Fatal," he said.

"¿Le preparo el desayuno?" she said, setting down his coffee in a small blue cup on a saucer.

His maid Luz Marina was a heavy-faced woman who smelled of some cheap, acrid soap that the poor used. He knew she was from the slum and that it must be peculiar to organize a wine cellar or serve drinks by a swimming pool, to iron and fold his clothes that came straight from London and Milan. He did not know if she was stupid or smart. She embraced him when his wife was killed and offered to box up her things. His wife had once caught her using the bidet in the master bedroom, which seemed like a firing offense to her, but Rafael said that after ten years, Luz Marina was family. There had been other servants to raise their children, but his wife saw them as projects for betterment, paying for their educations so they could become nurses and hygienists and schoolteachers. A tiresome mission in her life, a thing to brag about at church. Luz Marina had resisted betterment, and this pleased him.

The sky was still dark in the windows, red lights blinking on the slopes surrounding the city, the slums dim. It had been five years since he set foot in Urabá. Since then, he had only seen it from above, a neon green carpet threaded with brown rivers and dirt roads, when flying to Panama City or Houston, looking through the tiny oval window at his river, his canals, his banana bunches protected on the stem in blue plastic bags.

"Señor?" Luz Marina said. "Would you like eggs?"

"Speak clearly," Rafael said. "I don't understand you."

"Eggs?"

"Yes, please, and more coffee. Turn on the radio. The whole country is on strike."

He stared at her hands that seemed like bruised papayas, swollen and clean, her day starting an hour before usual. He imagined her in a banana field, a good woman who knew her place, who could swing a machete and slide a banana stem onto her shoulders, hook it to the cable, drag it straight to the packing area. He heard his daughter coughing. Luz Marina stared at him. I'll go, his eyes said. He walked down the hall and found her, her body bursting at the seams with puberty, a new smell in the room, her light brown hair tangled around the pillow and strewn across her pale face. Since his wife died, she was often sick with strange aches in her bones, coughs, runny noses, and acid reflux that had no cure. Her lips were cracked, covered in gloss. The rims of her nose were red from her picking it.

"What is it?" Rafael said.

"Sit with me, papá. I can't go to school today."

She rolled over. He rubbed her back and neck, but he did it carelessly, the way one would massage a dog or a bolt of fabric. She asked what was wrong. She could feel it in his touch. She turned on the lamp, and in her eyes he saw that he was wrecked. She pulled his hand from her shoulder and sucked in her bottom lip.

"Another strike," he said.

"Do they ever work?" she said.

"Who?"

"The workers."

"They've been tricked by their leaders," he said. "Or they trick themselves. Please sleep. I have to go to a meeting."

Luz Marina called down the hallway that his breakfast was ready. He left his daughter, walked by an early Botero still life of oranges cut into halves. He crossed the living room and touched the arms of his chairs, looked at the coffee table with the little stone sculpture at its center, and he saw how fragile the world was. He felt it orbiting around him, his wife's properties sold to support the plantations, the bankers assessing the price of his art collection and his vacation house near Jericó, always a relative number, the credenza emptied out of its silver and porcelain.

"These eggs are cold," he said.

Luz Marina tossed them into the garbage and scrambled more with bits of tomato and green onion, oil pooling orange with the tomato juice. She served them and they were still tasteless, like putting textured objects in his mouth. "Bring me aspirin," he told her. "This is the worst huevos al perico you've ever made."

"Perdón. Would you like me to prepare them again?"

"You think I have time to watch you make more eggs? Everyone wants money. Would you like a raise, too?"

"No, señor. I am content."

"You are the only one."

*

Before sunrise in Medellín, the planters dressed in suits and drove to the gray, modern office building with windows tinted a reflective blue on Avenida el Poblado. Rafael would make phone calls to the governor, a friend from childhood, to remind him that Urabá, this northern tip of the province of Antioquia, belonged to the people who put him in office, and Ernesto would call their lobbyists in Bogotá so that the senators, many of them friends, were aware of the money at stake. One planter had to cancel a vacation to Florida to show his kids Disney World. Another canceled a tryst with an ex-toothpaste model at the Marriott. Another received a call from the widow of a murdered manager. She sobbed for five minutes straight, saying, "Lo perdí, lo perdí, lo perdí, lo perdí," so that finally he held his phone away from his face while his own wife grabbed his arm like she would fall down in their bedroom, saying, "What are you going to do?"

3.

ONE GUERRILLA TOOK OFF his camouflage in a row of banana trees outside Currulao, handed it to a man on a motorcycle, and changed into jeans and a green T-shirt. He walked casually into town to stand behind the counter of his bakery. He looked deranged, his wife said. His hair stuck up like a brown weed on the the back of his head.

On his fingers was the smell of gasoline and gunpowder, as his group had exchanged fire with some soldiers on the road to Nueva Colonia. He served a customer a cup of coffee and a piece of bread wrapped in a napkin, and he felt the urge to vomit. He walked into the alley behind the bakery, a muddy place with garbage strewn in puddles. He leaned over his knees and drool fell from his lips. He took off his shirt and washed his face, neck, and armpits with laundry soap under a spout connected to a tank of rainwater. It tasted like plants. He sat down against the brick wall and felt the kick of his rifle and saw the body of a young soldier hanging off the side of a truck and bleeding from his eyes.

Back inside, he toweled off his head, checked his face in the mirror of the small bedroom connected to the bakery, and saw that he was the same man, Hugo Rodríguez a.k.a. el Caimán, a fierce nickname, though his comrades just called him "the baker." He returned to a counter without customers.

"Where is everyone?" he said.

His wife Yenifer just stared at him, working her hand through the knots in her thick brown hair, ordering an oily-faced teenage girl with a pink baseball cap to sweep around the tables. She said they had baked too much bread the night before, knowing that there would be a strike today.

"They're scared," Yenifer said.

"Of me?"

"They say the bridges are out on the road to the ocean. They burned down the chemical warehouse in Apartadó and stole a plane."

"Claro," he said. "Tuvimos éxito."

Yenifer was too thin despite the bread she ate with every meal, her wide face as shiny as a bronze coin, her body quick and not especially sensual to her husband whose eyes were elsewhere. He stared inward at the guerrilla insurrection or out at the soft hairs on the thighs of Nanci, the teenager who helped at the bakery.

Yenifer would remember his word, "éxito," when she was dragged to the outskirts of town to identify his body. She would find it broken at its joints and crammed into a black plastic garbage bag in the same way one might purchase a small pig, butchered into more manageable cuts. She would not be histrionic or in tears. She would wonder how he had lived so long with everyone knowing who he was, and she would say, "Sí, es él" to the police lieutenant who had no pity for a guerrilla widow, the same lieutenant who had been refused service at the bakery by her husband.

Hugo flirted with Nanci, touching the fake gold necklace that hung between her breasts and asking her what she had heard about the plantation fires. She crouched to check the laces on her shoes, knowing they were fine—her father, a banana worker at Finca San Jorge, had told her to keep her distance from the baker. A neighbor walked in and asked if they had heard about the burning of the supply warehouse for the cacao producers near Turbo. This was welcome news to Hugo, who did not know the full extent of all their targets. He had a jaunty step as he handed this man a plastic bag of bread and patted his shoulder in farewell.

Some businesses were shut down for the day: the barber shop, the butcher shop, the little hardware store. Hugo smoked a cigarette behind the counter, ashing on the floor, and opened a bottle of beer. He looked at himself again in the mirror to see if he was still the same man, and he said, "Things are changing," with an optimistic tone that would haunt Yenifer.

A few neighbors started to appear. Currulao was a guerrilla town, a union office just up the street, and during strikes the banana workers never knew whether to sleep all day or to drink. It was not a payday, so this soured it, as most men had debts at the bakery and the two cantinas up the street.

"Te fío," Hugo said, handing out bread and cookies on credit to the wives of the workers who came up short.

In the afternoon, the day got hot. As the sun fried the zinc roofs and dusty road, smoke blew in from the chemical warehouse and tasted like poison. A fellow guerrilla, dressed now as a civilian in a white shirt and sport pants, entered the bakery and passed Hugo a note with instructions for the night. The insurrection would continue, even as the 17th Brigade sent out patrols and received more soldiers from battalions in the south. Hugo would not sleep that night. Yenifer would have to do all the baking, and though she would not argue about it, he knew she would protest in other ways.

He entered the bedroom and stripped down to his underwear, pulling back the single bedsheet and lying on his back. He could feel Yenifer looking at him through the back doorway, tossing pieces of mango into a blender with water and ice. Her body looked tightly wound up and dry in the heat. She seemed not to need him at all. The radio in the bakery was playing salsa. A customer coughed and asked the price of cheese. Hugo rolled over a few times, the heat drowning him, his heart beating faster than normal, the taste of vinegar in his mouth.

Yenifer handed change to a customer and wished him a good morning. She was bitter, but not against the guerrillas. Her father had been a banana worker until he joined a union—was blacklisted and told to leave the zone. He fled to the south to work in the mines near Segovia, where he died in a flood. Her mother married a policeman who wanted nothing to do with the daughter of a disgraced worker. Three of her brothers worked at Finca San Jorge and the other two as braceros, loading barges in Nueva Colonia. Yenifer knew the planters did nothing out of goodness. They saw Urabá as fertile soil and a deep enough gulf where ships could anchor and head north with the most ordinary and profitable thing the country had ever made. She had dropped out of school in eighth grade, right when the classes were getting interesting, when she could read and handle longer math equations, and had gone to work in a restaurant in Apartadó. The family who owned it fed her well and gave her a small room to live in. Then the guerrillas left the owner's son dead and shoeless in a ditch on the road to Carepa. The owner, an older man who had seen Urabá as a place to get away from the cartel violence in Medellín, was so depressed he could not get out of bed. The food was undercooked and oversalted, the beer served at room temperature, the music all sad boleros every night. They had to close.

Her friend Orejas, a coordinator at Finca la Bella, got her a job in its cafeteria, where men reached across the counter to pinch her nipples, snag the waist of her underwear, and came up behind her with machetes to beg for blowjobs. When Orejas was looking, they behaved, but he could not always stand beside her. Even Mr.

Morris, the gringo owner, would call her into his office on a pretext of ordering supplies, and the next thing she knew his fingers were in her mouth. There were strikes then, too. The cardboard boxes unmade, stacked flat. The cooling tubs dry. The scales read zero. Her paychecks were barely enough to put clothes on her body and buy a cheap bicycle to get to and from her brother's house. Mr. Morris was found in a drainage near field three, his bright white body turned black in the sun.

It was after that she met Hugo, who was fifteen years older than her, who had just opened his bakery. She thought he would change, grow milder over the years, be faithful to her when he knew how good she was. But he loved his own face in the mirror. He loved trimming his mustache. He hired teenage girls to help at the bakery and found reasons to touch their waists and backs as they reached for bread in the display case. He had a lover in Apartadó and a child with a clandestine woman in Carepa. This was normal. That's what her friend Mariana José said, but someplace there had to be better men. "You're lucky," Mariana said. "You can eat beef every night of the week, you can put butter on your bread and eat cookies with chocolate for breakfast. And if he gets killed, it will be your bakery."

Occasionally, Hugo pulled down the metal curtain of the bakery and danced with her to romantic salsa. He praised her skill with flour and numbers. He cooked dinner and bought her random books on lizards, birds, the life of plants and the science of bananas. She read them all as if they were poetry, wanting to see inside of the stems and leaves, the grains of soil varying drastically from the flatlands to the slopes of the mountains.

But with all the food Yenifer ate, she could not gain weight, and she felt like a whore without the camaraderie of other women. Sullen today, she ordered Nanci around while her husband napped in the bedroom. When Nanci was done wiping down the glass of the display case, Yenifer told her to wash the potatoes in the back alley and pile them next to the onions so people would want to buy them. Nanci stared at her, waiting for Hugo to step out of the bedroom to tell Yenifer to ease up, it was the first day of the strike, a day to be kind to the workers. Yenifer repeated what she had said, and Nanci bowed her head, picked up the sack of potatoes and a bucket and lugged it into the back alley.

It was no day to celebrate. The planters were not going to watch their bananas rot all week and spend whatever it cost to build new tubs and conveyor belts. The government was not going to fix the bridges just so the guerrillas could strap dynamite to them again. Yenifer would tell Hugo that they had gone too far, that a general strike would be hard enough, that there was no point in killing so many managers or blowing up the gringo's chemicals next to the gravel runway. Everything you do to them, she would say, we will pay for in double.

"Yenifer," Hugo yelled from the bedroom, "tell Nanci to watch the counter and bring me a beer."

"Nanci is washing the potatoes," she said.

"What for?"

"They sell better."

"Poor little girl! Tell her I want her at the counter, and bring me the coldest beer there is."

She told Nanci to put down the potatoes that she was dipping in a bucket of water and setting in a basket.

"Basta, niña," Yenifer said. "Quiero que estés adelante."

Yenifer entered the sweltering bedroom. A single box fan blew in the corner. The room reeked of yeast and bread baking, the buttery smell of comfort. She listened to him brag in a whisper about a gunfight with the military, and could see in his clenched fist and wide eyes that he was sick from it. He wanted her to tell him he had done well and right by the people—men had to die for change, crowds of men had killed and died since the beginning of time, since Cain and Abel, since the founding of the republic—but she did not say any of these things. She loosened his fist and handed him the beer, which he drank on his back, sucking it out of the bottle with an open throat. His eyes watered from the carbonation. He set the bottle on the floor and tugged at her apron as if to tear it from her body. He seemed disappointed that she wore no bra. He stared at her boney chest and kissed her ribs, and within a few minutes it was like it always was and would be forever if he had lived.

She wondered if he was thinking about Nanci at the counter or his lover in Apartadó, or if he was thinking about the chemical warehouse exploding. As she followed his mind up the dirt roads, she began to enjoy it. It was almost too hot to breathe with the door closed, but he was inspired by some idea of himself. She heard the gas truck passing with its bell and a customer asking for a small package of coffee and a bird chirping right outside the window as if in the room with them. For a minute, she loved him. When it was over and he began to sleep beside her, both of their chests and hair soaked in sweat, just when she might nap, knowing she would have to bake all night and continue sweating beside the hot oven, he pushed her out of the bed and onto the cement floor. He looked at her naked body like it was an animal's or a piece of furniture. He said she was drowning him with her heat, that she should go help Nanci at the counter and make sure she wasn't stealing.

She leaned over to kiss him and he slapped her lightly on the cheek, fine, but it was shitty to feel it. "You want more?" he said. "Por favor. Let me sleep."

She realized he had not kissed her to start, her legs hurt from standing all morning, and she would not miss him if he was killed.

She would sell the bakery and move to Necoclí and open a restaurant by the beach because she knew what men liked to eat, and
there would be an ocean breeze and no more bananas.

*

Near Currulao, there were others like Hugo, taking off their
camouflage and untying the bandanas that hid their faces. Some
were campesinos, mechanics, plumbers, schoolteachers, electri-
cians, cooks, but most were banana workers and small farmers
who knew these fields well, whose relatives and friends had fallen
apart out there when their bodies gave way. They handed their
rifles to the full-time guerrillas who strapped them to motorcycles
and mules and disappeared up the trails into the hills, toward the
hidden encampments where the men dressed in street clothes visited for meetings but did not live. Nor did they wish to. They had
other lives. They had cows to milk, fences to mend, crops to bring
in, and chickens to feed. These part-time guerrillas lived in tiny
villages that did not exist on maps. There were no stores, no clinics,
no banks, no plazas, no schools, nothing but the community of
farmers who staked out their land within these gaps in the jungle
and in between the larger plantations that ate up the landscape.

In a way, they arrived to nothing. Their wives and children were
crouched in cow shit and pulling up weeds from small gardens. Just
like that, these men ceased to be the heroes of the movement. They
drank water from bad wells. Their clothes were faded and full of
holes. Some were so poor they had to borrow shovels from neighbors or dig with sticks and their hands when they planted. But still,
to have a double life and a war nickname gave them more than they
could get any other way.

4.

THE CONFERENCE ROOM AT the banana corporation had always seemed like an aquarium to Rafael. Two glass walls overlooked the city, and on the inner wall hung a map of Urabá, the land cupping its blue gulf, one finger leading to the Panama Canal and the other up along the Atlantic Coast, the plantations color-coded for the two dominant unions, and a skeletal tree-shape of gravel roads, rivers, canals, embarcaderos, all of it bisected by the north-south road to the ocean.

At the center of the table were the bottom-feeders who struggled to pay the mortgages on their land, whose stained bananas often ended up on the national market, whose drainages were clogged with weeds, men too cheap to fumigate often enough to prevent the plagues from decimating their fields. Closer to the heads of the table were bigger fish who besides bananas owned cattle, trucking companies, supermarkets, mines, and were waiting for the little fish to die so they could buy up their land. There was not enough air in the aquarium. Just steel pots of coffee at the center of the table, some sweet rolls, and jugs of water.

As a big fish, Rafael sat at one head of the table, Ernesto Echevarría at the other. In 1960, their fathers were the original banana men who flew into Turbo and pointed at maps in the municipal office, buying up jungle and pasture, forcing out the scattered colonos, the men and women who had migrated from the east and homesteaded small subsistence plots and had no idea they were living on green gold. Ernesto Echevarría could fit every other fish into his mouth. He was a small man who seemed big, his eyes the bright blue of ink, his reddish hair curly on a balding head. He walked to the map on the wall and pointed at the hardest-hit areas, mentioned the union's demands as if they were new—an eight-hour workday, a thirty percent raise in wages, better housing—all of it a fantasy, Rafael thought, in a country where no one, not even him, worked less than twelve hours a day.

"Is anyone enforcing the eight-hour workday?" Ernesto said.

The planters looked at one another, shrugged.

"Rafael?" Ernesto said.

Rafael's vision blurred, heat radiating in a rusty stench from his neckline, his collar probably already stained, his tie too tight on his neck. He made eye contact with every man at the table as a way to keep his balance. He told them there was a phone call scheduled for that afternoon with the gringos in Ohio, who had been exploring the creation of a Colombian subsidiary with local management. The investment could be massive. Improved infra-structure at the canals, new roads to the more remote plantations, and all this might mean access to other markets, like Eastern Europe where those people had never tried a decent banana. "In light of this," Rafael said, "our response to the strike should be careful. The timing is inconvenient."

In each face, Rafael saw square hectares, debt, corruption, men who would lie to him, who hated his slow speech, his old name, older than theirs, his long sloped nose. He knew their secrets. Nico-lás Patiño had sold a plantation to Pablo Escobar who did noth-ing with it. Fernando Londoño had married the whitest woman he could find to cover up the blood from his indigenous grandmother, but all his children had straight black hair and cacique noses. Beside Ernesto sat his oldest son Luis Alberto, a pale, fat manchild with a sweaty face and hands, who had fallen in love with his maid and spent a year in a psychiatric hospital in San Diego.

"This board is too passive," Fernando Londoño said. "You propose patience, but I don't have it. Half the country is eating shit and would kill for these jobs. Cede once, cede forever. It's like fighting with my ex-wife." He stood up for drama. Rafael did not look over his shoulder when he came up behind him. Every man at the table ran his own kingdom and hated cooperation. Every man seemed to be biting his tongue to not scream at the idiots around him.

"We go to Tolima and Magdalena Medio for new workers," Londoño said. "We build them cement houses and soccer fields. We start over."

"Listo, Fernando," Ernesto said. "We heard your perspective."

Rafael realized he would get the votes. Certain men jotted notes, a vague hope in their eyes that the gringos might save them. They divvied up the names of senators and ministers in Bogotá to call.

"I'll talk to our friends in Córdoba," Ernesto said, staring at Fernando Londoño and Mario Zuluaga Espinal, alluding to the paramilitaries. "It won't be like last time. We have standards. If we lose this harvest, that's our year."

Rafael felt cold and without memory, like nothing had ever happened but this day over and over. He flexed his legs to get some circulation. He had inherited this life, just nineteen, on a visit home from Princeton. His father had a flat pink forehead and white hair, always bored in the city, wishing he was at a cattle auction or watching bananas rise in a new field. His father hung up the phone and ordered Rafael to sit down to look at a contract. He said the gringos did not own any land but they owned everyone's bananas as soon as they were off the stems. "We all knew it was coming," his father said, "but not like this."

They were sitting on the back patio of the family home in el Poblado, a white-washed colonial with old European furniture, a piano no one played, two maids who seemed everywhere at once. His father was eating pork rinds and staining the contract, not the actual contract, but a list of terms. The grease spots expanded and dirtied the paper. His father had tears in his eyes. "As high as you get," he said, "you still have to kneel to these people."

"What do you say?" Ernesto said.

"Excuse me," Rafael said, as the whole table had turned to stare at him. "The gringos will come anyway. If not Urabá, they'll go to Magdalena."

"Magdalena is a wasteland," Fernando Londoño said. "Un mierdero with no rain."

"Then they come on our terms," Rafael said.

"Who negotiates?" Fernando Londoño said.

"I do," Rafael said.

5.

As a child, Orejas watched the banana workers swinging their machetes in the fields around Turbo or climbing onto the company buses, like his father with his tough hands and burst fingernails and cuts on his forearms and occasionally a gash in his leg from an errant machete swipe. By the time his father arrived home drunk, raving about how he was going to el monte to join the guerrillas, to take back what had been stolen from him—the land, the heads of cattle, the automobiles, the sunglasses, the good rum from Caldas—he had spent every last peso on beer. It was not even worth it to say he was robbed. No one would believe him. Orejas's mother beat him over the head with a broom. His father beat her back with his fists, never hitting her face because she was beautiful, ageless despite the birth of six boys. The next morning Orejas would see her washing clothes in just her underwear and she looked like a leopard with greenish bruises down her back and stomach and arms. Other nights, his father would come home with a hen and a crate of eggs and a sack of potatoes and yucca. They would have a feast. Those nights, in the years before his father disappeared, were happy but might not have existed, as if Orejas had made them up to feel less disappointed in his boyhood. What he remembered most was that his father was always worn out, his feet dirty, his eyes bloodshot and his breath terrible with hunger.

Orejas loved the birds along the river, and for a time he
thought he could sing. It was the romantic salsa on the radio, but
his father told him to quiet down, and the priest never chose him
for the choir because Orejas was too dark and would stick out.
Orejas thought maybe he would be a doctor because the doctor
in town drove a jeep; neighbors stepped aside on the road and
paid for his beer and asked him questions about the body, and he
obliged by drawing out their organs on napkins and feeling men's
sides and prescribing the little white pills that could cure everything. But when he told his father this, his father shook his head,
and said that as much as he wanted it, no child of his would ever
be a doctor.

"Best not to live in the clouds," his father said. He gazed down
at his bare, deformed feet, airing out after a day in the heavy rubber boots, and he said everything they needed was on the ground.
The ground in Urabá, especially near Turbo, was fertile. There were
rivers everywhere you looked. Drop in the rhizomes and up came
the banana plants, and the people were not slaves anymore. His
father had lived through the early days, working eighteen-hour
shifts, sleeping on a collapsed banana box. Now he had a cement
house and earned extra pay as a banderillero who held up a long
metal location pole in the banana fields so the fumigation planes
knew where to spray.

*

Even then, the guerrillas were everywhere. By day, they were
farmers and laborers, working the fields with everyone else, but
at night they kidnapped policemen, took unused land from the
plantations and gave it to landless farmers. A shopkeeper kept a
cache of rifles in a hole beneath his shelves and would not sell to

the police or the military or the mayor. A schoolteacher handed out flyers at the cantina and met workers at a boarded-up house in Apartadó. Men came from the center of the country, Santander and Bogotá, and educated the people to no longer accept the conditions of their lives. Orejas looked east up into the green Sierra de Abibé and imagined the guerrillas moving on the narrow foot trails, setting up tents and kidnapping inspectors and hauling out sacks of marijuana to be shipped north from Turbo along with the bananas.

The communists, his father said, were men with a vision. They could talk to the owners of the plantations and open the ledgers and show them what percentage should belong to the workers risking their lives in the drainages or hauling a dozen stems on the pulley with a rope tied to their waists. If the owners did not listen, they would spill their blood. If you cut the rich, gold flowed from their veins. They looked at all the people like they were negritos or indios who should be grateful for wages higher than anywhere else in the country, for the grid of the new roads and canals and the cable system, implemented for the good of the people and the economy.

"Ya no. Not anymore," his father said. "They can't force us to work through the night."

"Ya no, ya no, ya no." He said this about a lot of things, as if his life and the life of Urabá had turned some corner and would never look back at the eighteen-hour days and seven-day weeks and rotten hammocks hanging in buggy barracks and the women giving birth right there in the dirt because there were no hospitals yet.

"Don't ever repeat what your father says at home," his mother said.

"Don't repeat what anyone says," his mother said, "or try to understand it."

"Open your mouth too much," his mother said, "and they'll slice a hole in your neck and yank your tongue down your throat and out the hole. The planters are not playing games."

"But I don't have to worry about you," his mother said. "You're the quiet one. The quiet ones will live forever."

Later, when his father disappeared, there were multiple stories. Orejas did not believe any of them. The neighbors said he had fallen in love with a prostitute from Montería and had gone to try his luck there. Others said he had jumped on the back of a horse and rode up into the Sierra of Abibé to join the guerrillas and that he was shot in the head while stealing cattle. They said he had slept with the young daughter of a banana worker, who chopped his skull into two halves and dropped them into a banana canal. Yet another said he was living in the jungles of Chocó, working an illegal gold mine. Orejas knew the truth—men disappeared all the time. Their women replaced them or became widows with no body to mourn.

*

At thirteen, Orejas started at Finca la Bella, riding into the fields on the workers' bus beside his father. His father showed him how the bananas reproduced. They walked the rows together, his father short with long arms, a sharp machete hanging off his belt, a man who moved slowly, but when he grabbed something to lift it, his strength was shocking. His father taught him how to look at the mature banana plants with buds and rhizomes sprouting off the sides of their trunks. The tricky part was selection. Which bud or baby was the one to get rid of. The point was to create parallel lines into space where the chosen baby plant would have room to spread its roots, receive light from above, when the big plant died.

They had to kill all the babies that grew above the scar line on the plant, too high for the soil to reach it. There were names for all this. A killed baby was el hijo desmadrado, the unmothered child, or el cacho chivo, and his father made him memorize these names.

"Form una hilera," his father said. "Line, line, line! If you master this, you'll rise at the plantation ahead of all the others. The capataz walks the rows and in a second he recognizes good lines."

As his father spoke, he rotated a full circle, pointing at every line of plants, as if they were sewing together the universe.

When a still-too-young plant gave birth, they had to cut off all the baby rhizomes and chop them into fertilizer. "Think of it this way," his father said. "A girl your age gives birth. What happens to her? She atrophies. What kind of a life is she going to have with a baby at thirteen?"

On Orejas's birthday, his father took him to el Copelón to celebrate. They washed up at the cooling tubs, changed clothes, and drove to Apartadó on a borrowed motorcycle. They sat at a table by the door in a cantina with pink and blue lights. When Orejas downed his third beer, his father told him he had a gift for him. He pushed him away from the table to a woman behind a curtain. She wore a spongy bra and a red leather skirt, and there was a gray birthmark on her cheek, barely covered with makeup. She told him to take off his jeans. It was a narrow bed, no bigger than a military cot, and she lay down on her back and lifted the skirt. She kept the bra on. Her hip bones angled out from her sides. Her legs were scratched with dried blood, her toenails bright red.

She pulled him onto her, and in a way he felt like he was being pulled onto himself. She grabbed his neck and shifted him until he was fucking, listening to the voices of men talking through the curtains and the love songs that were even louder here. He smelled the ammoniacal urine of drunken men, the woman's breath rotten from cigarettes and beer. She would not look at him. He stared at her bra, and then it was done. He lay on the filthy cot while she checked her makeup in a mirror. "You're the best lover I've ever had," she said.

Out at the table, his father asked how many times he had done it.

"Once," Orejas said.

"Go back," his father said. "What kind of a man does it only once?" His father pulled him onto his lap and wrapped his arms around his chest and said, "You're the best lover I've ever had," in the same voice the woman had used.

Orejas realized that all the men at the table had been with this woman, as if they were all eating with cupped hands from the same soup, and he felt sick to his stomach. The men were passing him around and patting his back, and his father filled and refilled a little plastic cup with aguardiente for each drinker. In a short time, Orejas was on the floor. He would sit up occasionally to ask for more liquor until the owner came and said they had to get him out.

His memories of that night were in pieces. He was on the motorcycle again, sandwiched between his father and another man, and then they were out in a banana field, his father threading a rope under Orejas's crotch and waist and up under his armpits. They attached him to a pulley on the cable, as if he were a banana stem to be sent downslope into the packing area. Orejas vomited, and his father stepped back and insulted him. He punched his ribs and groin. Someone kicked him in the butt, and he began to move. He heard the grind of metal that he knew was the pulley clicking against steel. He was flying along the cable, crossing a river into a plantation.

"Feliz cumpleaños!" his father yelled.

When Orejas awoke, he felt pain in his back and arms. Light was breaking on the horizon. He looked down, and there was el Río

Guadalito. He could hear the fumigation planes in the distance, and he could see the fog of spray approaching him. He swung his body until he was away from the river and touched the ground and ran forward and lifted his legs, and the pulley took him up the rows at a high speed. When he saw the roof of Mr. Morris's house and Finca la Bella in the distance, he knew was going to live.

*

When Orejas was seventeen, his father returned on a horse at night. His mother was in bed, asleep with his two younger brothers. At the time, she was working all day cooking and tending the counter at the cafeteria of a banana plantation outside Turbo—she arrived after dark with pots of food for her children and collapsed in bed. Orejas slept in a hammock beneath an overhang at the back of the house. He heard his father's throat clearing, the clank of the coffee pot as he lit the stove, as if he were just coming home on a normal day. Three years had passed since they'd last seen him. Orejas felt his father's gaze on him from the back door, then his hands touching his head, his cheeks, his chest, as if checking him for money. Orejas did not open his eyes. He listened to his father sipping the coffee on the little plot of dirt behind the house, then walking to the chicken coop, calling the hens by their names, Josefina, Raquél, Tata, Pepa, but those hens were long dead.

His father carried his little brothers outside, setting one on the ground, the other in the hammock on top of Orejas. Then Orejas's mother was short of breath and moaning. No one said a word. The moon floated above the fields. A truck passed on the larger road a kilometer away. The neighborhood dogs barked. After, his mother followed his father out to the back where he was scooping up Orejas's little brothers to return them to the bed. His mother seemed to be pointing at them, whispering that they were his boys and he should own them. His father fixed more coffee. He asked about a leak in the roof, climbed up there to repair it. He caressed Orejas's face again, kissing the tops of his eyebrows and telling him what a good job he was doing taking care of everyone. Then he was on the street, giving water to his horse and galloping toward the river.

*

A month later, Orejas joined the guerrillas.

He knew all the power in the world was on paper, in ink. The managers kept ledgers and opened envelopes full of documents. On TV, the rich read books with colored spines, books on tables, on shelves, on laps, on napping faces. He could read most signs, or words he had seen a thousand times before on the crates, like Embarcadero Zungo or Destino España, and he was an expert at getting other men to read from documents, but if you handed him a full page of words, he was lost in it. Men said everything twice and loved their voices. If you listened, you didn't need half the documents in the world. Being the quiet one was easy enough.

But that's not why he joined the guerrillas that night in the schoolhouse with no roof, just a sagging tarp and some plastic stools, standing next to the baker whom he hated, who would marry his friend Yenifer. He had been drinking since noon. A single lightbulb hung from a wire. The comandante called them "compañeros" and painted a dull vision of paradise in which the workers ran the plantations and "la oligarquía" was dead. It sounded like fantasy to Orejas who knew that the men in offices always came out ahead. Workers chimed in with their grievances. The whole place smelled like beer. The lightbulb swayed. Orejas stared at it and tried not to yawn. He had no interest in a revolution. But once he saw everyone's face, it was a risk to back out.

At first, he ran easy errands, snitched on the managers at the plantations, delivered messages, and one night he joined a raid to steal cattle from a rancher in Necoclí. He grabbed a nice cut before they kicked up to the comandante. He wore a red bandana over his face, though his giant pink ears were impossible to conceal. On a visit to a camp in the sierra, they taught him to shoot a rifle and set up an ambush along a road. Even at point-blank range, he missed the targets. Not everyone was built to kill, the comandante said. The full-time guerrillas were campesinos who slept on muddy slopes and ate rice and lentils every day and went crazy at the sight of a woman. It was all a mystery to him. It was like playing a game for which no one knew the rules.

He rose up the ranks at Finca la Bella, as if being a guerrilla had made him smarter. He tested soil for expansion of the fields. He drove a pickup to the headquarters for supplies and bought a motorcycle to get to and from work. His parallel lives met and split and met, and when the guerrillas accused a worker of being a snitch, Orejas was glad that it was not him on their list.

6.

THE CONVERSATION WITH THE American banana men from Cincinnati took place in a fog of distrust. The gringos had all the data of what they were getting into but none of the nuance or the history. Rafael and Luis Alberto Echevarría sat huddled over a speakerphone in the aquarium. Both had studied in the United States, but their English was rusty; Rafael leaned too far forward with his hands behind his ears and Luis Alberto took chaotic notes on a legal pad. The outline of the subsidiary was in order and the terms clear, so Rafael focused on the subtext, always braced for the gringos to make some outlandish offer to test him.

"How is the weather?" a cheerful gringo voice asked.

"Do you say here or in Urabá?" Rafael said, wondering if the gringo was referring to the guerrillas or the empty ships in Turbo, or the yearly rainfall, or maybe it was a straightforward question about the weather in Medellín.

"Where are you again?" the gringo said.

"Medellín. The bananas are in Urabá."

"Well, both," the gringo said.

"Limited rains in Urabá today," Rafael said. "Then very hot. Great weather for bananas, as you all wish. How is the weather there?"

There was a long silence, as if the men needed to confer.

A different voice said, "Beautiful fall day in Ohio. The leaves are colorful. We like it here."

Rafael felt subservient in English, his voice too high and tentative. He wanted to speak English the way the Germans and Israelis did, to be assertive and obnoxious. He never had to raise his voice to be heard in his world.

"First quarter high profits," Luis Alberto said, as if he were having a parallel conversation, each word enunciated with such precision that it became incomprehensible. "Second quarter even better. The markets share possibility is grand. Opportunities do abound here."

"Could you say that again?" a gringo said. "Maybe it's the reception, but we do not understand."

"I am saying that our production is unsurpassable, and the bananas are the tastiest in not just Latin America, but the world. Once you try, you will not go back."

"Come again?" a gringo said, and Rafael put one arm across Luis Alberto's chest as if they were in a crashing vehicle. Let me handle this, it said.

The small talk ended. They went over the area of land that the gringos wanted, including both established plantations and virgin land. Rafael circled options on the map of Urabá. Luis Alberto read off the yields of the past five years, all things they had sent them via fax, but everything had to be confirmed a hundred times with the gringos. They assumed Rafael and Luis Alberto were savvy mafiosos, living surrounded by bodyguards in buildings with bulletproof glass, smart in all the ways that mattered in their world, but ignorant of global trade and law and the picky appetites of American and European consumers. Their numbers surely exaggerated. The condescension was mutual. Rafael thought of them as naïve, out of their depth, clueless about Urabá, and yet they controlled the entire fruit industry in the Americas, they had cleared the jungles, laid cement for ports and tracks for railroads. Not these men, but their grandfathers. So, you had to be careful. Seeming naïve was part of their charm, but the gringos understood the cost of violence.

By the end of the phone call, with just a brief mention of the strike, "a minor setback," Rafael said, they had agreed on initial numbers. The gringos would be opening a headquarters in Medellín. They would not officially own the land, but they would own the bananas on the stems, and it would all be done with their capital.

Did Banana Bolívar seem like a good name for the company?

Yes, Rafael said. It sounded patriotic and unifying. It was very good.

Rafael and Luis wrote down numbers, the timeline, they talked dates for a trip up to Cincinnati, and by the time the sun touched the western mountains and the aquarium filled with an orange light, everything seemed possible.

"You take care now," a voice said.

"Take care, too," Rafael said. "Goodbye."

They might have celebrated if they trusted the gringos, or if the guerrillas had not paralyzed the banana economy that morning.

"Too easy," Luis Alberto said. "We have the best fruit."

"Maybe cede to both the unions," Rafael said. "The market opens up in eastern Europe and Russia, and we get there first."

Luis Alberto wondered if he looked handsome in the orange light. He was thinking about his girlfriend, Graciela, feeling quite sure that she had been fucking the TV actor the night before. He could see her facedown on a bed, the pink bottoms of her feet in the lamplight. He saw the appeal of the actor. He had the indigenous look, large, panoramic eyes, high cheekbones, and a tight body, whereas Luis's chest was pale, a paunch growing under his soft pecs, and he had a sweating problem, which for some women was unbearable. Graciela complained about the smell of her sheets and said he tasted like acid.

"Are you listening?" Rafael said.

"Perdón," Luis Alberto said. "Don't you think the unions and the guerillas are the same thing?"

Luis Alberto did not respect Rafael. It was his soprano voice, or his contorted posture, a bit of a maricón, he felt. He did not have good instincts for business. He overpaid his managers, and they still got murdered. Yet he always came out ahead. Sure, it was unlucky when Rafael's wife was killed, but now he was going to make a fortune off his land and this new arrangement with the gringos, and with that new money he would be confident and could hook another wife, a younger one. They would have more kids and he would behave normally again. There was a religious calm in his bearing. He seemed at ease in the world, like he had nothing to prove, and like the whole operation was a minor event.

"I trust the guerrillas about as much as I trust the military to do its job," Rafael said. "We pay. We've always paid."

"Money speaks."

"Right."

"The problem," Luis Alberto said, "is when the guerrillas know the gringos are coming, they'll just want a larger share."

"Maybe." Rafael looked at the thousands of fingerprints on the glass table. "No secrets here."

Luis Alberto saw himself walking out of the room, past the secretaries to the elevator. He could be at Graciela's office in fifteen minutes. He wanted to see her pink feet. He wanted to smell her hair to see if she smelled like the actor. He would know just from her face, if it was relaxed, post-coital, if her voice was smooth or bottled up. Or maybe he was just telling himself a crazy story. He could not separate his nightmares from reality. He would cover his body in deodorant to limit the sweat and bring her a bouquet of white roses.

"You seem distracted," Rafael said.

Their eyes met, and Luis Alberto thought how unfortunate it was that they would have to travel together. He imagined Rafael jumping from his balcony and dying. That would solve it. Death solved everything, but Luis Alberto would never kill. Except Graciela. It would be easy to do, twenty or forty thousand pesos to a teenage sicario, but then hard to live with afterward.

7.

A few weeks into the strike, Orejas crossed the fields on a flood-ed dirt path and stashed his motorcycle in a drainage ditch. He walked with his machete out and tightened the string propping up an off-kilter plant, even if it was going to be dug up. The air tasted like jungle. More birds than usual explored the fields, dipping down to eat fruit. As he neared the Finca la Bella packing area, the cable was ruptured in its braid, severed from the posts and footbridges. One canal bridge had been dumped into the river, so he had to enter the rows to look for a narrow where he could jump it. They would haul in coils of new cable and join it with the old lengths they could salvage.

He emerged from the row and crouched behind a barrel of chemicals in the packing area to listen. No one was here. No bananas were allowed to move. All the buildings had collapsed in the fire. The cafeteria was ashes and mutilated pots. Water puddled in the main office, a white cement structure reduced to a collection of charred objects, a file cabinet, a desk and chair. In the packing area, tubs were ripped open on the sides, the conveyor belts curled up into melted fibers.

He had no love for the owner, Rafael Restrepo, whom he knew only as a cold voice on the telephone, but at least he paid his salary. The destruction in the light of day hurt his eyes. The stiff cables would cut his hands as he welded them together. The new packing area roof would rise up on his shoulders.

He heard a noise at the gate and ducked into the fields. He took a shortcut to get out and pulled his motorcycle from the drainage. He followed the main road north and crossed the river on one of the metal bridges the military had constructed to replace the one the guerrillas had blown. He turned into Currulao, as he had a thousand times in his life, this village where he had grown up, where he still had friends, and he stopped in front of its only bakery. A red stenciled sign above it said, *Pan y Más*.

"Y ese milagro!" Yenifer said, standing at the opening of the bakery with a broom in her hands. She kissed his cheek and pinched the bone of his elbow.

They spoke with an old familiarity. When he was nine, she was abandoned and stayed with him and his family for a time. His mother fed her, gave her a place to sleep in exchange for taking care of his brothers, and from the beginning they had an understanding. She was his oldest friend. He stopped here just to see her, to stand stiff while she kissed his cheek, to hear her voice and to watch her move around the bakery and serve people. Each word carried a dozen others that only they heard. She slipped him the coconut cookies he loved and milk that was about to turn.

"¿Qué va a tomar?" she said.

"A beer."

The bakery smelled of old coffee simmering in the aluminum urn and the plantains spotted brown on the ceiling hook. He walked to one end, where there was an old phone encased in a blue metal box. He dropped in coins and dialed Don Rafael's office and spoke with a receptionist.

"¿De parte de quien?" she said.

"Samuel Yuletis."

"He's in a meeting."

"Just a message then," he said. "Tell him there's nothing to save at Finca la Bella. We have to clear it all and rebuild the packing area. All the cables are cut."

A door behind the bakery counter opened, and Hugo greeted him.

"Medellín," Orejas whispered, covering the mouthpiece with his palm.

"Well?" Hugo said when Orejas hung up. "Are you the new manager?"

Orejas downed his beer and looked at the stains in Hugo's armpits, a tattoo of a condor on his forearm. He was trigger happy. He had killed a policeman the night of the insurrection and wouldn't shut up about it. He led Orejas behind the counter and closed the bedroom door. The walls were decorated with a cheap poster of the Eiffel Tower and another of a Swiss valley with a turquoise lake. There was an unmade bed, a shelf of baking supplies, a line of clothes strung up on banana rope. Everything smelled like sweat. Hugo pulled out a piece of paper hidden beneath a bag of flour. "Read it, hermano. Bad news."

"Just tell me," Orejas said.

Hugo stared at him. Orejas said he didn't have time for games, so Hugo relented and said it was an intercepted letter from one of the comandantes. They were negotiating peace with the government. No one would go to jail. The government was promising money and land for the end of the war. They wanted to protect the banana zone.

"It's a fraud," Hugo said. "We disarm, and they hunt us down, one by one. Like always." He said a group of compañeros was planning to stay in the mountains. It meant disobeying their leaders, but for men like Orejas and Hugo, it would be suicide to pose at some peace ceremony in Apartadó and get blessed by the bishop.

"Read this, if you don't believe me."

Someone banged on the bedroom door.

"What is wrong with this woman?" Hugo said. "Make up your mind, hermano. We want to know who's who."

Orejas took the paper and with his thumb traced the lines of text that could be an advertisement for televisions for all he knew.

"There's no agreement yet," Hugo said, "but it's coming, and that peace, compañero, it's going to be worse than war." The knocking resumed. Yenifer said she needed the bathroom. "Leave us alone, woman!"

"I have to go," Orejas said.

"Do you have a roof for the house yet?"

"Not even close."

"How many walls?"

"One."

"My cousin Bernardo is selling a roof in Chigorodó. Tell me when you get there. Are you with us?"

"Of course."

"A man like you, Orejas, gets to the other side, no?"

8.

No one could sleep. Rafael would lie awake at night until his phone rang. It was always another planter. Londoño or Echevarría or Zuluaga. Voices in the night. Not much comfort. They talked loans. They talked interest. They debated killing all the union leaders in Apartadó or flying to Bogotá to meet with their military contacts and even the president, but none of this was useful. The government was negotiating with the guerrillas and did not want to mess it up by putting pressure on the banana unions.

The strike entered its forty-third day. Every field he owned was overgrown, the plants damaged by friction, spewing snot, covered in bugs. He had laid off his workers and stopped paying his managers, including Orejas Yuletis, who had risen fast, who, according to the gossipy widow of Gerardo Reyes, was not just a man with big ears (Rafael had never seen him) but a snitch for the guerrillas. Rafael had even borrowed a small sum of money from a narco neighbor upstairs whose walls were plastered with Boteros so everyone would know he could afford them.

"What do you think the solution is?" he said to Luz Marina, who was sweeping around the living room while he, unshaven with ash on the chest of his pajamas, sat on the sofa and smoked through a pack of cigarettes.

"Señor?"

"The reason I am here and not at the office. The reason I am flying to the United States tomorrow like a beggar. What is your opinion?"

He saw his wife standing in the door, late as usual and on her way to hail the same taxi over and over that dumped her body in Comuna 12, her life worth just a few thousand pesos and the rings on her fingers. She would tell him that Luz Marina was an idiot.

"Don Rafael knows best," she said.

*

In Cincinnati, he felt naked, stripped of his name. It was winter there, and the gringos were stalling. He intrigued them with the history of Urabá, from the fierce Kuna rejecting the Spaniards with poisonous arrows in the sixteenth century, to a region of cimarrones and colonos who wanted nothing to do with the rest of the world, to the founding of the most prosperous banana zone on the continent. He explained the futility of the Colombian military, how they could patrol within a hundred feet of a guerrilla camp and not see their enemy. The military lacked bullets for their guns and gas for their trucks. The guerrillas were mostly disguised as civilians anyway. Who knew how many of his workers were betraying him? All his words seemed wrong. His accent seemed like a joke. He was sure one of the gringos, a man with a small head on a rosey football body, was laughing when he spoke, or laughing later in the break room when Rafael had been sent out to the skywalks to explore downtown Cincinnati without having to face the cold air, traversing all of it twenty feet above ground to arrive at his hotel, where he stood in front of a fake fireplace with perfect orange and blue symmetrical flames behind a thick glass display. The illusion of it. The gringos could not last even a single day in his life.

"Stick up for yourself," he whispered in English. "Be a macho."

That night he met with a gringo who had a wolfish, hungry face, who wore a gold earring in one ear, silver in another, and who was completely fluent in Spanish. His mother was a Spaniard, he said, or not quite, a gringa who lived in Madrid where he had spent much of his childhood. His name was Jay Harrison. He treated Rafael like an old friend, like they might visit a strip club in the suburbs. He drank fast and caressed his own face and ran long fingers through his blond hair. He said he had always wanted to invest in Latin America. "Es el futuro," Jay said. "It's not here. Ohio is already in the post-rapture." The steel boom had long ended. The towns were depressed places with unhealthy food, drug addiction, suicides, and no potential. The problem, Jay told him, was that the Colombian planters had surrendered to the guerrillas, that they were barely investing in their plantations at all, and the only way for this deal to work was for everyone to put in capital.

"Give us some good news," Jay said. "No one wants to be the first to stick his toe in a violent pool."

PEACE
1991

9.

HUGO AWOKE FROM HIS SIESTA, drank two coffees at the counter of his bakery, sold costeño cheese to the butcher who carried a brown baby that looked nothing like him, and watched night fall. He paid Nanci for the week, loaded a canvas bag with what remained of the day's bread, and gave Yenifer instructions for that night's baking. Yenifer walked him beyond the front door, the streets of Currulao barely lit up with the yellow streetlights hung from wires at the corners, and he kissed her. It was a full kiss, his teeth against hers, his head tilted into hers, pulling her into him, and for a moment she pretended like none of the other things had ever happened. He had not grazed Nanci's waist with his thumb to touch a stain on her jeans or told her to leave the bathroom door open so he could watch her piss, Nanci laughing uncomfortably, Yenifer walking in to ask him a question about the old flour they were using. He looked at her with a curled lip, his teeth out, like she was a fly that had buzzed into his ear. Yes, she set all that aside as he twisted her wrists behind her back, enough to give her a little of the pain she liked, and then lifted her up against the brick wall. He was hard, but there was a blink of fear in his eyes. He released her. She felt annoyed with herself. This was not affection, it was endless arousal, Hugo a boy with pretty dolls to undress, and along with her pleasure from the kiss was the hope that he might enter the night and never return.

She watched him advance up the dark street with puddles from the day's rain, the sack of bread over his shoulders. She could see doubt in his steps; some nights it was better to be a baker, not a hero, and go to bed early. A stray dog scratched itself and checked with her for scraps. The cantina was closed. A neighbor's radio played loudly with salsa. She watched her husband's figure pass the final lights at the edge of town.

She locked the metal door of the bakery, running a chain around the handles inside, just in case. She was alone now, and anything could happen during those nights. The air in the bedroom was heavy. The box fan just shuffled it around, and the whole brick structure would be like a kiln when she turned on the oven. She opened a beer for herself, something he would laugh at or tell her she was wasting their money, women should only drink beer on holidays. She gulped, holding the cold bottle against her neck and leaning into the open refrigerator. She set the empty in one of the plastic crates and was about to remove a second beer when there was a knock at the front door.

It was as if someone had taken a live wire and held it up against her spine. She put the bottle back in its slot.

"¿Quién es?" Yenifer said through the locked door.

"Soy yo."

She opened only the little square through which you could shove a liter of milk or bread late at night, and here was this girl Nanci, hair smashed down on the side of her head, and something was wrong with her mouth that seemed detached from her face and bleeding. But Yenifer was already saying no and closing the little metal square. It was cruel. It was not what a neighbor should do in these times, but there was momentum to her refusal.

"I'm sorry," Yenifer said to the door, "but there's nowhere for you here."

"Por favor, Yeni. Por favor. No tengo a nadie."

Maybe Nanci thought she was a TV actress escaping her family. She was just a poor girl. Someone had to make her realize this. She had looked at Yenifer like she was old cheese, a joke to the neighborhood, yes, that was the look, she was always on the verge of laughter, as if she were about to explode with it and destroy Yenifer who had been laughed at enough, called ugly, called a man's toy, a witch who could not even get pregnant. This girl's problem now was a man, maybe her crazy father or a lover.

Yenifer walked away from the door and bent down to light the oven.

"Por favor, Yeni!" Nanci said.

"Go away, niña. I can't help you."

"I don't have anywhere to go."

Yenifer righted herself against the counter and burped from the beer. She would probably regret this. No. She would regret it more if Nanci settled into their house for the night, then another and another. She should go home and get on her knees to apologize, and of course they would let her in. Everyone had to get on their knees, especially the poor, and it was good to learn this young. She would come to work the next day, as was the routine. But to be so unkind was not easy. Yenifer, too, might have to knock on a door someday, and the person behind it could tell her to go away.

"Pobre niña," she said, opening the square and looking out onto the empty street.

*

After mixing the flour and kneading the dough, Yenifer opened a second beer, a risk, as Hugo kept a tight inventory. Right as she popped off the cap, the lights cut out. The refrigerator stopped buzzing. The box fan in the bedroom went still. The strong light bulb above the counter flashed silver and went dark.

"Mierda," she said, sipping the beer as if it were the last cold thing on earth. "Lo que faltaba."

The oven ran on gas. The dough was everywhere, and so she rummaged around a shelf in the bedroom and found a small candle, the sort to light in the alcove of a cathedral, and she carried that to the counter. It was not enough. She lit it and searched for another, finding nothing but matches. She worked fast. She slid her first tray of buns into the oven, and she stripped down to her underwear, which was soaked, sweat falling off her chin and nose and even the tips of her hair, dripping into the dough. She mixed sugar and butter into the cookies, eyeballing the measurements— these things she had done a thousand times seemed mysterious in the candlelight. She shaped the little balls and discs with her palms and did not waste a single grain of flour.

If Nanci were here now, Yenifer could have put her to work, scraping the cookies off the tray, shaping more buns, sweeping the floors and wiping down the display cases. If Hugo and his guerrillas had caused the blackout, and surely they did, she wanted him to know he was sabotaging his own business. They would probably be without electricity for the next two days until the power company repaired the towers. They would lose everything in the refrigerator. The beer would not be cold.

She pulled out the first tray of bread and slid in the next one. She sat down on one of the plastic chairs, but it stuck to her legs. So hot she lay down on the cement floor. She felt some vibrations through it. A truck stopped before her door. The headlights seeped through the window frame before the truck turned onto the road to the ocean. Her feet were swollen, her legs hurt deep in their bones. Time stopped during a blackout. Sometimes you could sleep through it, but with no fan, on these hot, rainy nights, it was impossible. Her uncle who lived in Bogotá once told her that during blackouts everyone got robbed. That he had climbed into a taxi and did not know where he was in the city, that the taxista had stopped at the door to his apartment building and said, "This is it," and her uncle said, no, it was not it, and yet it was. A city with that much light made no sense in the night without it. He had climbed up sixteen flights of stairs in the dark, trying to feel the numbers above the doors. He had feared he would be trapped on the staircase, but when he got to his floor, he just knew.

Yes, she thought, everyone found ways to get through it. When little, she studied in the light of the doorway because their house had no windows, and at night used a streetlamp a block away. Her older brother, a banana worker with his milky eyes damaged by some chemical, said, "Are you showing off to the neighbors?" In her hands was a book about famous buildings in Europe, the size of the rooms, the pools, the balconies, the lobbies, with glossy pictures of Paris and London and Munich. She had found it on the teacher's desk, dropped it down the neck of her blouse, and then felt the stiff cover glued to her chest all day.

"The teacher gave it to me," Yenifer said.

"Gave it or lent it?" her brother said, and looked weary, lifting his battered hand as if to slap her, to send her right back with the book to admit she was a thief. "You'll never stay in a hotel."

In the years that she was homeless, her clothes in a little canvas sack, she hoarded magazines and newspapers and that one book. She read parts of it. She lived in each hotel, swam in the pools and tried out all the beds. It was a relief to pull it out occasionally and look at the symmetrical lines, the titles, the styles of architecture, the time and materials for each building. But probably her brother was right.

Her candle went out. She found the wall and worked her way around the counter to the oven. Nor was Hugo the hero in his life. Nor was Nanci in some drama out there. No one was a hero. Yenifer, too, could be turned out on a whim. Used up. Fucked enough. She would show up at Orejas's mother's house in Turbo, and she would hang a hammock for her and say she could stay for a time.

She withdrew the hot tray of bread, touching a bun to see if it was hard on the outside, yes, it was fine, and tomorrow the customers would also see the bread in dim light, so it did not matter. She loaded another tray with more buns and shut them in the oven. At the sink, she held her head under the faucet, wetting her hair and her neck and tossing water onto her chest. Within a few minutes, the hot air from the oven seemed to catch fire on her skin, and so she moved away and lay back down on the cement floor, pressing her wet cheek into it.

There were gunshots up the street. She lay as flat as she could. She heard a bullet hit the wall of the bakery.

There was banging on the door again.

"¡Por favor! ¡Por favor, Yeni! ¡Me van a matar!"

Yenifer unwound the chain and stepped away, as Nanci pushed past her like she was a second door. No light on the streets at all. Someone was sprinting away toward the road.

"Help me close this," Yenifer said. "Fast."

They ran the bolt through the door and padlocked the chain. It was dark. The gunshots continued up the block. Occasionally one would strike the brick of the bakery walls. There was a bang when one hit the door.

"What is happening?" Yenifer said.

Nanci was crouched there, sobbing, and Yenifer pushed her toward the counter and away from the door, both of them slamming into the plastic tables, sitting behind the counter with their backs against the refrigerator. Heat from the oven blanketed them. It was normal to be baking during a war. To worry about cookies and buns.

"Whoever they wanted to kill is dead," Yenifer said, after six shots sounded in quick succession.

And who was he? She asked Nanci, who said she wasn't sure. She said there were men in military uniforms and others in civilian clothing. Yenifer lit a match. Smoke rose from the oven. The bread was burning, but she saw blood on Nanci's face, much of it dried up, her nose broken to one side, cut badly, her left eye swollen shut, and one of her teeth dangling by its root. Yenifer did not ask who did it. She did not care. Maybe Nanci had laughed at the wrong person.

"What did you do?" Yenifer said.

"I?"

"I have no ice. Do you want to clean your face in the bathroom? It does not look good."

Nanci just whimpered, and Yenifer ran her fingers along her fleshy arms and back to be sure she had not been shot or stabbed. Nanci was dry and complete—she was not going to die. "To the bathroom," Yenifer said. All this while smoke rose from the oven. By the bed Yenifer found Hugo's towel, and she told her to wash out the blood first with a lot of water and to not stain the towel. She turned on the faucet. She guided Nanci's head under the stream to get water into the eye, and held it when she resisted.

"Here's soap. Put it in the cuts. Do you want me to rip out your tooth?"

"Don't you dare!"

Yenifer found a clean T-shirt for her. Nanci sat on the toilet, as she had in the afternoon when Hugo wanted to watch her. Yenifer listened to her sounds, she was obviously sick, and closed the door so the smell would not get into the fresh bread.

"Take your time," Yenifer said.

She was pleased to see her suffer and be her only salvation. She moved back around the counter and into the smoke. She had been offered a second chance to be good. This was rare in life.

10.

AT LA PICARDÍA, Orejas spent his evenings among the working women—Paleta, Esperanza, Consuelo, la Bombona, Blanca, Paloma, Flor, la Pelada, Petra, Virginia, Aurora, Tita, Amapola, la Barbi. He made them write down his expenditures in the same way he would make a seller mark down a box of cornmeal or socks. One night it was Paleta with her stick legs and distended stomach, or la Bombona with her machine laugh and ox tongue everywhere on his body, or Petra, a towering Black woman with a blonde wig and big hips and a scientific gaze, or la Pelada who wore a new wig every night, tea-colored to blonde to jet black and shaved her body to a smoothness he loved, or Amapola who was usually drunk and high on pills, who smelled like old tires, who made growling noises that echoed in his head, and he longed for her most of all. In the dim light, they were all beautiful.

Tonight was dead. The women were moody and broke, only a few customers passing through town, as the guerrillas had taken the embarcaderos and stopped work at all the plantations near Apartadó.

"Where does it end?" Amapola said, just the two of them sitting at a table.

In the gap between his long days at the plantations and his nightwork with the guerrillas, he found rest at la Picardía where he slept for a few hours, breathing through his squeaky nose and filling the room with a smell that reminded the women of wet soil in a cow pasture. No one could sleep beside him. They were paid to lie still, to resist going through his pockets, to review their lives and circle around to this same bed every time, the unclean sheets, this peculiar guerrilla with flung-out, veiny, pink ears who remembered every detail of your body, your face, your hands, and everything you said to him about your life, and though any money was good, not every woman could bear the existential drain of lying beside him. Often he would sleepwalk, and they would have to each grab a limb and wrestle him to the floor until he calmed.

Amapola sat on his lap and stole sips from his beer. He received a message from a kid on a bike, wide-eyed before the women. Orejas asked her to read it, but she could not read, so they called for la Bombona.

"It just says go to the office," she said.

"Got it," he said. "Gracias, mi amor."

The lights went out, but no one heard the transformer blow. The madame lit candles, tipping wax to stick them places. In candlelight, the madame had extra lines on her face, and Amapola had lines all over her body, like some disease creasing her arms and up her neck. She was happier in the candlelight. Orejas saw the whole brothel burning, the green felt on the pool table curling up black, the disco ball a bright flame, the floor on fire and the women all running for the door with their clothes in their arms. No one would save anyone.

*

Orejas picked up rifles and drove north from Apartadó, saw the lines again near Currulao, where he made a U-turn and parked.

Hugo climbed into the front seat while two other men jumped into the back of the pickup, tapping the window, "Hola, Orejas." Without looking at them he knew their voices, and he looked up at the lines of the headlights to the road that itself was a line. He saw his mother sitting in front of the fan in her little house in Turbo, her hair jumping above her. She would open the door when he arrived later. All the neighbors would see him and not see him. What they were about to do was not necessary, he felt, yet another office to burn, supposedly the one the gringos had bought, this fire being their welcome and warning, but he had a good feeling about tonight.

Apartadó was in the dark. His headlights grazed the sides of the brick buildings, the gas station, the cathedral, and all of this made sense. It was like going backwards into time, back to the Spanish Colony or back even further to when this was just indigenous Kuna and Emberá walking trails and guiding canoes along the rivers. Naked people, fornicators, Orejas thought, warriors. Nothing had changed. Just a mix of incompatible people and all the jungle chopped down for bananas, and lines drawn across it in every direction, and him following the most important one, this north-south shipping route through the heart of the plantations.

"Soccer on Sunday," Hugo said.

"Where?" Orejas asked.

"Apartadó. Andrés Botero is going to play."

"Barefoot like last time?"

"There's talk of him getting a call from Medellín. Listen, slow down, hermano. This road falls apart up here."

"Botero is not fast enough for that league."

"They feed them beef and goat milk every day. They make them run the hills. He has heart and that kid grew up hard. If he gets the call…who knows."

Orejas sped up. It was a pleasure to feel the wind against his face, to make small adjustments to the plastic wheel and to ignore Hugo, who was a terrible soccer player, barking orders, tripping everyone with his red cleats, attempting impossible kicks from half-field and sending the ball into the canal where they'd pay some poor kid to swim after it. It was magical to see Andrés Botero run with a soccer ball stuck to the tips of his toes, then stop, shift, spin through defenders and find a line to the net.

"Can you get real defenders?" Orejas said. "I'm not going to scream instructions to guys who don't listen."

"I have gloves for you."

"I don't need gloves. Look at my hands, hermano."

"The best goalies wear gloves."

Orejas turned onto a new gravel road through a banana field. Cables caught light from somewhere. "I'll play," he said. "What time?"

"Five."

"Hot."

"Better than noon."

They tied bandanas over their mouths. Hugo shut off the radio, and they pulled up to the white gate of the gringo headquarters, the security guard walking up to the driver's side. Orejas put a gun to the man's head as Hugo ran around the front of the truck, bound his wrists with thin yellow banana rope, and opened the gates. On a plateau of grass was a white building with a gravel lot, the start of a soccer field, and a warehouse for machinery. There was another guard at the office, and Hugo disarmed him, tied him to the low branch of a mango tree. Time sped up. Orejas circled the building and felt airborne. He was breathing fast, tasting salt in the bandana. He felt a poke in his groin, a biting pain from an old hernia he would probably die with, a little lump that Amapola pressed on with her thumb, and he would say, "Stop, that's my intestine," and she would put her mouth against it.

One of his other men split open the metal door with a crowbar, and they went desk to desk, shoving papers, telephones, calculators, a fax machine, two computers, and a typewriter into canvas sacks, hauling all this out to the truck. Orejas entered with a gas can and irrigated the desks, walls, chairs, and a few stacks of unused paper. An insect bit his cheek. He slapped himself, looked out the window and into the banana fields. One of the other men spray-painted the walls with the black letters—*FARC*.

"And the warehouse?" Hugo said.

"Not tonight," Orejas said, patting his pockets. "Does someone have fire?"

He heard a boot slide into the gravel by the gate and he saw the glint of steel in the dark. He heard twenty men breathing at once, or holding their breath at once, their fingers flicking on trigger guards. Just a flash of light at the opening round. The gravel itself seemed to ignite, and he felt a bullet tear through his calf. He dove behind the office, Hugo beside him, saying, "La puta madre!" Orejas slung his rifle and ran for the fence. He swung himself over the barbed wire, cutting his hands and thighs, tearing apart his shirt. When he fell, his rifle strap tangled across his neck, choking him as he rolled onto the muddy bank of a canal.

*

Orejas's leg stiffened from the bullet wound, but he could walk. He stayed off the roads, finding paths through a pasture, working his way north to Carepa. He pressed down on the barbed wire with two hands and swung his bleeding leg over it. He seemed to be on someone's dairy, the grass shin-high, lumps of cow shit here and there, a sack of feed hanging from a tree and a trough of water outside a barn. How far had he walked? He saw a mule grazing and ran toward it. She was passive, bowing her head under his hands because he knew cattle, and he led her toward the house to find a saddle. He wouldn't make it home to Turbo tonight, but if he got back to la Picardía before dawn, Amapola would send for a doctor to take the bullet out of his leg.

He saddled the mule and tried to climb onto her, falling down on his stiffened leg, and yet the mule did not run or kick him. He looked up and at first he thought she was a hallucination—a young woman standing there with a machete, asking him what he was doing. His bandana had fallen and his face was wide open. Who was she?

"Mujer," he said. "Can you make a tourniquet on my leg?"

"How?"

"I am not going to hurt you."

She snatched a T-shirt from the clothesline and wrapped it around his leg and tightened the knot, wiping her fingers on the grass because they were stained with his blood. She handed him a plastic cup of water from a barrel below the roof gutters. He drank half of it, poured the rest onto a cut in his arm.

"I am not stealing your mule," he said.

She reached behind her to touch the clothesline and glanced at the door to the house. Orejas repeated that the mule would be back by the end of the week. A few seconds later, he was galloping out the gate, and looked over his shoulder to see her father standing in the pasture with his hands on his knees. Orejas listened to hooves hit the packed dirt, his whole body convulsed with pain, and he could feel mud flying up without seeing it, and then he was on the outskirts of Carepa. Not safe yet, but close.

11.

THEY SPOKE ONLY IN SPANISH at first. They were sitting in the aquarium at the long glass conference table at the corporation headquarters in Medellín. A map laid out with black dots for the plantations not for sale and green dots where the plantations were for sale, some failing, some bankrupted, and Jay's company's subsidiary would acquire many of them. Location was everything— how flat, how far from a canal or road, how close to the port—and time was everything, too, a clock ticking the second a banana left its stem.

Jay wore a black, pin-striped suit, a little tight at the shoulders, his blond hair slicked sideways with gel, the silver hoop earring in one ear and the gold hoop in the other, and small silver-rimmed glasses. He looked more like a lamb than a wolf in Colombia. He touched his face with long fingers right before he spoke and these fingers slashed at the air, his arms raised to weigh contrary decisions. Also on the map were red blotches marking guerrilla-controlled zones. A red blotch all over Apartadó, Chigorodó, Turbo, and red up the coast toward Panama, and up into the mountains to the east toward Córdoba where no bananas grew but the cattle industry thrived. The red blotches looked to Jay like a rash in the landscape, he scratched it, looking to Rafael who got hot when he talked about the guerrillas, naming the leaders, Bernardo Gutiérrez and Francisco Caraballo, and the numbers, 4,000 men, about 1,500 in uniform and the rest hidden within the population. He wished them the worst, apologized for wishing any man dead.

"What do they ultimately want?" Jay said.

"Just power. All of it. Oh, and all our land."

A servant brought a tray of coffee and pastries. Neither man looked at her; they were staring at the map. Jay saw her brown hands flash across his line of sight, heard his "gracias," and her "a la órden," and then he poured cream into the coffee, sipped it, hot, too strong. All of Medellín was in the wall-sized windows. Green mountains and new brick buildings. Jay liked it far more than Managua or Tegucigalpa, these banana cities half-destroyed in earthquakes, reeking of open sewers even in the rich neighborhoods, cities without centers or firm delineations.

Rafael ran his finger on a line north from Medellín to Turbo and told the story of his father and other landowners fighting to get the highway built in the 1950s, to connect Medellín to the ocean. That road was a conquest and took twenty years. Hell to build, it began in the mountains north of Medellín and then carved through jungle flatlands of Urabá. Without this strip of asphalt, Urabá would not even exist.

"So what's the strategy?" Jay said.

"Excuse me?"

"Your fax. You said there was a way to manage the guerrilla problem."

"Time for a break, friend. We are late."

*

"So?" Jay said. They were resting on a bench after their first set, the lights glowing over the orange clay tennis courts, this private club at the heart of the city, high fences all around to keep the others out.

"Maybe you don't need to know," Rafael said.

"I can forget things."

"So you *want* to know?"

"Yes."

"We do what Córdoba did." Rafael used the handle of his aluminum racket and drew the dip of the Gulf of Urabá, the thin neck of Panama, and then a line east along the Caribbean coast to the state of Córdoba, digging a dot for the city of Montería. He explained that Córdoba was like Texas but with hills and excellent pasture. The ranchers there got fed up with guerrillas kidnapping them and stealing their cattle, so they formed private armies. Colombia was not like Central America, where you called the army to protect your land from subversive groups.

"So we hire these private armies to protect our plantations?" Jay said.

"It's complicated—they came before the mayoral elections of 1987 and things went ugly."

"How so?"

"Imagine."

"I'm not imaginative. I'm a businessman."

"There was a massacre. Well, two. It scared the people, which was the point. But it backfired—the guerrillas recruited these scared people for their cause, and then we had the strikes. So it has to be done right. We exterminate the guerrillas down to the last man and woman. It was bloody in Córdoba, but now people are happy. The paramilitaries have built schools and allocated land for the campesinos. Beautiful projects, long overdue."

"That's our strategy?" Jay said.

"Let's play another set, and you think about it," Rafael said, spinning the bright yellow ball, bouncing it up and down with an angled racket. "We'll get stiff if we keep talking."

They played their second set with the map carved into the clay by the bench, and even though Jay was hitting cleanly, every time they switched between odd games, he would look at the map and avoid stepping on it.

"It's not so easy," Rafael said, when they rested after the second set. He scraped hash marks into the clay with his racket. He said they would have to target the guerrillas passing as civilians, men without uniforms, workers at the plantations, yes, the key was to weed them out. He drew out the letters EPL and put an X over them. He snuffed out the entire map, grinding the heel of his white tennis shoes.

*

Lawyers arrived from Cincinnati to go over the contracts and bills of sale with the Colombian lawyers. In a matter of weeks, the subsidiary, Banana Bolívar, was real, a silver-plated sign on the door on the tenth story of a modern brick office building in el Poblado. They laid carpet to dampen the noise and set up gray cubicles with tinted blue glass enclosed offices and meeting rooms along the edges, Rafael's office in a corner, not large, not ostentatious, but with a couch and a map and a glass desk. Beyond that a cafeteria with black modern tables and a view of the entire city, where women in white smocks served the coffee and refilled the cream and sugar. Every day at dawn, the salesmen met with private English tutors to work through textbooks and practice conversation. Midmorning, a shoeshine boy showed up and went office to office with his polish and brushes.

The office had a youthful spirit of competition. The export

salesmen were the busiest and the best paid. They tore off their blazers by midday and wore headsets, speaking English with the British, the French, the Germans, and Spanish with the Spaniards, as they sold fory-five-pound boxes of bananas. Jay liked to walk across the room and touch shoulders, backs, and to sit in the cafeteria and be especially kind to the women in white smocks who served him coffee, who recoiled at first when he handed them tips. "You are the heart of this company," he would tell them. He was handing cash to everyone—the notaries, the lawyers, the governor's office, union leaders, some of it official, some not, so the subsidiary would surge ahead.

Jay had gone to college with men who took helicopters from New Haven to New York for dinner or to fight with their parents who did not love them. They languished in Tuscany or the Hamptons or some private island in the Caribbean, supposedly on the verge of a breakthrough where the whole world would see them emerge from the shadows of their fathers. Too many of them had looked at Jay with pity because he had to start from nothing.

At night in his quiet suite at the Marriott, he closed his eyes and traveled with the bananas. He dug a ditch for a new drainage. He fired a worker for showing up late two days in a row. He stood before a guerrilla messenger who retrieved an envelope of money, and Jay said, "Your time is up." He said, "Comrades, let's join the free market." He climbed atop a white container and watched the Atlantic turn from green to blue and the waves shake the boxes, a sailor leaning on the railing for a cigarette, the sun hitting the containers, the bananas safe, his hair blowing in the wind. It was not his job to consider all the stages, but the more he understood how each problem got solved, the quicker he would find his angle within it.

12.

AT FIRST LIGHT, YENIFER swung open the wide metal doors of the bakery. She brewed coffee in the large steel percolator and drank her first cup, which dried out her eyes—she hadn't slept more than twenty minutes slumped over a plastic table. The bakery was a mess, the chairs tipped over, flour everywhere, and the bread was deformed, still raw on the inside while one batch looked like burned humps of earth.

Nanci lay in their bed. Yenifer had helped her clean her cuts, but one of her eyes was swollen shut, her cheek ballooned and purple, so she could not work. No one wanted to look at a girl in that condition. When Hugo arrived, they would have to throw her out.

The neighbors gradually emerged from their houses, wary, hanging wet laundry and smoking cigarettes. The banana buses passed, so full there were workers in the aisles. A woman raised her hand at Yenifer and mouthed a quiet "Buenos días," as if it were still too early to speak. Divots from bullets marked the bricks.

"Buenos días, Yeni," the butcher said, always a drop of dried blood on his nose or forehead. "Y Hugo?"

"He's running an errand. Is your meat going bad?"

"All of it, Yeni."

She served him a coffee and set a broken cookie on a plate, even though he hadn't ordered one. He sat down facing the street in the gray shadows of the bakery. A few other customers bought milk, looked at the bread, and asked if it was discounted. By noon, a number of men were sitting at the tables, drinking coffee and talking about an attack on the banana office in Carepa.

"Where's Hugo?" Nanci said when Yenifer passed through the bedroom to grab change for a customer.

Yenifer tilted her head toward la Sierra de Abibé. "He's up there. They probably kidnapped someone. Or he's with his whore in Carepa."

*

Late afternoon, the butcher built a fire in a lot beside his shop. When it had burned down to hot coals, he laid a rough grate across it, and upon that steaks and hamburgers and halved chickens and pork chops. He played loud music and announced with a megaphone that the meat was free. People dropped what they were doing and ate with their hands, children appeared out of nowhere, loading plates with meat. The smell of meat cooking traveled to the villages outside of Currulao. Those who arrived too late insulted the ones who had eaten two or three helpings, but the butcher opened a bottle of rum and poured little shots in plastic cups. The people bought beer from the bakery, and Yenifer contributed bread.

"I am not going to eat that meat," she said to Nanci. "I don't trust the butcher."

When it was dark, they started with the baking. Yenifer locked the doors with the chain and lit the candles she had bought earlier. Nanci helped her. With one eye she proved to be no clumsier than she was with two, but it was nice to have someone sweating beside her, kneading dough, cutting it, scraping out the mixer bowl.

"It never stops," Yenifer said. "You have to make it every night."

They were sitting at one of the plastic tables, Nanci's hair plastered to her head, her one eye blinking, her cuts black in the candlelight. The final batch of bread was in the oven.

"Do you want a beer?" Yenifer said. "It's not cold."

They drank in silence. Yenifer pulled out the final tray and shut off the oven, and she said they could share the bed. She was already hallucinating with the noises on the street, imagining Hugo knocking or being shot against the bricks of the bakery. There were rumors of selective killings in Apartadó, that the military had set up a checkpoint by the cathedral, that they were searching houses. She knew that Hugo had papers, ammunition, some grenades hidden behind the flour. She wondered if she should bury these things behind the bakery or ask a neighbor to store them. She tested the chains on the door. She blew out the candles and lay down beside Nanci on the hard mattress.

The box fan was motionless on the floor. Yenifer felt like a screw that had been turned too many times. She was spinning there, staring up at the ceiling, listening to Nanci breathe through her nose beside her, and Yenifer said, "If he's dead, I am not going to be the raving widow."

*

The next morning, the butcher stopped by again. Rumors moved fast. Likely it was he, weeks later, who would say that Yenifer had killed her husband, buried him deep in a banana field near the ocean. She packaged the butcher's bread, and right then the radio burst into static, the lights all coming on at once. A green and white police truck rolled up and parked right in the door. Five young patrolmen came inside to order coffee and eggs.

"Let me know if I can help," the butcher said, taking his breakfast across the street.

"Buenos días," one of the policemen said.

They sat with their rifles at an empty table and stared at the road, as if challenging anyone to question their presence in Currulao. They talked about nearby bridges being rebuilt so the banana trucks could pass, how they would have to patrol these bridges now, every night. The power went out again, but in a few minutes it was back on, and the policemen cheered. One of them stared at her as if to memorize her face. Another one asked Nanci how she got beaten up, but her answer was to disappear into the bedroom.

"Señora, we found something that's yours," said a short policeman with a square face and no chin. He stared at Yenifer's chest with disappointment. He reached out for her arm and she grabbed his elbow, but his hand was not something she could halt, as it pulled her away from the counter by the back of her neck and told her she was coming with them for questioning.

*

She rode in the front seat of the police truck. Sweat dripped down her neck and itched where he had grabbed her. She wanted to spit in their faces but her throat was dry. The truck swerved on the gravel, turning up the back roads and crossing through the heart of Finca la Estera, the sky upside down as one of the police pushed her under the dashboard. They took a decline onto a mud plain and crossed a creek at high speed, smashing through the water and up the embankment. They entered the gates to Embarcadero Zungo, just the empty loading docks and an open warehouse without shipments.

"Get out," said the policeman with no chin.

He climbed down from the truck and slashed a plastic bag with a razor. Hugo looked small. Knees and elbows. No clothes. The black hairs around his nipples stood out like they were electrified. In the background, workers marched across the fields. They were slashing at everything, stalks, leaves, weeds, stems, knocking it all down like hurricane creatures. She did not kneel. She twisted her ankle, turning away, and she held out both arms to stay upright.

"Llore, señora," said the policeman, nudging her toward the bag. "Llore."

The smell was of shit and decomposition. A policeman called her a cold whore with no feelings. A banana bus passed behind her, covering them in a veil of white dust. The workers looked out the windows at yet another body. Fuck the guerrillas, their eyes said. Fuck your husband who burned down our plantation.

"Not all men are good," the policeman said, "but a decent widow should cry for her dead husband."

*

That evening Yenifer sat on the bed for a while. She picked up one of Hugo's dirty T-shirts and tasted salt, fried plantains, and the perfume of another woman. She kept the collar in her mouth and sucked on it. She would not have to wash it. Her knuckles ached just thinking of his thick jeans and stained shirts.

"Estoy sola," she said. "Estoy bien."

She brushed her teeth with water in the bathroom because the toothpaste had been squeezed flat. She was not so old. Her eyes bloodshot but without wrinkles. A large mosquito bite on her forehead. Otherwise her skin was smooth and pale. Her hair had grown long. It looked like brown grass growing out of a stump.

She raised it into a ponytail, rubber-banded it, and saw her head get smaller. She found tweezers in a drawer and she plucked her eyebrows to nearly nothing, and then added a line of dark makeup. She was not fit for a magazine cover, but it was a face you could look at. She once told Hugo how she wished to return to school, first to get her secondary school certificate and later more. Maybe study agronomy. She could wear one of the white collared shirts and drive a pickup for Banana Bolívar. Orejas said they were beginning to hire women for the packing area and the office because they had good eyes.

"You're a grown woman," Hugo had said and kept saying, for not even the dead shut their mouths. "You won't fit in the desk. The children will throw pencils at your big head." He said all the flesh on her body had gone straight to her brain. It was genetic. Bad luck. He had chosen her as a wife when he should have hired her to run the bakery while he opened a second one.

*

"Hugo murió," she said to Orejas over the phone. It was noon. He was at Finca la Bella and promised to stop by after work. Nanci was serving coffee at one of the outer tables to four men who were laughing so loudly that Yenifer had to cover the phone so as not to seem at a party.

"When?" he said after a long pause in which she could hear his breathing, and then another phone ringing, as someone yelled in the background.

"They just told me."

"And his body?"

"I saw it. It was in pieces."

There was a pause while her voice floated in the mysterious

space of phone lines. She could see him looking at his workers packing bananas into boxes and sticking a finger in his mouth to pick food from his gums.

"Come stay with me," he said. "I'll help you sell the bakery. No reason to stay in Currulao."

"We're busy today," she said. "People have money again."

"Close it."

"I can't afford that."

She wavered for a second, his voice kindly telling her what was next in her life, as someone always had, that she would be targeted, that the guerrillas would not protect her. The phone call was expensive. A faint dial tone sounded after every minute, marking the cost. They both seemed to realize this, and so they said goodbye.

*

When night fell, she bathed herself, undoing the ponytail and wiping off her eyebrows in front of the mirror. Nanci entered the bedroom and stood behind her. It was different now. They were alone in the bakery. Orejas had stopped by and changed the locks on the doors. He had never loved Hugo, whose name he pretended not to know, calling him only "el panadero" or "tu panadero."

"The building belongs to you, Yeni," he said, "and it's a brick structure at the center of town. It's more than some people get in their entire lives."

He told her to get rid of anything related to the guerrillas. The police would be watching. She said that someone had already stopped by to get some papers, boots, some boxes of bullets mixed in with the sacks of flour, and a couple rifles she did not know existed, strapped to the bottom of the bed. She gave Orejas bread and some fruit to take to Apartadó where he had finally raised the roof on his house and was sleeping alone, fixing things at night. He said there was a young woman, not from la Picardía, but a decent one from Carepa, and he was in love with her. He turned back on his motorcycle and told her to be careful, to watch the town for these first days and see how the people treated her.

"Claro," she said. "I've always watched."

*

"I have a good hand for cutting hair," Nanci said.

"Did you check the locks?" Yenifer said.

"Yes."

"Front and back?"

"Yes."

"I made a bed on the floor," Yenifer said. "I don't want those rumors. If you want to go, it might be better for you. Everyone knew Hugo here. I'm no one."

"Are you going to sell it?" Nanci asked.

"Not yet."

"Do you want a haircut or not?"

"Fine," Yenifer said. "The scissors are dull."

Nanci brought in a plastic chair from the bakery. She buttoned one of Hugo's white dress shirts backward over Yenifer's chest to collect the hair. She flicked water from a cup onto her head, combing out the tangles, and then snipped the uneven tips. Yenifer looked ahead at the Eiffel Tower and wondered if it was time to take down these posters, find new ones that would not remind her of Hugo.

"How short do you want it?" Nanci said.

Yenifer shut her eyes to feel Nanci's fingers pulling, measuring, and though it was only in her hair, she felt the comb run the length of her body. She heard the pleasant clash of blades, the radio in the kitchen, she looked down from the observation deck at all of Paris, she would keep the posters, and said, "Whatever you think, mi amor. I want to look different, but not so much that people talk."

13.

As Orejas neared the barn, the mule quickened her pace, recognizing the smell of the pasture. He tied her to a stanchion, patted her neck, and saw in the daylight that it was a large cement house with almost twenty cows in the field, a long clothesline with a rainbow of clothes, a fenced-in chicken coop, a roof antenna for TV. They were rich.

"What are you looking for?" the father said, kneeling behind a cow with a bucket of milk. His wife, a tall, brown woman with dark curly hair, held a shovel against her bare shoulder, and Orejas saw it all, this square-faced colonizer from Medellín buying up cheap land and falling in love with his negrita.

Orejas noticed a line of sick plantains, the edges of the leaves black and mottled, struck by the moco plague. He said he was the manager at Finca la Bella, south of Turbo. He could get them a pesticide that would clean it all up. The oldest son trotted across the field with a calf slung over the saddle of a horse. Another son stepped out of the barn with a machete. The young woman Orejas had returned to see set down a bin of yucca mush she had been tossing into a pig pen and looked hard at him.

"We don't want your help," her father said.

*

Her name was Gloria. Their courtship was short. Orejas did not take her to church or out dancing at a cantina. He showed up at her father's farm on Sundays and worked. He fumigated the plantains with a pesticide stolen from the plantation and reorganized the field into shorter lines with better drainage. He ate with the family, large bowls of beef soup, potatoes, yucca, and plantains. In her father's eyes he made no sense.

"You're a worker," her father said, "so why get mixed up with these others?"

Gloria had the eyes of a daydreamer. She was quiet like him. She half-listened to the world around her, but when she spoke it was interesting. Crooked, small teeth crowded her mouth, and she was ashamed of them, never smiling, and he learned that the kids at school had made fun of her, called her Bocachico, and later she told him to never bring home that fish. When he said it was a beautiful mouth, she kissed him. She seemed to know his whole life, the fires he'd lit, his nights at la Picardía, his religious desire to be saved by her, as if she were the Marías of the church painters, the ones with the rainbow halos and baby Jesuses, but thank God she looked nothing like those Marías with their thin European noses and paper white skin. Gloria was tall like her mother, a head taller than Orejas. Careful, her look said. You can lose me easy.

*

They married at the farm rather than the church. His mother cried and wore her old wedding dress because it was the nicest dress she owned. His brothers bought him cloth diapers for the baby. Gloria was pregnant. Orejas screwed in hinges for a door and installed the final block of cement to complete the fourth wall of his house in Apartadó. He did all this in a stupor after twelve-hour

days at the banana plantation. On a night of a heavy rain in October, Gloria lay against him with a lagoon of sweat on her chest.
He was too exhausted to sleep. He listened to the water pound the
new roof, splattering in the open windows and dripping through
the edges of the door.

"What if you gave it up?" Gloria said.

He let her question float in the dark. She deserved more than
this house. She wanted actual land where she could grow things, a
farm by a river, beasts in pens, but he said they had to start small.
She did not want to be a banana worker's wife who waited at the
door all night for him to arrive drunk. Not him, he told her. He
was a manager. Same thing, she said. She wanted to work, too. Her
father would help, but they had to take risks. That was the only way.
Love was good, she said, but without money it was not enough.

14.

In February of 1991, EPL guerrillas signed a peace accord with the Colombian government. Jay spread a copy of *El Espectador* across Rafael's desk, a large photo of Bernardo Gutiérrez with his bushy mustache and long nose, Humberto de la Calle beside him, a piece of paper with the treaty. In the corner of the office, a small TV showed guerrillas lined up with a flea market assortment of shotguns, M-16s, grenades, and pistols, and each time a weapon was handed over, the government officials raised it up for the cameras and set it on a table.

"You don't look happy enough," Jay said, loosening his tie and setting it on the chair, looking at the map with the red blotches and thinking they would erase them or buy a fresh map, that the guerrilla camps would be overgrown with new bushes and grass, how the old caches with camouflage and weapons could be planted with things for people to eat, how these men who tore people from their beds at night would sleep normal hours in their own beds.

"See those red marks," Rafael said. "They leave a hole. Someone always arrives to fill it."

"The bishop is there," Jay said, pointing at the screen. He sipped from a glass of whiskey, no ice, and it made him a little sick, the way good news here could never just be good. There was always a shadow. "He's praying. Children are singing a song about peace."

"The bishop is a communist. He'll be dead in a year."

*

In the bathroom, Jay washed his face, dried it with a paper towel and sat in a stall and prayed for himself. He heard a toilet flushing. Someone was brushing their teeth at a sink, and Jay could feel each individual bristle against his own gums. He did not want to ask too much from God. God knew Rafael Restrepo's heart and would guide him in the right direction. Even in the bible there was violence, but in the end God sought harmony among all his believers. Jay heard a voice, just a whisper, maybe water in the pipes or air in the vents, the door whooshing open, a quick moan as a man urinated. But it might be God's voice, deep, easy, loving, telling Jay he was doing good.

*

Rafael found himself talking to his paintings or calling employees who were below him and telling them he would need them at the office tomorrow, a holiday. Wind rattled the loose glass door of the balcony and rain was falling diagonally. He walked around his living room to look at his art. He fixed his eyes on a Roberto Matta with a black background, like a runway with floating lines that might be birds or humans or satellites, everything spiraling around an axis of light. There was a balance in the chaos. He put a rare version of the Berlin Philharmonic playing Beethoven's Fifth Symphony on the turntable. It was something he could not have done when his wife was alive. She hated the Romantics. With her, they would be at her sister's house in Río Negro, eating steaks on the back patio and talking real estate, or at the movies, she loved the American comedies that were a torture for him. The phone rang at the start of the second movement.

"She'll live," Ernesto said.

"Thank God," Rafael said, lifting the handle of the record player to silence it.

What followed was a continuation of a conversation in Ernesto's office. Rafael imagined Graciela, an employee at the banana corporation, covered in bandages, receiving blood and fluids through her wrists, her mother crying beside her. Luis Alberto had hired a sicario to kill her because she had refused his love. Yesterday, she had been driving to see her parents in la Sabaneta when a sicario came up beside her on a motorcycle and shot her through the window. She wrenched the wheel to one side and ran him over, smashing into a pharmacy, right through the counter and into the shelves of pills.

"What's your next move?" Rafael asked.

"Her parents are on board. She'll sign what we give her and get a promotion. Do you know her? She must have some brains to have refused my son."

"We're on the phone, Ernesto."

"No one is listening. If they are, they'll regret it."

"And your Luis Alberto?"

"He goes away. Bogotá, or maybe Miami."

Everything could be cleaned up. Luis Alberto had an alibi; he was seen swimming laps at el Club Campestre on the Saturday afternoon when it happened. The woman's parents were Ecuadoran, middle class, the father a car salesman who owed money all over the city. The sicario, a poor kid from some comuna, could be silenced. The police already set a price to not pursue it.

Rafael thought about his own wife's body. A piece of plastic over it. One leg broken to the side—for some jewelry, some money, a trip to the cash machine. A paramedic taped her eyes shut because they were open. She looked fierce in the morgue and even in her coffin when they painted her face, her eyelids, and put her in a dark blue suit. "Don't let them praise me at my funeral," she had once said, knowing that Rafael was not religious or sentimental. "No one should pretend I was a saint."

"Miami," Rafael said. "Bogotá is too close."

"He's my blood," Ernesto said, "but I have to say, between us—I've raised an imbecile. He said she put horns in his head with some actor. Are our gringos happy?"

"The gringos are always happy."

Jay Harrison was at the Marriott with two other Americans who had flown in that morning for an early audit to show they would be watching everything. Ernesto didn't like the audit. He wanted Rafael to hear that nothing would change. He was bigger than the gringos, who only half-comprehended what they had gotten into. If the guerrillas or this poor woman Graciela could see him tonight, they would hang up their gloves.

Rafael heard Luz Marina in the kitchen, balling arepa dough for tomorrow's breakfast, and he said he had to sleep. Ernesto stayed silent for a minute, breathing into the receiver, like they were again kids on a beach in Cartagena, Ernesto wrestling him into the hot sand just to show he could win.

15.

THEY REARRANGED EVERYTHING in the bakery. They split the tables for an aisle to the counter, and they angled the counter outward to create space to cook in the back. They painted the walls a light ocean blue that made the room seem cooler than it was. Yenifer bought two cheap burners to heat up giant tamales wrapped in banana leaves and soup made from beef bones. She got rid of the merchandise whose margins were tiny, and bought batteries, razorblades, soap, aguardiente, rum, and candy, which she could sell for higher prices. They began to offer a cheap lunch with meat on Saturdays and Sundays. They baked more sweets, loading the display case with coconut cake and cookies with powdered sugar and homemade arequipe. They changed the brand of coffee to a slightly cheaper one that tasted the same. Yenifer bought flour and sugar in greater bulk. Nanci was still clumsy in the kitchen, she struggled to add and subtract the larger orders, but her face had healed, and certain customers came just to see her, to feel her hand on their shoulders and to hear her voice—"¿Qué más, vecino?"—as she served them.

The gossip varied. In one rumor, both women had killed the baker and were lesbians, and their passion made the sweets taste better. In another, the bakery was a front for the guerrillas who were using it as a weapons stash and Yenifer was selling Nanci to some of the comandantes, including Orejas, who frequented Pan y Más more than was normal, likely the lover of both women, and with this money Yenifer had improved the bakery. The "más" in "Pan y Más" meant sex. Yenifer provided Orejas with information on everyone who entered; she was always listening, just watch her little eyes moving in her big head with a new, flashy haircut every month.

No one said anything risky in the bakery or anywhere in those years. They stuck to safe topics like the quickest way to travel to a certain village, the best recipe for sancocho, and the weather—it was always hot, and the November rains were as bad as October's, bad enough to flood the new gringo plantations where they were hiring workers to redig the drainages.

Some called it a bonanza. A land grab. New investors. Men from Medellín roamed with bodyguards and disappeared after a day. The gringos moved fences in Carepa and at all their plantations, buying up the smaller planters.

The ocean-blue walls at the bakery made everyone suspicious. Some said the bread was sweeter, fresher, but one woman insisted it was stale and that she would no longer buy it. Crass men joked that all the bread tasted like pussy. Others complained they had to work harder to be able to feed their children the cookies and cakes they begged for. They accused Yenifer of inflating the prices, even when she had lowered them. Some were proud to have a nice bakery in such a rundown village like Currulao, but others said she was wasting her time, that everything would fail when the war heated up again.

The truth was less exciting. Yenifer paid la vacuna to the FARC guerrillas who had stepped right into the empty space of the old EPL guerrillas, and Currulao became a battleground. She knew nothing would change. Orejas, one of the dissidents, appeared with his wrinkled eyes and large ears sticking out from a red baseball cap, as if he were stepping out of a wall in the bakery. Not there and suddenly at her counter. She would not hear his motorcycle or his feet on the cement. Just his breathing, leaning in to eye the cookies, waiting for her to notice him or not waiting at all, taking his time and absorbing the whole place, carrying out a quick but thorough inventory of what it was worth.

"Me asustaste." Yenifer would kiss his cheek and pinch one of his ears.

There was a new formality to how Orejas spoke, like he was always in a meeting with the other managers at Banana Bolívar. He sought words that belonged in a dictionary and not in a bakery, but she liked the words. She liked seeing him look up at the ceiling and pretend he was someone else, that he could read a dictionary or write out a report on the health of his bananas, when in reality he brought her documents, and after hours, when the metal curtain was down between them and Currulao's ears, she read aloud to him. It only took once. She read in a quiet voice, Nanci in the back room. Orejas would have killed her if she said anything funny about what was going on. He could read a little. He recognized certain words that were everywhere, and he knew the language of bananas. Yenifer believed he was smart, even when the teacher would joke that he was a deaf-mute. His intelligence did not belong in a classroom but in the physical world, among the lines, as he always said, that connected everything, the shipping routes, the lines of workers asking for shifts and the other lines of workers claiming they were sick from the fumigations. All of it needed someone to solve daily problems, large and small, to keep the peace among workers, and unlike the managers from Medellín, he had started at the bottom and knew every rung.

"And Gloria?" she said.

"Sick," he said. "The baby is due and she can barely move."

"You can stop living in shame."

"I've stopped."

"You're still a dog."

Yenifer knew he visited la Picardía, but he told her he did not visit the rooms, he just drank in the company of the women.

"Why lie to me?" she said.

Orejas helped her sell Hugo's two cows to his father-in-law. He offered to open a bank account at la Caja Agraria in Apartadó, saying it was not safe to hide money in the bedroom wall, but she took what little money was left after her expenses, and she shoved it into an unused drain of the bakery. Orejas told her not to trust anyone in Currulao and lent her a .38 caliber revolver and told her to keep it under her bed. He drove her out to his father-in-law's dairy in Carepa and tried to demonstrate with it. He was a terrible shot. He made her shoot at a post and her ears rang for days. "It's not a big gun," he said, "but it will kill. People say Hugo promised the bakery to another woman in Carepa and she's with an esperanzado. She walks around talking about you."

"The esperanzados are all dying," she said.

"Not all of them. They're forming their own group."

"Por favor," she said. "Everyone wants what I have."

*

One morning, the butcher sat at a table alone, sipped his coffee and nibbled on a coconut bun. A fumigation plane passing over had accidentally sprayed the whole town, and the air stunk. Everyone was spitting and rubbing their eyes. Yenifer directed a fan to blow air out the door. A heavy shipment of bananas was moving past them on trucks to the canal. The sun was angling light across the street with long shadows, the heat still bearable.

"I heard you're selling the bakery," the butcher said.

Nanci was sweeping around him and knocked a plastic chair onto its side.

"Tranquila, niña," the butcher said, accustomed to her clumsiness.

Yenifer had been making a list of what she needed to buy from the market in Apartadó—*plátano, carne de res, huevos, papa, zapallo.* Nanci walked around the counter and touched her waist in the same way Hugo used to touch her waist.

"Who said that?" Yenifer said.

The butcher drank down his last bit of coffee and stood up to pay her. "Let me know when you have a price. I'd rather negotiate with you than your father-in-law."

*

Yenifer's mother used to say if you were poor, someone always poisoned the well right as you were about to get ahead. You fell sick. You were bound to a bed. All your work was burned to the skies in a few days. You had to be ready to lose it.

*

The butcher came every morning with little spots of dried blood on his forehead and earlobes and on his forearms, sometimes in a clean shirt, but most days it was a blood-stained T-shirt that had been washed for years by his poor wife and it had turned a yellowish brown that was hard to look at. He ordered the same thing: a coffee with a coconut bun. He smoked one cigarette, ashing onto the floor. He looked around at the dimensions of the bakery as if he already owned it, as if he had already painted the walls white and moved the counter back to where it used to be and turned the bedroom into storage. He paid with precise change and wished her a good day.

No one knew where his money came from. His meat was not flavorful or cheap, and if a customer was short a few pesos, he never gave credit. He drove a truck with a large cargo trailer, and there were rumors that he only bought the old and sick cattle from the auctions and ranchers north of town. Gradually, people noticed that the land they stood on was all his. Yenifer saw his influence like a slow flood, every few months it spread from one house to the next, until the whole block in the center of town was painted with his name for the mayoral election.

Gradually, too, the bakery began to have problems. The roof leaked one night, ruined a day's worth of bread, and stained her poster of the Swiss valley, coloring the sky yellow and the turquoise lake brown. The water pressure was gone, and they would have to carry buckets in from the spigot in the back alley. They lost electricity with more frequency than the rest of the town, almost always at night when it was time to do the baking. The bricks themselves seemed to bleed with moisture when it rained, and the cement floor was cracking corner to corner. Certain customers, loyal to the butcher or in debt to him, stopped buying bread.

One night, as the women were baking, Nanci said, "You could talk to the guerrillas."

"He's in with them," Yenifer said, "or he wouldn't run for mayor."

"He's going to win."

The bakery was hot as usual, the outer brick holding the sun's heat from the day, worse in January and February, the drought months, and the inner brick radiating with the oven's heat. Yenifer slept in her underwear with the box fan inches from her face, no sheet on her body, and every so often she would walk to the bathroom and toss water on her face and neck. There was no remnant of Hugo in the bedroom. They had cleaned it, stuffed his clothes into sacks and given them to a poor farmer, about his size, who sometimes bought cookies. They did not miss him, but it was impractical to be without him. Tonight, she would have liked his strong arms around her waist, his belief in the world, even if he was a minor player in it.

No one said his name. No one told a single story about him. Occasionally, a friend from Córdoba would stop by, and she would say he was dead, but the friends did not seem sad. With Hugo the butcher would have left her alone. The two men would have sat at a table with beer and in a roundabout way it would have been decided that if the butcher wanted to buy the bakery and consolidate his land, he would have to kill Hugo. Hugo had five brothers, so there would be repercussions. She imagined herself picking up the .38 caliber revolver and walking up the street to knock on the butcher's door. Maybe his wife would open it. Yenifer would ask to speak to him and put the barrel of the gun to his neck and pull the trigger. No woman had ever killed a man in this town, though in Turbo a woman stabbed her husband in his sleep for having relations with her sister and managed to sink his body in the harbor. But Yenifer knew she was not protected, and la vacuna she paid the guerrillas only protected her from them.

"I could kill him," Nanci said in the dark, as if hearing her thoughts. "Or even better, I know someone who would do it for us. It would cost a little."

Yenifer pretended to sleep, letting Nanci's words float there in the dark like colorful swirls of gasoline in water. It was unnerving to have Nanci get into her head like this. Too much time together doing the same things day after day, hearing her on the toilet at dawn, her coughing, yes, she always coughed in the morning, and she spooned an unbearable amount of sugar into her coffee. Nanci chewed bread on one side of her mouth; her teeth hurt, she said, having lost the one loose tooth that first night. She was terrible at washing clothes. She never wrung them out sufficiently so everything was rigid and itchy with soap. But she also stroked Yenifer's hair affectionately throughout the day, she spoke to her softly, she did all the baking one night when Yenifer was sick, and in the end they were used to each other. Being alone was no treat. Both women knew this. Just the sound of her own breathing in the bakery at night, the sound of the world outside and no one to share it with, would drive her crazy or into the arms of a man who would hurt her.

"You are not going to kill the butcher," Yenifer said.

16.

THE SUN SET OVER DOWNTOWN Cincinnati in a smoky, winter light. Jay's mind was floating there above traffic on the superhighway bypassing the city from the airport. The taxi took I-71 north and dropped him at his apartment building near the Kenwood Towne Center in the suburbs. He froze in the mirror of the elevator. It was not easy to be home. It was a fake world here, the buildings hollow, the streets empty. He ate a frozen pizza alone at the kitchen counter, looked at his notes for tomorrow, and made a phone call.

"Come over," she said. "The conditions are good."

She was a neighbor, married, a Baptist pastor with a rigid but pretty face, prematurely gray hair, and muscular arms, whose all-loving presence at the altar contrasted with her morbidity in bed.

"Pray for me," he said in the bedroom of her apartment that was white and clean as a hospital and decorated with black and white photographs of the woods in winter. No alcohol in the cupboards. No stereo. "I'm nervous about my presentation."

She clamped handcuffs to his wrists, attached the two keys to a chain on her neck, and laid him across the bed in the best position.

"It's hard to fail in America," she said, stuffing a gag into his mouth.

His mind flew elsewhere, going over the slides for his presentation, answering hypothetical questions in the dark, his boss,

Craig Washburn, staring at him without expression. At the end of it Craig Washburn said, "Can I talk to you?" and there was a restructuring and Jay was out. Or Craig Washburn demoted him back to Central America. Told him he was too new with too much riding on Colombia. As the pastor stormed him with her body, he was in Guatemala City, laughing at the jokes of a colonel with gold teeth, an anorexic wife who barely spoke and who told him that Americans were the most loving people she had ever met, and Rafael Restrepo entered the room, too, wearing a white tennis sweater with a cigar in his teeth, an orange flag to mark new land. Jay could barely breathe through the gag. He felt like it was raining in the room. A deluge of water rushing through the bed and through her body as her saliva dripped onto his face and chest.

"I don't do prayers for you," the pastor said later. "Touch me. I'm solid as a rock. Are you here or are you still on some plane?"

"Medellín," he said. "It takes me a minute."

"Look at me, honey. Forget it."

"What?"

"Don't think I'm deaf to the silence because that's actually when I hear you. You all pray for money. It irks me. Do you think God answers?"

"Sometimes."

*

The next morning Jay talked to a room of executives who saw him as expendable. He showed them slides of the new packing areas, banana barges, and tubs with green bananas, but what they really wanted to see was a production line that looked like the Andes, soaring away from its axis and becoming new additions to their houses, new cabins on Lake Erie, new wives, better offices.

No one asked him about the conditions of the workers, the dissidents in ditches with no shoes, or their nervous accountant in Medellín who flew north every two weeks to pay la vacuna to some comandante in Apartadó. Jay's wrists were raw from the night before, hair-thin cuts on his wrists, a sore throat, the pastor using him, and he was more with her now than before. That was his life. Six hours behind, living on delay. Someone's watch ticked audibly. Jay's sciatic nerve fired with electric pain and his feet were sweating. He wiped his eyes with his handkerchief and felt the words leaping from his mouth and hitting the men in their suits.

He stood with a map printed all over his face and suit, camouflaged into the landscape, pointing at the areas for further development, what was still jungle, what was failing under its Colombian management, and then he switched slides and showed the shipping routes with times. Galveston 9 days. Long Beach 13 days. New York 10 days. Rotterdam 19 days. Depending on weather in the Atlantic and Caribbean. He switched slides again. "These are our plantations. Don't look now, but they are outyielding their equivalents in Ecuador and Guatemala. This is prosperity. La prosperidad ya viene, caballeros."

"Good Spanish," Craig Washburn said. "What's the friendly union?"

"Sintrainagro," Jay said. "Sin-trai-nagro."

"How friendly?"

"Very."

Jay said Banana Bolívar paid its workers higher salaries than the other plantations, gave them new boots, clothes, and machetes every six months. A small but key detail. He discussed the new security program and how that had been integrated into their hiring practice and training. Their eyes glazed over with boredom. A man stood up to stretch his back. Knowledge was boring.

"Thank you, Jay," Craig Washburn said.

It was time to sit. When he did, Ed Kennedy, VP of finance, leaned into him with cough drop breath and said, "I bet you've met some hot señoritas."

Jay wished to tell him there were ships weaving across the globe, packed to the brim with bananas, and that what least interested him was women with no other option, but he said, "The whole country is a brothel."

Jay received a substantial bonus during this early bonanza. He bought tailored suits and silk ties. None of this was necessary for his survival. He did not waste money on a new Mercedes. He did not buy a brownstone house in the hilly Mount Adams neighborhood in Cincinnati. He was not interested in symbolic wealth objects that only depreciated in value. He extended his lease at the apartment complex with heated parking. He celebrated by eating at TGI Friday's at the mall, and then walked its central corridors to the melody of "Rudolph the Red-Nosed Reindeer," found himself staring at happy teenagers holding hands. Outdoors he took a walk through the parking lots that were so vast there must be some greater purpose to their creation.

"It went well," he said on the phone.

Just silence on the line, and she said, "Wrong number."

*

"When are you going to marry, Jay?" Craig Washburn asked. He was the one who hired Jay based on a strange CV that involved stints in life insurance and a Mexican oil company. Craig was a Yalie, too, and assumed this meant telepathy and smooth collaboration between men. He was an irritating person to play tennis with. His style was math-based, mechanical, playing the court as it was offered. When he read the newspaper, he folded it back exactly into its original form. He loved to hear his own name, and Jay was aware of this.

"Craig, when I was seven years old I walked in on my parents," Jay said. "I saw my father's testicles swinging, etcetera. I never want to do that to a kid."

"Your father was doing his duty."

"Maybe," Jay said. "They got divorced."

"I'm in charge of risk in Colombia, not you. Are we hiring guerrillas on our plantations? Do we know?"

"It's not like the people have guerrilla souls, Craig. They have run Urabá for twenty years. Big families. Small towns. Everyone knows everyone."

"We can't know, OK? It's not your job to give them peace. It's not your country. Not yours. Not mine. That is not our country."

"It's not."

17.

ON A MONDAY MORNING, the butcher did not come for his coffee. Yenifer hoped he had died in his sleep or was dragged out by a paramilitary death squad. Then, no one came. Neighbors who usually bought bread or drank coffee before work must have taken some other route. Just sun on the roof. Just the radio. By the afternoon, all the bread was stacked in the display window, untouched. The coffee steamed in the urn. Nanci had swept, and they ate their soup at the counter.

"I'll take bread to Apartadó and sell it on the street," Nanci said.

"Fine."

They packed a basket for her, and by seven o'clock that night, Nanci returned with it empty. That night they decided not to bake. They opened early with what was left of the day-old bread, the coffee brewed, the refrigerator humming. No one entered. Neighbors looked at the bakery and everything in it like a bomb was ticking. When the children ran out from school, they stood on the street and pointed at the two women and elbowed each other.

Yenifer saw Orejas's motorcycle on its stand but did not see him until he was standing at the counter, having been watching her for God knew how long. Yenifer kissed his cheek and served him a day-old cookie with a coffee.

"Do you have a second to talk?" she said.

He looked around at the neighbors who were watching him. He leaned across the counter and reached into one of the open cigarette packs by the cash register and shook one into his hand and lit it. He stared at the flame on his lighter for too long.

"I want you to kill the butcher," Yenifer said.

"He's with us."

Orejas closed his eyes as he inhaled, the smoke flowing out around his face and over his ears. He said the butcher's brother was a comandante in Necoclí. No one could touch him. Orejas looked at her from somewhere beyond the weekly stops, like they were still awake as children in his mother's house, eating raw eggs they had stolen from the neighbor's coop. He seemed to have grown bigger since the peace accord. He wore a white Polo with the company symbol and his arms and neck were all veiny muscle.

Nanci stood in the doorway of the bedroom. He checked her out, his eyes stopping on the crease between her breasts and her knees and then her ankles, and he said, "You want my advice?"

"What if we closed the bakery and opened a cantina?" Nanci said. "The workers don't want bread. They want beer. We sell this oven and buy a decent stereo. I can get the men to come, and I know music."

"How does this help me?" Yenifer said and saw her life transformed again. A bakery was a decent business, a quiet one. A cantina would bring the worst kind of men trying to drink for free or threatening her in other ways. Hugo always said there was more money in a cantina, but eventually you ended up with blood on your hands.

"Later you sell to the butcher," Nanci said. "It's what he would do with the bakery, but he doesn't know it yet. Yes or no?"

"Maybe," Orejas said, turning his back to them and gazing across the street at the butcher shop to see if some sign would

indicate the level of his power. He reached over the counter for another cigarette and left a puddle of sweat on the display case. Nanci
pointed where the tables would go, a small dance floor where he
was standing. She told him that if they got one plantation to come,
then another, they would have steady clientele. Play the right salsa,
sad stuff, romantic songs. There were women in this town. There
was love in Currulao. Her brothers worked at Finca la Estera, and
they could bring people. Yenifer wanted to grab her by the collar
of the shirt and throw her onto the street.

"Yes or no?" Nanci said.

"Let's talk numbers," Orejas said.

"It's not your decision," Yenifer said, and her voice sounded
crazy, like a bird flying in through the door. "It's my business."

                                    *

The butcher maintained his boycott, but it was not enough
against the banana workers, who heard the romantic salsa the way
they used to smell the bread, and once a man was sitting and calling for his friends, the room was full. The plastic crates of beer
were stacked to the ceiling where the oven had been. The refrigerator emptied and filled. Yenifer kept the .38 pistol under the counter and went over the numbers with Orejas to see if she was going
to get screwed. Nanci allowed men to pinch and poke at her legs
and ass but never her upper body. Occasionally she received a kiss
on the hand, an arm grab, a wedding proposal, and men fought
over her when none of them had her. She called it a pig pen, and
that stuck. Pan y Más was painted over and the cantina became el
Chiquero.

Yenifer realized a building could change identities as easily as
a man. Kids buying cookies and soap became men on their knees

begging for one last beer on credit, a man with his head cracked open on the edge of a table, another man sending his son to retrieve his gun at the house, another man sending his teenage daughter for his, and then everyone else clearing out. On the street one man dead, shot, the other man running off to get on a motorcycle and then drive off the road and into the river. Two dead. Customers. Both without identification because when you ran out of money, Yenifer took your ID and put it in her pocket, and you could have it back when you paid. The dead did not pay.

Orejas was present on Friday and Saturday nights, the money nights, in and out of the cantina without anyone knowing where he was, sometimes alone on a chair in the far corner. If a fight broke out, he would appear in the middle, making sure no one was murdered inside the cantina. Not all nights were bad. Sometimes everyone was in a high mood, an accordionist would stop by and Orejas would sing the songs he knew, which were many. On Sundays he took his cut which was large enough that Yenifer and Nanci cursed him as he sped away on his motorcycle.

Without Orejas, the men would have burned down the cantina and kidnapped Nanci, who now lived with a cousin in Apartadó. Orejas made it clear from the start that two women could not live together. The workers burned through their paydays. They slept beneath the tables and awoke, and Nanci served them. Their wives showed up occasionally and smashed empty bottles on the cement. A wife demanded milk for her babies. Nanci's sister showed up and screamed, a lump in her belly, her husband knocking her down with one punch while the other men held him back and told him, "Tranquilo," and this might repeat every Saturday for eternity while you filled your pockets with their money.

18.

OREJAS REALIZED THAT THERE WAS no revolution. He hauled sacks of cement and a crate of bricks to his mother's house. He paid his brothers to construct the second story on her house. They would paint the house gold and put bars on the windows. That was the revolution. One man improving his house. One man giving his mother, a woman who had begged in plazas, eaten wormy fish, and somehow found a way to buy shoes for her kids, what she had longed for. Rafael Restrepo had asked him to rob a couple trucks from the gringos, "Don't say a word to anyone about it," and this too was the revolution. "I'm going to get mad at you on the phone," Don Rafael said, "but it's all show."

Everyone, top to bottom, was taking their cut. There was always somebody above you, and with the extra money Orejas bought a delivery truck with a seven-meter container on the back of it. Everything stunk because it had belonged to a salt-fish seller from Montería. Orejas and Gloria scrubbed it with bleach and vinegar, but it didn't matter. On his days off at Finca la Bella, he picked up freight at the port, the slaughterhouse, from wholesalers in Montería, and he began driving a circuit around Urabá. He delivered anything—TVs, fertilizer, billiard tables, flour, beer, cassette tapes, clothes, plantains—and he moved people who were escaping the violence. He drank beer in little stores. He chatted with farmers and pastors and other guerrillas. Every bush, ditch, and power line held a distinct memory for him. People would ask him to deliver to a small village, and he would say, "Conozco la ruta," and in his mind's eye he would see the rutted fork in the road, the spit of dirt where the women washed clothes in the river, a chapel wall speckled from bullets, a woman with beautiful feet standing next to a scale where farmers weighed their plantains. Then gradually these objects changed color. The fork in the road had three men standing at it, "Qui hubo?" The spit of dirt caught corpses killed upriver in Pueblo Bello. The chapel was full of people hiding, and the signs of businesses changed. The paramilitaries were quiet about it. They moved at night when Orejas was off the road. They crept westward into Urabá from Córdoba. He heard that the banana planters were paying for their protection, that the guerrillas were already in trouble.

"I'll build you a third story someday," he said to his mother, but instead he put down money for a plot of land outside Necoclí. Gloria wanted a farm.

His mother raised her hand to slap him but cupped one of his large ears in her palm, shaking her head at the reality of her son calling the shots in a neighborhood where kids used to rob her on the way home.

"I didn't ask for the second story," she said. "What can I do with the third?"

"Rent it out," he said.

19.

DURING THE WEEK, Nanci turned the cantina into a one-chair barbershop for local women, learning to braid Black women's hair
and offering lower prices than the other shop in town. Yenifer took
classes at el SENA in Apartadó. No one threw a pencil at her head.
She bought the books to finish her high school degree, passed the
test, and within six months she was enrolled in an accounting program. It was not agronomy. She would not study the life of plants
or fruit trees or flowers. That was not her destiny. She would study
the life of numbers. She could hold a lot of them in her head while
her classmates wrote them down. The teacher made her write them
down, too. You could not blurt answers all day. So she made notes
and learned a new kind of patience when the numbers were wrong,
and even with her talent for it, the numbers were often wrong as
the problems got harder. So hard, the teacher wrote them on the
board and they were wrong and so he had to look at the book, and
even then he did not get to the right numbers. He said the world
was easier than the book. The book was designed to give you the
hardest problems, whereas in the world you were mostly counting
bananas and weighing banana boxes and measuring the volume
of bananas within a certain area adjacent to other areas. Or you
calculated distances and times, and there were solid equations for
all that. She learned to take a sum of money and whittle away at it

with the cost of business, and to doctor this number for the inevitable bribes and extortions every business in Urabá suffered, so that the number kept its dignity but also lost it at the same time. She sat at a desk and sweated over her papers and tapped the rubber keys of a calculator.

This is what I am, she thought. This is me with a taste of something. It might have been happiness, but she never would have uttered this word, not even a whisper to herself in the mirror at night, in the bedroom that stunk of old beer and vomit and urine. To have uttered such a word in those months would be suicidal.

After class, she took a crowded bus back to Currulao. The muddy streets and the rundown cantina depressed her, and she suspected that Nanci was earning money on the side by sleeping with some of the men. Under Yenifer's bed, in the bathroom, and in a compartment along the wall were boxes of camouflage, boots, belts, rope, old and new machetes, bullets, and arms coming in from the port in Turbo, being distributed all along the road to the ocean. Orejas had organized it, and in exchange she did not have to pay a weekly vacuna to the guerrillas.

One Friday night Orejas did not show up. Someone said he had been called into el monte for a confrontation with paramilitaries in Córdoba. That same night, Nanci did not return from the hair salon where she had begun work in Apartadó.

That night the men's teeth were lit up by the dance lights. Their fingernails, too, a neon red in the dim light. Yenifer shoved the .38 into the back of her jeans under her shirt. The butcher came to drink. He wore clean clothes, but he stank of blood and viscera and ground up bone. He drank alone and steadily. When it came time for him to go home and pay her, as the rising sun crept above the sierra, he told Yenifer to sit down, and she stood, and he told her to sit, and she stood, and then he pounded his fist on the table, and he put a revolver to her cheek and cocked it, and told her to either sit or try to draw her gun from her underwear. She sat with her hands on the table. From his back pocket, he unfolded a piece of paper, the title for her lot. The ground they were on. This rectangular slab of concrete. The four thick walls of brick and the shitty zinc roof that leaked. The back alley where men pissed all over the wall and vomited. It had been notarized in Apartadó. It carried the seal of the municipality and the state of Antioquia. The title carried the butcher's name, Vicente Navárro Rondón, and the date of his purchase which was July 13, 1991.

"Basta de pendejadas," he said, and folded the paper back up. She could go to the municipal office and they would have a copy on file. She was his employee, he was not dumb—she could run a business—but things were going to change. He wanted to bring in a couple women for the back room, the men were sick of seeking out the few clandestine women in town.

She felt his knee touching hers. The .38 dug into the gap of her butt. The butcher unfolded his title for her land and folded it again so she could see once more his name in the greenish light and his greenish teeth still lit up sharp by the same light, and the title that looked more official than the one Orejas was storing for her at his house. The butcher ordered a beer and told her to clean up and change clothes. She should find somewhere to live. No one wanted to look at her anymore, and Orejas was no one, possibly a snitch for the planters who loved him, and he was not going to live long. "What about you?" he said. "Are you a snitch?" One thing he hated was women who fucked each other and thought they had brains. That was what offended him the most, he said. Women with big heads and noisy mouths. Women with money in their pockets. He was liable to change his mind, he said, to cut her into pieces the way the police had cut Hugo into pieces, and toss her into el Río Zungo. He said all of this in a roundabout way while she served him another beer and he stood up and closed the door. She was alone with him. The gun in her jeans was dripping sweat. Then he was describing how she and Nanci had sex and how it made him sick to think about it. Only a man could cure them, or he himself could do it. She interrupted him and said she believed in God, so he could kill her now.

"Is it necessary?" he said.

A week later, she lost everything.

*

It was that easy to banish someone from a place like Currulao. The lack of loyalty from the neighbors, the women whom she had given credit for years at the bakery, the men to whom she had sold discounted booze and forgiven debts, none of them would even look at her when she packed her things into Orejas's box truck. She rolled up the posters of the water-stained Swiss landscape and the Eiffel Tower, and the bare walls of the room looked ugly, a deadend with no window to anything. The butcher came out to shake Orejas's hand, believing there was some camaraderie between two men before a fallen woman, and Orejas kept his hand in his pocket. "Usted se abre, pero ya," Orejas said, and he trembled as he drove because he did not have a plan. He drove her to Policarpa, a claustrophobic neighborhood with narrow streets, the odor of shit in the open sewers, and he installed her in the little apartment he had built next to his house, just a single room with a little mattress.

"You eat with us," he said. "Gloria loves to cook."

Years later, she would wonder at her coldness that morning, her lack of gratitude. She should have kissed his cheeks. It was as if he were somehow part of the other men who always wanted to do you favors that were only for them. You did not realize it at the time. You thought this one is the exception, the good one, but then down the line he threw it in your face somehow. He came for payment. Or it was just her pride—she felt like Nanci, sleeping in someone else's house for free, eating their food, asking permission to use the shampoo in the back patio shower. She hung only the poster of Swiss mountains, but it did little to brighten the room. Gloria, who had grown thick after their second baby, gave her extra clothes to wear. "It's all temporary," Gloria said. "Orejas is going to get you a job at Finca la Bella, and once we build the farm in Necoclí, you can have all this."

"I am sick of bananas," Yenifer said.

"What else is there?" Gloria said. "Once the boys are in school, I'll probably work there, too."

That first night, Yenifer sat under the single light bulb hanging above her small room and calculated on paper what she had lost. She jotted down her weekly profit from the cantina, from Nanci's little salon, and multiplied this by four weeks per month, twelve months in the year. She would do this the rest of her life. Hay que mantener cuentas, she thought, putting each note into a little bucket which was the first of many buckets, her own caletas that seemed meaningless at that moment, notes for herself that would become the most valuable thing she owned. Like this she began to live a parallel existence where she slept in this stuffy room and yet continued to live on the main street of Currulao, raising her curtain to mop the cantina and pay Orejas, and in that life, she saw the butcher before he saw himself that night. She uncapped a bottle of beer to serve it over his shoulder, she put the pistol to his ear and squeezed.

20.

In Cincinnati, Jay sat on his desk and gazed at a tiny brown strip of the Ohio River below. He paced the halls, using the skywalks to go to other buildings, to stand there in the sun, faking it, yes, faking all the time that he was busy, on his way to an urgent phone call with Colombia. Others were doing it—sitting at length in the bathroom stalls, extending lunches, hoping for delayed flights, lingering in the hallways to talk football. They were, Jay realized, trying to stand between units of time. He was used to it, having grown up in Michigan, where his father was an economics professor, and gone to high school in Madrid, where his mother worked as an art historian and taught at la Universidad Complutense. Back and forth to a tiny green room in a flat off la Gran Vía, back to the drafty attic room in Ohio that smelled like a freezer. Spanish to English. Olive oil to margarine.

In Medellín, Jay and Rafael played tennis at dawn or under the lights at el Club Campestre, a private club in the heart of the city. Rafael played a finesse style suited for the clay courts, while Jay played a hard-court power game, trying to kill the ball, hit it flat, hit corners and lines so the chalk would jump. Not much business talk here. They sat between sets and sweated and drank water. Rafael mentioned the girlfriend of a dead neighbor was selling the apartment on the thirteenth floor of his building for a price so low it was a gift.

The place was too large for a bachelor. Six bedrooms. A kitchen with white granite counters and diamond light fixtures over the buffet. A jungle theme in a dining room with leopard-print wallpaper. The bedrooms were all green, leafy wallpaper with mirrors, bathrooms with gold faucets and pink marble.

"This is a narco apartment," Jay said, raising his arms to touch the gold flake ceiling. "So garish it's almost beautiful."

"Paint the walls white," Rafael said. "I know a man who can sell you furniture."

Jay found ways to extend his time in Medellín. There were always problems to solve at Banana Bolívar. As production rose, trucks disappeared, a fumigation plane shot down, a worker drowned in a canal, new contracts with Saudi Arabia, a new policy to not hire the dissidents from the Maoist guerrillas because they were being cleansed from the zone.

Jay liked being seen with Rafael at el Club Campestre. Men would ask him for favors at the pool or on the footpath to the tennis courts. Women smiled at him across the clubhouse bar. Servants bowed nearly to the floor in his presence. In the entrance were black and white photos of Rafael's parents and grandparents. When they were alone and naked in the steam room, Rafael told him about his wife's murder. Jay stared at him, trying to find the right word or phrase, "Lo lamento, hermano," and grabbed his elegant hand and hoisted him onto his feet for an embrace, erotic at a distance but it was brotherly, simple, the right thing to do. Rafael cried as they emerged into the chilled air of the locker room. Men looked up from their own dicks and thighs to examine Rafael, the old aristocratic dick, a slight bend in the shaft, and the gringo dick, absurdly circumcised. Was he Jewish? Rafael once asked. He was a Baptist but not such a good one.

In the morning, Jay would stop by Rafael's apartment, drink

coffee and ride to the office with him in an SUV with a driver and bodyguard up front, the two of them in the back watching the city through thick tinted windows, the pedestrians peering at them and wondering who they were. Jay loved watching the gray-dark city slide past. In the evenings, he would drink scotch in Rafael's living room on what seemed like an old American electric chair with no straps, a wood frame with a red leather cushion, while Rafael lay on a chaise lounge, and they listened to bleak music, Brahms, Mahler, Bartók, and stared at the paintings on the walls. Rafael told Jay about his plantation nightmare. He was thrust into the thick of a banana shipment going out after dark. There was a riot. Workers ran bare-chested through rows of bananas. There was blood on their faces. A dead manager hanged decapitated from a cable. One of the workers was carrying a giant radio, a boombox, and there was loud vallenato.

"Maybe in another life," Jay said, "you were one of those men."

Rafael stared at Jay, as he sometimes did, like he was the greatest fool on earth, there were no other lives, only this one. In these moments, Jay would look at his watch and wish to leave. Say no to dinner with Rafael and his maid. The space between them was too great, and he would be better off upstairs in the crawl space the narco had designed for hiding from the police.

Later, Jay stripped naked in the center of his apartment, set the pieces of his suit on a chair, and gazed at the painting he had bought with Rafael in Bogotá, an Obregón barracuda and his other acquisition, a cheaper one, a drawing of a body by Luis Caballero Holguín, whom Rafael referred to as the Colombian Mapplethorpe, bodies cropped at the neck, men tangled up together with erect penises in some act of violence. He wondered at the objects around him, the baskets woven from corn husk from el Chocó, the balled-up sock in the bathroom, the empty house where he seemed to be drifting, a life constructed quite suddenly. He closed his eyes in bed and saw himself swimming in the blue Caribbean water, a distant white sand beach, perhaps Las Islas Rosario in Cartagena, a fisherman in a white and red boat tossing nets, a little boy straddling a log and paddling himself out to sea, and Jay was that boy, in Cartagena, in Valladolid watching his mother give a lecture, in Michigan watching a yellow leaf fall from an oak tree onto his father's porch, in the steam room with Rafael, and for what?

21.

OREJAS GOT YENIFER A JOB as a receptionist at Finca la Bella, and months later she was promoted to shipment coordinator for Banana Bolívar. She walked every morning to catch the plantation bus with the workers and began to see the bananas in a different light. They were not just fragile bunches in blue bags, ripped down by the winds—they were volume and number, they were counted containers stacked on barges, with a mass of men involved at every level to care for them and take advantage of their journey. Her managers realized she could do anything. She tapped numbers on a calculator with a roll of paper to print receipts. She made purchases for the larger plantations. She managed payrolls and handed out paychecks. At each plantation was a ledger, and she filled the columns with neat print, not unlike the ledger Hugo had kept at the bakery and had to show to the guerrillas. She locked the ledger in the drawer of a desk, or the manager would take it from her at the end of the day and store it in the gringo office. Orejas helped her purchase a cheap lot in El Bosque, a new squatter neighborhood near Carepa, where she paid a cousin to construct a one-bedroom house. She painted the walls white. She hung in the same arrangement from the bakery her posters of the Eiffel Tower and the Swiss landscape, wrinkly from the humidity, torn at the edges, as if they were still her windows into a better world.

It pleased her to position her chair before a blue lake in the green bowl of a mountain and sip coffee after a long day, no Nanci, no Orejas, her door locked against the rumble of the neighborhood, the screams of women beaten by their husbands, the motorcycles, the constant violence that belonged in the night and had always belonged in the night. She might not even be able to sleep without it. Orejas rented out his house in Apartadó and moved to his farm in Necoclí. He was rising during the boom. She was rising. She would look back and remember that year, 1992, as a good one for her. She bought a used motorcycle and named it Miki and no longer had to endure the long rides on the buses that were often stopped at guerrilla barricades.

On Sundays she visited Nanci, and they walked around Plaza Martina. It was hot, and Yenifer made them cross to the shady side of the street. Nanci wore black jeans and a tight purple tank top whose pink seams were zigzagged along her ribs. She walked straight, her hips still. Sweat dripped off her eyes to her jaw. She said she had been visiting the guerrilla camps for extra money, un chicharrón, even if it was dirty, a hassle to get up there. Though it bothered Yenifer to see her friend's face smothered in makeup, her legs exposed in tiny skirts, she did not blame her for seizing the moment and making her money. The boom would end. Yenifer had helped her to open a bank account and deposit just enough to keep it open. The prostitutes were flush and some were buying property in Medellín to escape the drudgery of el Copelón. In a year, Nanci said she would quit and open a hair salon right there on Plaza Martina.

"Avoid the camps for awhile," Yenifer whispered, looking around to see two kids eating ice cream, checking out Nanci. "I know things."

She steered Nanci to an empty part of the plaza, a few meters from the ice cream parlor but concealed by a market hut, a little triangle of shade. "Where I am," Yenifer said, "the gringos are moving things. Lots of new men from Córdoba stop by the plantations and they're arming the esperanzados. That's what I see. All those roads are changing."

"I know things, too," Nanci said. "My clients talk. God, do they talk."

It was hard to imagine change in Plaza Martina, the guerrillas in every business, including the ice cream parlor with its cool pink walls and white counter with a fan blowing their hair above their heads. The clerk served Nanci an extra scoop of mango ice cream, "Te lo convido," he said, and licked his upper lip.

"Qué asco," Yenifer said when they were back out at the plaza, the ice cream dripping down their wrists in the sun. "You look tired, niña."

"And you? I just started resting."

They walked once around the plaza, but it was too hot in the sun. They turned onto a narrow street where every so often the metal doors and brick walls were spray-painted with the words FARC. The street curved at a right angle up along the riverbank. Clotheslines extended off the roofs with bright skirts and blouses, a few painted faces in the open windows, and at la Picardía, Yenifer kissed Nanci's cheek and said, "See you next week?"

"You need a haircut," Nanci said, picking at the hair over Yenifer's ears and pinching the frayed ends.

"Not today."

"Are you scared of the girls? Don't be, Yeni. Most are decent. A little crazy, but no crazier than us."

Rather than cross the dance floor, they took a dark side hallway, then climbed a set of stairs, past the little shared rooms, all the way to the roof where shiny, tight clothes were hanging. A green plastic roof covered part of it, and a tall Black woman with hair the color of orange juice was in a hammock, opening one eye, asleep.

"Yeni, this is Petra. She's famous, but I bet you've never heard of her. Now sit. I'll get my scissors."

Yenifer had come to warn her friend of the great change coming, but now Nanci was clipping a dirty white sheet over her neck, spraying water onto her head, the fine-toothed comb stuck in her knots, though it felt good to feel each strand of hair tugged at the roots, straightened, wetted, then sliced by squeaking scissors.

"You should dye it blonde," Petra said, sitting up to swat a fly from her leg. "I have some good stuff left over downstairs."

"Bring it," Nanci said.

"I did not say yes," Yenifer said. "It's my head."

"Don't be tedious."

There was no mirror to see what was happening. Nanci was cutting too much hair, and Yenifer could feel it landing on her shoulders, everything in layers and clipped to one side, "a modern cut," Nanci kept saying, and Yenifer closed her eyes to keep from crying, letting her do it because it was nice to be touched. Nanci rubbed her neck every so often and even kissed her cheek. She did not laugh. No one liked a laughing stylist. Yenifer's head felt lighter, and then the dye squeezed like toothpaste onto her scalp. They put her out in the sun to sweat. Nanci smoked a cigarette with Petra, gossiping at lightning speed about people Yenifer did not know. The minutes passed, the dye taking hold. Then Nanci brought up two pails of water and washed it out, combing her, squeezing bunches of hair with a towel.

"The new Yeni," Nanci said, handing her a mirror.

"I look desperate."

"I would say pretty. You're just not used to it yet. Let's paint your eyes a little."

"Do it!" Petra shouted.

"A little," Yenifer said.

Petra was standing there and they were turning her into a whore. No, they were helping her, Nanci's nails combing and combing, wiping bits of hair from her ears, then rubbing gel into it, standing away and smiling. "I don't even recognize you."

"Is she new here?" Petra said.

"Don't be stupid," Nanci said. "She works in the bananas."

*

No one made fun of her haircut. You could not go wrong with blonde hair, the managers said. Only Orejas said he preferred the natural color.

One day in October, when certain roads got washed away in the rain, a shipment disappeared completely. It was not registered at the embarcadero. A few weeks later, the serial numbers of the container reappeared in the log as shipped to Germany. She looked back through old ledgers and saw patterns of payments or oddly reduced shipments, bribes to the port officials and street gangs, numbers that added up or did not add up at all, as if there were a black hole at the center of every plantation ledger. Alone in the office, she wrote down the numbers, at first as a way to prove her own innocence, knowing, as everyone knew, she would be the first to be fired when the owners started asking questions, and these numbers might be valuable.

"Everyone is taking a bite," she said to Nanci. It was a Sunday. They sat under the green plastic canopy on the roof of la Picardía, a deep puddle at the center. Rain fell in waves, splattering onto their legs, so they took off their shoes. She had brought her own dye and Nanci was combing it in thickly and clipping her hair above her head. "At every level. Even Orejas. I'm not sure how much he takes for himself."

"And you?" Nanci said.

"I am honest."

"The idiot!"

"Well, I am writing it all down. I use bits of paper, or I even roll up my sleeve and write it on my arm." At home she transferred these numbers to notebooks and buried them in buckets in her back patio. Her caletas.

Nanci wiped her hands on a towel and came around to look at Yenifer square in the face. "Why risk it?"

"Someone will want to know these things."

"I know who."

"Who?"

"The ones who are coming to take all this away. Los paracos."

Nanci wiped some of the dye off her forehead with a rag. She walked over to the stairway leading inside and made sure they were alone. "I'll tell you what I hear. You write it down and put it in one of the caletas. If it serves you, you pay me for it."

Yenifer regretted saying what she was doing aloud, even if she trusted Nanci who saw profit in it. She held the mirror to her face and noticed that the upper part of her cheek was twitching. She touched her hair, and Nanci swatted her hand away.

"How many caletas?"

"There's so much money," Yenifer said. "You would not believe it by looking at the workers or this shit town. Or me. Or you. Look at our clothes. But if you add up the numbers, you realize we are in paradise. Someone is getting rich."

"Whose paradise?" Petra appeared on the roof. She laughed irritatingly after she spoke, lit a cigarette and sat down with them.

Nanci squeezed Yeni's head, rinsing dye to change the subject.

"Does she cut your hair, too?" Yenifer said.

"Everyone's," Petra said. "She's not cheap."

"There's money in the dirt," Nanci said, "and in the sky. The weather, right? And all these assholes in Medellín we've never met. They keep it all."

"Do I look ugly?" Petra said. "The men were just walking away from me last night."

"I'll cut it," Nanci said. "You need a trim."

"I'm leaving," Yenifer said, drying her head with the towel and checking the new color in the mirror, more of a dark gold than the yellow of last time.

"We have a deal then," Nanci said.

"What deal?" Petra said. "Doesn't she pay you?"

"Don't be a snitch," Nanci said. "Yeni is my sister."

22.

SOMETIMES THE GRINGO came up behind her while Graciela was in her cubicle, his hand landing right between her shoulder blades, touching the hair on the back of her neck. It sent a surge of electricity down her spine. The tang of lime in her mouth. She would glance over her shoulder, sucking in her lower lip beneath her upper teeth, and it was a relief to see this tall man with mismatched gold and silver earrings, who had been nothing but kind, sitting in on meetings where he was not exactly welcome.

She sat in the bathroom stall to avoid Ernesto Echevarría, who every Monday morning at seven met with Rafael Restrepo in the corner office. She touched the scars on her chest and shoulder. Three years had passed since her "accident," since the Echevarría lawyers stood on both sides of her hospital bed, the plastic tubes in her nose and arms, and convinced her to sign the settlement. She still felt gunshots break through her body and the motorcyclist beneath the front wheel, and then the car hammering into a solid wall, the seatbelt like wires around her chest and waist.

"Hijueputa," she said to an imagined Luis Alberto when she sat in the bathroom stall, when her nerve-damaged shoulder ached from the cold. "Maricón de mierda."

Ernesto Echevarría never failed to say hello. He stood at the edge of her cubicle, his red hair bright and curly under the lights.

He looked at the scar tissue on her shoulder and at the center of her chest, and he seemed satisfied. No one knew that her phone rang occasionally at night. It was a mint-green phone that matched the walls of the apartment she had purchased thanks to the settlement. It was supposed to simulate a garden with three bedrooms and a view of a creek, plants everywhere that gave her air to breathe, a smell of potting soil and the herbs she planted on the balcony.

When she answered, it was silent. She could hear his breathing. His onion sweat dripping on her back while he fucked her before the "accident." She knew Luis Alberto was in Bogotá managing money, or he was in Miami taking a business seminar, and after her "Aló, aló?" she listened for a second and hung up. She measured distance. She knew where each of the Echevarrías lived in Medellín. She drove by their buildings and supermarkets and hated them all.

She could have moved away, taken an easier job in Manizales or Pereira. In the stall, she heard distant gunfire, that strange tide of static in her ears that came every single day when she was tired and sometimes even pulsed in her nerve-damaged shoulder. When she rode in taxis, she sat in the center seat, turning her head for the motorcycles that were everywhere. She saw blood on certain men, and her therapist prescribed a light dose of valium so she could sleep and calm herself on bad days. He said there was no blood on anyone. She let him have this lie. She wore fruit-patterned neck scarves, but by midafternoon, when men undid their ties, she too slipped the knot and left her neck exposed, the scar-darkened skin an embankment on a beige field. Rafael Restrepo appreciated her and like the gringo was flirtatious, but never crossed the line. She found him arrogant and lost in his own old world of Restrepos and Uribes and Londoños who never really heard what anyone said.

She felt picked up by some wind and dropped into a day-by-day routine she found pleasantly boring. She lived a narrow life and saw only a few friends and always during the day. For the long nights, she purchased a special reading pillow to prop herself up in bed where she ate her meals and watched TV or just sat in silence to relive the day. She would stand up in the middle of the night and walk room to room in her nightgown, the floor cold on her feet, the windows open to the night air.

One afternoon, the gringo asked her to dinner at a new steak restaurant, and she said no—"I'm busy."

"Still busy?" he asked a week later.

"Yes, very busy."

Salespeople sat in their cubicles and punched numbers into their phones and everyone they reached wanted more bananas. It was 1992. Production was rising. A year of bonuses and new offices across the hall. Graciela stood from her chair and met others in the hallway to discuss raises. Rafael and the other executives sat in long, celebratory meetings, the gringo jumping over a chair, spilling red wine down his chest, a secretary sent out to buy him a new shirt. Graciela went to the bathroom stall, and even if they had done nothing to her lately, she insulted the Echevarrías in whispers and avoided the party.

One morning, she received a call from a Spanish buyer who said there was a storm on the horizon. He was forced to cancel a large order.

"What's coming?" she said.

"Quotas," he said. "The European Union is fucking us."

"When?"

"Find a new job, Graciela. There's nothing we can do unless the gringos intervene. It's going to hurt."

SURPLUS
1993

23.

JUST LIKE THAT RAFAEL was standing in front of the planters in the aquarium, the only difference being that Jay was here, his long legs crossed, a newspaper in his lap, the giant headline—"The Banana Wars"—with a photo of the Colombian president waving his fist at Europe. There was no strike. The plantations were thriving, the cables intact and the workers calm. The unions did not know what was coming. The managers on the ground did not know. But everyone in this room was staring at the maps on the wall, staring at the newspaper, the memos from Bogotá, and just up the road was a massive surplus of unsold and unsellable bananas, layoffs, and, as always for the small fish, bankruptcy. In Rafael's mind it was simple—Europe had failed the world. They couldn't compete with the Latin American fruit industry and put draconian trade quotes on imports, cutting them in half. The age of quotas had been over. Now, with the slash of a pen and a raising of hands in a conference room in Belgium, they were back, and they had no idea they were killers. Rafael's heart beat unevenly, and he pushed on a little blister pack of tranquilizers in his pocket, trying to ease one out. He saw ships circling the Atlantic with containers of bananas that no one could buy. He saw Spanish shoppers looking for the Colombian stickers, the perfect yellow arc and unblemished skin of a cavendish grown on his plantations, and in England some wealthy bureaucrat with the black beating heart of the empire in his chest, importing from his own plantations in Angola or in Kenya, because that's all it was, a scam, no reparation for the ex-colonies, no, just them buying from themselves, a short-term, anti-future, anti-progress policy.

"How does Europe fill the void?" Jay asked.

"Impossible," Rafael said. "They import stubby, tasteless shit from Jamaica and Africa for double the price."

Jay stood up as if to leave, his tie loose on his neck, his eyes pink. We'll talk later, his eyes said. Where was the gravitas of the gringo? Rafael knew he had been on the phone all morning with Cincinnati, a shock that they did not control Europe. Not even Bill Clinton could save them. This is how we feel all the time, Rafael wanted to say, but would never say because everything in his brain was off limits to Jay. He had to present total calm.

"It won't last," Ernesto said, reaching for Jay to make him sit for the remainder of the meeting, but Jay was not beholden to the king of the Colombian banana empire. He shoved papers into his briefcase and walked out.

It was like waiting for a hurricane, Rafael thought, as the men gathered their things and left him and Ernesto alone. Just a gentle breeze today. A few leaves spiraling down. The birds still chirping. The Medellín soccer team was leading its division. Tepid sun in the great glass of the aquarium. The office was bustling with daily work. The bodyguards of the planters waited below in the entrance of the building, smoked cigarettes, and opened the doors of SUVs for their bosses. The swimming pool would be clean and blue at el Club Campestre, surrounded with widows in bikinis, the daughters of the great oligarchs, some trying to catch his eye—until tomorrow, when the rumors would abound that Rafael Restrepo was again in a hole. The bankers would avoid his greeting in the locker room. He would sit alone naked in the steam room.

"The gringo looks scared," Ernesto said, "like he might lose his job."

"He won't."

"You don't see how bad this is."

"I see it. I might even buy some land."

"Don't buy land, Rafa. It's too soon."

Rafael approached the glass wall because just the idea of Banana Bolívar ceasing to exist might give him a heart attack. Not a bad way to go. His children would survive on the trust. They had land to sell, a small life insurance policy. Only his maid would be out on the street. Poor Luz Marina. He leaned into the glass, and he tapped with one finger, as if the world were the real aquarium and this room were outside of it, and if he broke the glass, the room would flood with water and he would drown.

*

In the narco apartment, Jay lay alone in his bed, a gothic, iron monstrosity he had bought at a furniture store in Bogotá and shipped across the mountains. It was a banana bed. The iron bent out like leaves. He almost cut himself getting into it. Two bars looped across it like cables for stems. The sort of bed his pastor would love. He turned on a reading lamp that burned too hot and looked at the numbers that would never unify him. The plagues were under control. The weather that year was flawless. Their only hope was natural disasters in Central America and Ecuador.

Jay closed his eyes and saw the world crashing down. He put on a sweater, turned on the light, and began pacing his apartment. He paused for a moment before the blue, fierce barracuda and waited for answers. He could sell it. He averted his gaze from the

tangled-up bodies of the Caballero drawing. That one should be
the first to go. He sat on the long balcony, looking northward to
the bananas he had never seen. Once the surplus was in full swing,
when the ships stopped coming, they would order the workers to
chop down all the plants and grind them into fertilizer. Rafael said
the guerrillas would hide in those fields, tying up their hostages and
burying their money. Rafael had screamed at his maid that night,
asking her what the hell she was cooking that smelled so horrible.
It was food for herself, Jay thought, some country stew with organ
meat. Rafael looked like a crazed child. He was holding a bottle of
scotch by the neck and his maid crouched over her knees afraid of
him. Later, Rafael apologized. He told Jay it was going to be ugly
for a few weeks, but then they would have a conversation.

*

They laid off half the Medellín office at Banana Bolívar and
two-thirds of the office in Urabá. They closed entire plantations.
They sat down before the large map in Rafael's office and wiped
their fingers across green stretches of banana, all to be eradicated.
Rafael made phone calls and they fired managers, accountants, re-
ceptionists, drivers, loaders, mechanics, and hundreds of workers.
The numbers were blood on paper. They looked like people's lives
with no backup. No one needed to say they were all but recruiting
for the guerrillas.

"They want to sell us this," Rafael said, touching a wasted spot
on the map, looking at the door to be sure it was closed.

Jay sat with his feet high on the desk. No tie. It was a time of
no ties. His black shoes were slightly scuffed, as the boy who used
to visit the office every day to shine shoes for the executives had
also been asked not to come.

"We can't afford it," Jay said.

"You and I," Rafael said. "Not the company."

Jay pretended to breathe like a normal man. He looked over his shoulder into the empty office. It was five in the afternoon, well before when employees were usually expected to go home. Rafael said it was simple. They would buy land from bankrupt planters. Not just any land. They would choose lots near Apartadó, land that might be zoned for housing someday, and land up near the coast in Turbo. They would fire all the employees at these plantations and clear the fields of bananas. They could bring in cattle to graze. The price of beef was stable. But more importantly, they would rent out much of this land to certain parties in Medellín who needed a clean place to deposit money. "We have a liquidity problem but for them it's the opposite." He said Orejas, the manager at Finca la Bella, would be involved. He had contacts with the guerrillas, and so even when things got really hot, they would be allowed to operate. The guerrillas had non-aggression agreements with certain parties in Medellín.

Jay felt a burning sensation in his throat, like he should make it all explicit the way one never did here, just lift it into the air of the room. He stood up and stretched his legs. He stared out the window at a city constructed largely from such business transactions. All this narco money just floating around like dust. He saw it in the red brick and the new glass being shoved into the holes of the buildings. Cranes everywhere. New taxi companies. The first line of the subway almost complete. A construction boom at all times. The pretty landscaping. The overpasses. It was in the ice cream and parmesan cheese. So much money to be cleaned. Plantations like giant washing machines.

"I might lose my job in a week," Jay said.

"This is your job."

It was his destiny, Jay thought.

"How much do you want to know?" Rafael said. "Not every-thing, because no one ever means that."

"I certainly don't want to meet these people," Jay said.

*

Jay sat alone in a pew at church and watched his lover sermon-ize about the holiness of lepers in the Bible. He found it disturb-ing, as did others, who were there to hear about Jesus and transcen-dence. No one in the congregation looked like a leper. They were all white except for a Mexican family. Watches gleamed on wrists. New bright autumnal sweaters and smiles for everyone.

Jay found her beautiful. She had permed her gray hair that was positioned in two thick bushels above her shoulders, like she was carrying a giant hair package to a temple somewhere in Egypt or Syria. She was wearing a sleeveless dress of purple and pink and yellow strands that exhibited her muscular arms. Her voice rang clear in the microphone and there was such a beauty to clarity, Jay thought.

Jay mouthed the liturgy but did not speak. He did not like liturgies. He did not like God either, he realized, but there he was. He held the program in his lap and swallowed saliva that was de-sire, the hardwood pressing his back and legs until his hamstrings were numb. God forgave him. Just like that. God told Jay there was land and business and dispossession. At the final hymn, he stood and right before the first note from the organ, he realized he was a good man.

*

The next day Jay stood before a reduced group of executives in Cincinnati and talked about measures taken to cut costs, to access other non-European markets, but it was not going well. Asia had its own subpar bananas from India. He projected a map of Urabá and showed what plantations had shut down.

"What are the guerrillas up to?" Craig Washburn asked.

"Everything," Jay said. "We have a highly active guerrilla."

On the outside, Jay was confident. He said the guerrillas were still killing the ex-guerrillas, the esperanzados, who had formed their own armed group called Comandos Populares. The unions had split. No one had a choice. You were loyal to one group or another. On the inside, Jay imagined Rafael flying up to Montería in a little Cessna and landing on an airstrip outside the city, riding in an SUV across el Río Sinú and going to meet the head of the paramilitaries, a man the planters and then the people were calling the Messiah. Probably beef cows out there. Probably teenagers in camouflage training. Jay owned cattle, too, and land. Did Craig Washburn suspect this? No, the ruddy-faced executives at this table were not crazy enough to wonder what Jay was doing. At any moment, they would fire him. He would fax his resume to a hundred companies. Wrap a new blue tie around his neck. He was a budget actor at some dinner club in the suburbs. It amazed him the way the executives nodded their heads and understood only the surface. No one's son was beheaded in a field, no one's daughter kidnapped to go sleep with a comandante. No one felt the Escobar car bombs vibrate through the pavement and break windows. No one saw the streets flooded with poor people crying and praying when Escobar was murdered by the police a few months ago. No one had smelled Ernesto Echevarría's sour breath in the stream room. And what do I know? Jay thought.

"Can you give us a minute?" Craig Washburn said.

Jay walked up the long hallway to the bathroom and vomited in one of the stalls. Maybe some bad chicken from the night before. He washed his face in the sink. He went back to his office and called Rafael who said he had completed the purchase for three plantations in Urabá, if Jay could wire the money for his portion, or travel soon and deliver cash. Cash? Jay thought. Rafael said the paramilitaries in Córdoba would join the Commandos Populares in the zone. Now was the time to go. The unions were weak, the leaders ousted by angry workers. The guerrillas could not extort because no one had money. So they were robbing the woman selling empanadas on the street corner or the guy with a truck selling bricks. They were not popular. There was a vacuum of power in Medellín with the cartel fallen. A good moment, he said, and Jay wondered if it was the planters who killed Escobar.

"When are you coming?" Rafael said.

Jay sat atop his desk and stared at the green line of the Ohio River, Kentucky there, Cincinnati here, and all the little streets like tunnels in a beehive, and thought it was true—he could no longer stand in between things.

24.

OREJAS WOKE IN THE dark to realize he was alive still. He touched the vein on Gloria's neck and felt her pulse. She was smiling in her sleep, her arms extended above her chest and her hands rubbing together as if to apply lotion. He slipped out of the mosquito netting around their bed and walked across the tilted cement floor. Everything on his farm stood at a slant—the cows, the plantains, the fences, and the pot of water he set on the stove to boil. He breathed in the sour, swampy air of the bedroom, smelling his work clothes across the room.

He carried a machete into the field beside the farmhouse, watching for snakes in the wet, shin-high grass. The chickens were up, marching at him, and he kicked at the rooster to leave him alone.

"Mamá will feed you," he said.

He counted the heads of his cows—three white, the one bull black and skinny, old, barely able to do his duty—and checked on one that would calve any day. Would he see it? He checked the fencing around the pigs and circled the house, as he did every morning, touching the cement blocks and the windows covered in green mesh, the plastic tank that collected rainwater off the roof. A gray cat crawled out of the plantains. He caressed her head and let her rub against his legs. She had splintered claws and a mound of trapped pus on her forehead. He listened to the high creek clicking against its banks below, the neighbor calling in his cows. He waited for the footsteps of his compañeros ascending in the dark with covered faces, and he would say, "I am Orejas," and they would execute him.

"Bury me right here," he had said to Gloria one night, pointing to the corner of the pasture, and she told him to stop. A relative of hers had joined the paramilitaries in Córdoba, and she wanted him there. The guerrillas had no future in Urabá.

He drank his coffee standing by the stove. He looked in at his youngest boy Nórton in his crib, a cloth diaper pinned to his waist, the sheet tossed off his body. Even asleep, he seemed too curious, a kid who spent the day talking to the trees and staring at the texture of the soil, satisfied to look wherever you set him. Francisco, his older son, a serious, friendly kid, was fast asleep on a little cot by the door. Gloria sat up in bed, pulled on a T-shirt, and asked where he was scheduled to go.

"Finca la Bella," he said.

They had a shipment and no manager. If he was not home by dark, she should go to her uncle's in Necoclí, tell the neighbor to watch the cows. If it looked bad, she should drive the box truck to Montería and wait at a friend's hotel.

"I know," she said.

He pushed his motorcycle down the hill and started it on the flat road. The surplus was not a physical thing he could see in the dark, but once he was on the ocean road he would feel it—workers begging for a day's labor at bus stops, cows grazing where bananas had grown. Necoclí was swarming with the skeletal crews of laborers rushing to work. His single headlight drilled through the gray light. He breathed the exhaust of the buses and the trucks, weaving through them when the road straightened. As he neared Turbo, he veered onto a flat dirt road that forked before dead-ending at Finca la Bella. Rain had fallen. The road was carved up with puddles, the canal high on its banks, pulsing in the light.

Look who's the manager now, Orejas would have said to his father, awaiting the scolding because Orejas had fired more workers in the past few months than he had ever hired.

He passed through the gates, shut off the motorcycle, and covered the seat with a piece of cardboard so the sun wouldn't destroy it. All the flying insects and butterflies were dead from the spraying. He heard a hum that was the plants growing. Everything erupted at once with the grind of the pulley against its cable, the smash of a machete into a stem. The workers knew what to do. They did not ask him what was next. Orejas paid the night watchman and unlocked the office. Someone hit the tap for the tubs—first a pitter-patter and then a swish as the big metal tubs filled up with cold water.

He barked at two men to grab new carving knives. The conveyor belt spat out the folded, empty boxes. The first stems got sliced into bunches and were tossed into cooling tubs. The workers' hands struck fast with the blades, the stickers, the plastic lining the boxes. Orejas spoke on the phone with Rafael Restrepo whose voice ricocheted through his head every day with questions and invaded his sleep, as if they were talking all the time. Rafael said exporters from the United States had increased their order, but they should not put any stickers on the bananas or label the crate. All this was normal until he said, "Call me when the shipment's out."

Orejas spotted a flawed banana in a bunch, and one of the cutters heard his mind before Orejas even spoke and sliced it off and tossed it over the conveyer belt and into the bright green pile of bolejas. Later, kids would show up with a wagon and collect them to sell in the villages.

Orejas entered the cafeteria that used to be the house of Mr. Morris, the gringo who cleared jungle for the plantation twenty years ago, but now its walls were removed, the books burned, the furniture stolen, just a tarred roof with rough wooden tables where Orejas sat facing the new packing area, his eyes magnetized by the stems sliding along the cables. He drank his second coffee of the day. It amazed him how the problems they solved repeated themselves, and he remembered how at times, when he had been one of them, the grunts, the boxers and cutters and fumigators, the speed of it all would almost break him. The high stack of banana boxes running out. A truck waiting in the night. Mr. Morris's brutal capataz screaming at him to be more careful, to somehow see the blemishes under a low wattage light bulb above the tubs and cutting boards. Could he have gone a different route? If he hadn't joined the guerrillas, he'd be a lowly worker with no name. If he had disarmed when they gave him the chance, he'd be dead. All that fire. They could burn Finca la Bella a thousand times, and it would outlast him.

*

Yenifer unzipped a pouch of money to count into envelopes with the workers' names on them. Orejas noticed her foot was drawing shapes on the cement floor and that she stared too long at the tip of her pen. Her straightened blonde hair was darkened with sweat on her pink forehead. The face of education, he thought, and he wanted to have a daughter like her, but better, one who would not be risking her life on some banana plantation during a surplus but sitting in a bank in Medellín. Whenever he mentioned the butcher, apologizing for not protecting her, she would look high over his shoulder and tell him to stop living in that time.

"Are you sick?" Orejas said.

"What do you mean?" Yenifer said.

"Your foot."

"I saw a body," she said and told him about Don Jairo, the manager at Finca los Bongos, hanged from a cable with no boots on his feet. She herself had paid the vacuna to the guerrillas a week ago, so she didn't know what it was about. The capataz had tried to head her off so she would not see it. She tripped over a root and hurt her knee that was now swollen around the joint.

"I can barely count," she said.

"Do you want coffee?" he said. "Or a soda?"

"Coffee, please."

Orejas put his arm around Yenifer's shoulder, felt her hold her breath as if he stunk or should not touch her at all, and he kept his hand there anyway and told her to take the day off, go home once she finished the payroll, and she said, "I wish I hadn't seen it."

In a minute, he set down a little plastic cup of coffee for her, and said, "I'll be back soon. I want to see where they're cutting in field seven."

"Orejas," she said.

"What, mi amor?"

"They're going to kill you."

"I know."

*

Yenifer watched him sharpen his machete with a rod and follow the main cable under a plastic green canopy into the bananas. She loved him still. She imagined him appearing behind a lazy worker and cursing his mother. Orejas used to have some fantasy, despite all the rumors that were always true in some way or another, that his compañeros were loyal to him and that the quality of his work protected him from the planters. So he just continued like nothing was happening. He had done the worst thing you could do—he betrayed everyone, and it didn't matter whether he was actually giving names to the guerrillas or hiring paramilitary workers for Rafael Restrepo. Gossip made everything true.

The phone rang, and she picked it up.

"Orejas, por favor," said Wilián, a manager from Finca Paraíso.

"He's in the field."

"How far are you in the shipment?"

"Barely halfway."

"Tell them to rush. You won't make it."

"And you?"

"Don't be out tonight, Yeni. One of my drivers spotted a guerrilla encampment up the road from you. Let me know if I can send any help over there."

When she hung up, she pressed on her swollen knee and wished there were ice. She had seen other bodies, but Don Jairo's could have been hers. She had helped Jairo alter numbers on a shipment, a fifty-fifty share, and she didn't know if he was dead for this or something else. She opened the drawers of Orejas's desk. Nothing unusual here, but when she looked closer she saw a list of container numbers and instructions that pertained to some business with Medellín. Maybe Orejas did not even see it. There were things he was not saying. She lifted her shirt and wrote a few numbers onto her stomach. She saw the space between them widening, like a river swelling up after days of rain, and she was waving to him from the other bank. Her hands itched from the pesticides she never touched. She felt sweat running down her thighs and the chair soaked beneath her.

"Disculpe," a voice said, and Big Fernando, the capataz, leaned in through the door. "Orejas?"

"Field seven," she said. "What's the problem?"

"A truck is stuck by the loading dock. We need the tractor."

*

In field seven, Orejas smoked a cigarette in the shade and checked the sick roots of a young row of plants. It was two in the afternoon, hot. His sons would be back from school by now, Gloria taking her siesta with them, their cows grazing, the pigs fed, the plantains growing, and maybe her brother had stopped by with the new radio. Gloria would heat up soup for him and make coffee. She would feed leftovers to the chickens. She would work on the hole for the new bathroom. A military helicopter passed over field four, circled once, and headed toward the port in Turbo.

"Don Orejas," a worker said, arriving on la garrucha, hooked to a pulley on the cable, his red shirt black with dirt and sweat. "They need you."

"I'm going."

"Do you want the garrucha, jefe?"

"No, gracias."

Orejas walked from field seven into field three and saw the place where his father had once hung him from a cable over the river on his fifteenth birthday. You are alone, was the lesson. No wife or friend can save you from what they will do. Or maybe there was no lesson at all.

*

Orejas sent Yenifer home once they got the truck out of the mud. She told him about the guerrilla encampment, and he said,

"Nada que hacer. The shipment has to go." But he rushed the cutters and men in the boxing room when the sun set, and they knew why. Then he sat at his desk and handed out pay. The fieldworkers were filthy whereas the ones who had stood in the packing area since dawn were cleaner, their eyes bloodshot from staring. There was a bonus for all. No one reacted much to the extra bills in the envelopes. The illiterates signed their names as Xs, and he despised them, as he was among their kind.

"Come drink with us," Big Fernando said. "We'll be at el Feoucho's in el Copelón."

"I'm going home," Orejas said. "I have a cow that's about to calve. Maybe tomorrow."

*

When night fell, it was a steady paranoia in every object, a night bird flashing through the packing area, banana trucks on the road, but more than this it was between things, the gap between his hand and a length of rope, the sagging power line to the packing area. He could feel the guerrillas descending from their camp. He could see them changing clothes in the schools. They were watching him all day. They were patrolling Necoclí, waiting for the sound of his motorcycle, which was a new sound, not the cheap Suzuki but a Honda with twice the horsepower.

He had shut off the lights of the packing area. He helped the kids load the final bolejas onto the horse cart and locked the gate behind them. He unsheathed his machete and walked into the first field because he thought he saw a white shirt in the dark. A gunshot tore through the air. He crouched. The chiggers came up from the ground and bit his arms. He heard steps. He crawled into a drainage. Only a few meters from him, the boots passed by, men in camouflage with rifles on their shoulders, his compañeros, the red-yellow-blue armbands with FARC printed on them. He gripped the roots of the bananas, burrowing deeper into the weeds. He heard the rusty chain of the watchman's bicycle and the slam of the gate.

*

As Orejas pulled the withered cardboard off his motorcycle, the phone rang in the office. It was unsettling how Rafael Restrepo knew where he was at all times.

"Buenas noches, Orejas. How did it go?"

Three years ago, Rafael had flown in from Medellín to shake his hand and talk about the bananas that would now belong to the gringos, to explain the subsidiary and the larger office they would build near Casa Verde, a thing connected to but separate from the banana corporation, and there would be side deals between just the two of them, a flow of bonuses for Orejas that would not show up on any pay stub. They had this conversation inside the airport in Carepa, Rafael staring at the bananas along the runway, the teenage policemen half-guarding the doorways.

"I paid the crew," Orejas said, "and now I'm going home. Excuse me for being direct—guerrillas just walked through the packing area."

"How many?"

"Twenty or thirty."

"Have we paid?"

"Sí, señor."

"There's a change of plan for tomorrow."

Orejas could hear a woman talking in the background, her voice with a rich Medellín lilt, then the sound of pop music, and Rafael was smoking, clearing his throat—a high-pitched static flared up in the line. Orejas lifted his machete off the hook and checked the gates where the watchman was smoking. A faucet dripped over a tub. The single light of the packing area glowed like a yellow moon. He sat on the desk and braced himself for what was coming.

"Are you listening?" Rafael said.

"Sí, señor."

"You can't go home tonight. I want you to visit San Pedro tomorrow to meet with Comandante Borrego and collaborate with his organization. Yenifer Contreras will handle the shipment."

"To die or what, señor?"

"Excuse me?"

He heard the voice of a different woman in the background, saying "Don Rafael," reminding him that dinner was on the table, and Rafael was telling her to give him a minute, and for some reason Orejas was left witnessing this ordinary conversation between planter and servant in some mansion guarded by the police in Medellín, and in a few minutes Rafael would eat and nothing would happen to him. While Orejas would call his cousin's store in Necoclí and tell him to pick up Gloria and his sons, get them off the farm. Then he would sleep in this office with a cardboard box for a bed. He would hear the bananas growing, and if a car approached on the road, he would strap himself to a banana cable and glide into the fields.

"I have to go," Rafael said. "The game you've been playing, Orejas, it's not good in these times. I called our friends in Córdoba. My advice is to tell them everything and be loyal."

"Loyal, jefe?"

"You're a lucky man. So far."

25.

IN HIS MIND, THERE were three forks in the road. Orejas had walked each of them. He was killed by the paramilitaries at the border of San Pedro. He was accepted into their army in Valencia. He escaped alone into the Sierra de Abibé, unclaimed by either armed group, and met Gloria in Medellín to start over. Standing in the main plaza of San Pedro, he saw Café María wetted with gasoline and burning. Smoke blowing out the door and the tanks of propane exploding. It would spread to the buildings on both sides, and it pleased him to imagine the plastic light fixtures melting, the bulbs shattering, the people gathering in a half circle, so close they were sweating, to admire the flames.

"Sit," the man said. He was clean-shaven, ex-military, Orejas saw that in his posture, the way he set his pen adjacent to his notebook, the way his legs formed a right angle at his knee. "Coffee?"

"A water, comandante," Orejas said. "Please."

The man whose name was Borrego held up two fingers to the woman behind the counter and said, "Un agüita y un tinto."

A woman with a bandaid on her forehead was chopping onions. The sharp odor of that and the smell of chicken broth. A child, sexless, ran into the room on drunken legs, fell, rolled on the floor until the woman scooped it up. Orejas rubbed his swollen knuckles and wanted to begin right. What he wanted to say to the paramilitary comandante was that he had spent over a decade with the guerrillas and more than that on the banana plantations, accumulating nothing but data. Not written data. But faces and names and numbers all stored away in the rooms of his brain.

Orejas sipped from the water set before him. It tasted like fish. He looked at his motorcycle set in the doorway, the tank and the wheels caked in mud, all uphill to get here, and there was mud on his jeans. He saw the green flash of the hills, the little towns where the people looked shrunken, fucked by daily fear, the military checkpoint as he entered San Pedro and showed ID. It was a war zone. The guerrillas and paramilitaries were meters away from each other.

"So, who are you?" Borrego said.

"My true name is Samuel Yuletis, but most know me as Orejas."

"You're in the Fifth Front of las *FARC*?"

"Yes, comandante."

"Why bomb the bridges so the people can't get to work or take their crops to market?"

"It's a cruel strategy, comandante."

Borrego said the problem in the banana zone was one of identification. They had to kill the teachers because they let the guerrillas meet in the school. Were the teachers Marxists? Maybe, maybe not. But the schools closed and the children did not learn and became guerrillas. "It goes like this." He raised a finger and traced a circle in the air. "Do you know anything about Marxism?"

"Very little, comandante."

"Marx said a man is all stomach." Borrego rubbed his waist. "Freud said a man is all his dick. Plato thought we were all mind. None of these pendejos is right, Orejas. It's a combination. If a man were just hungry, we could feed him and it's over. No war. People want more."

A deep yellow scar curled off one eyebrow up into Borrego's hairline, making his head seem cracked. He had a school education, books absorbed into his brain that let him talk at a distance, but he did not know the bushes that marked trails into the mountains, a mule that seemed to be grazing but was waiting for a guerrilla to mount it, a huge tank of water that was actually gasoline, a truck that seemed to be full of beer but was carrying rifles and camouflage. You don't have the eyes for it, Orejas thought. He wanted to mention his grandfather, a fisherman in Turbo. He worked canals without fish. Orejas had bought him a motor and some nets to get away from the port and try the rivers along the gulf. He did better, selling his catch at the market. He and Orejas's mother yelled "bocachico" all day in their bell voices and wrapped it up in newspaper for those who could afford it. The salted fish sweated in big crates in the kitchen and the neighbors complained of the stench. Then the people along those rivers put a bullet in his grandfather's head for taking their fish. Not enough land for everyone. His grandfather's speech slurred because the bullet was stuck in his skull and somehow he had driven back across the gulf and walked to the clinic. He sold the boat and the motor. He smoked Caribes, up at dawn for nothing, standing at intersections where trucks passed and he might get hired for a construction site or a farm. He could build fences. He could dig pools to raise fish. No one wanted him. That was Marxism, as Orejas knew it.

"Who's your comandante?" Borrego said.

"Rubén Palacio."

"Why betray him?'

"I don't believe anymore. It's as simple as that, comandante."

Borrego slid his notebook across the table, handed his pen to Orejas and told him to prove it. Orejas drew an outline of Urabá, an upright rectangle with a concave at the top where the gulf was.

His coastline was crooked and inaccurate, but you could not go backwards with a pen. He drew lines until the paper contained a map of Xs for plantations and circles for guerrilla strongholds because he did not know how to write their names. He said them. It was his life in those lines. They split in every direction, up into the Sierra de Abibé and straight to this café, into the horse tracks and cattle trails of Córdoba. When he drove his delivery truck, he knew when muchachos with bags of meat had stolen a cow and butchered it in a field. He knew how much a man carried in his pockets to spend at a brothel in Turbo. He knew the names of the women who visited the camps and the ones who ran errands for the narcos.

Borrego leaned back in his chair and rubbed his face. "We have a training camp in Valencia. You'll meet the Messiah, and we'll see what he wants to do with you. He's going to ask you if you like music."

"And?"

"Say yes."

The woman with the bandaid on her forehead set down bowls of soup with chicken bones, claws, heads, beside chunks of carrot, plantain, and yucca. The soup needed salt and more time—everything was a bit raw, tasteless. They ate in silence, getting to the bottom of their bowls, and Orejas felt like something bad was about to occur.

The woman with the bandaid on her forehead was replacing the rubber gasket on a large steel pressure cooker, but she did not look at him. The door closed, and someone spiked a burlap sack over his head, cinched it with rope and wrestled him onto the ground. He went limp as they bound his wrists. Two men hoisted him up by his arms and walked him out a back door and shoved him into a pickup where he was lodged between a sack of dirt and

another man. He saw the sun sparkling through the mesh of the
sack, but he could not see anything else. The road bounced him
and the other man together. He felt the hit of each pothole as they
left the pavement of San Pedro, the spray of gravel clinking up the
wheel wells. He coughed the fine dust of hay and dirt, trying to
time his breathing against the other man's stomach.

*

The room echoed with rubber boots skidding on concrete,
spoons in bowls, teeth gnashing meat, tongues licking bones, voices of young men bullshiting, mocking the one with the big teeth,
the other with the little dick—"Show it," someone said, and then
the subject of women's legs and how to maneuver them, as if they
were eating women, and then a voice said, "Vamos, muchachos,"
a quiet voice of power. All at once boots on the floor, chairs scraping, the stacking of plates, spoons dropped on boards. Then quiet
except for the guard sucking on a cigarette next to Orejas.

"I have to piss," Orejas said.

"Vamos."

He felt a sharp hand under his armpit and his wrists were un-
bound so he could handle his own dick, no idea who was around
him but the sound of someone digging, the blade of the shovel
screeching into the clay, dirt thunking into a pile.

"Be calm, hermano," the guard said. "Someone likes you in
Medellín."

They sat again. Orejas felt dizzy in the heat, his eyes open
against the mesh of the sack.

*

Hours passed and there were knives chopping again, the odor of beef stewing and plantains frying. Boots clicked against the floor, the banter a little quieter in the evening, an argument over the name of a certain breed of pig. Both men were wrong. Orejas knew the answer. The voices seemed tired and pleased with themselves. That's how it was here, he figured. You got through the heat, and in the night you could relax.

"Who's this?" a new voice said.

"Orejas," the guard said. "Un bananero."

"Why is he here?"

"It's hot back there. We get a little breeze out here."

"Take him to a room. We have visitors."

Night was falling. Someone brought the guard his dinner and the smell of beef a foot away from Orejas made his mouth water. The fan rotated across them, but Orejas was done sweating, as if his body had run out. The guard apologized that he couldn't give him anything to eat. A helicopter beat the air overhead, and there were voices in the hallway.

*

Orejas sneezed when they took the sack off his head. The light flashed like fire. He saw whitewashed walls, a bulb dangling from the ceiling, three men in camouflage. The leader sat in a chair, his face rippling white, beige and green, blinking as he examined him. Orejas felt his bowels loosen and he clenched his back and waist to keep from shitting. His hernia ached from the pressure on his pelvis. He leaned forward and spit dust and dirt onto the floor.

"Are you sick?" said the leader who must be the Messiah.

"No, comandante. I'm fine."

The Messiah sat upright with his palms facing the sky. He was rigid, lean-bodied. Head-tilted. He handed Orejas a cup of coffee, and though what he really wanted was water, he drank it. The Messiah drank coffee too, and said in a voice both guttural and high-pitched, "What kind of music do you like?"

"Excuse me?"

"You don't like music?"

"Yes, but everything, comandante. I wanted to be a singer when I was little."

"Vallenato? Champeta?"

"All of it, comandante."

"I don't trust anyone who doesn't like music, Orejas. Do people like music in the banana zone? I would have looked at you yesterday and said you were a manager, an ordinary bananero with a small farm in Necoclí. Good cows. Two sons. A wife whose family comes from Medellín. The planters have too much power, Orejas. I'll be frank—they're the reason I exist. Borrego says you know where the rats hide."

"The camps move," Orejas said, "but I know where they go."

"We don't attack the camps. We lose in el monte, Orejas. We win in the towns. Do you understand? I want to know the route from the camps to the mayor's office in Apartadó where your compañeros have friends. Do you see it?"

"Yes, comandante."

"The military can't do it. You can lose your job if you are a colonel and you kill a guerrilla disguised as a human rights worker. Did you know that?"

"Yes, comandante."

"We can find that man at night." The Messiah leaned back in his chair. "You work for me now, not those fat oligarchs in Medellín. If you deceive me, I'll take care of you personally. Que quede claro eso."

"It's clear, comandante."

*

Later, Orejas heard gunshots in the hills. A cowbell rang out louder than seemed possible, and then a scratching sound like some animal was trying to get in. It was just rain against the roof. Men snored on all sides. They hung like swollen banana stems in their hammocks, this room a type of packing area with no walls. Orejas had shaken a few hands, saying his name, though no one was especially friendly. He was a snitch. He swayed in his hammock, sweating through a clean T-shirt, a mosquito net thrown over him, and when he stuck out his tongue, he tasted its funk. The guerrillas would haul away his four cows, his chickens, his TV, his stove, his bed. He had to get Gloria out of Necoclí. He saw her splashing a bucket of fresh water onto their sons in the bathroom of her uncle's house, washing off the salt from the ocean, scraping behind their ears and between their legs with a rag, kissing their little fingers and telling them to close their eyes for the soap. He sat up and hung his legs down to the floor. Mosquitoes attacked his feet. He whispered the names of the people he loved, and though he had ignored God for years, it seemed like God was right there waiting for him to speak again, and God said maybe, which was the problem. Orejas was still strung from that cable over el Río Guadalito. He felt everything—he stuck his finger into the soil among his plantains and pulled out worms that stuck to his palm, he ran his clean fingers through Gloria's hair and down her neck to her spine that was driven deep into her back and down over her butt to her thick legs and to her feet, and past that he touched the smooth hide of their best cow and the taut wire of the fence he had built and the smooth boxes of the shipment tomorrow at Finca los Bongos and the handle of the machete he would use to walk the fields and the greasy braid of the cables and the hard green skin of the bananas and the sweaty shoulder of a worker he would poke to give him instructions, but that shipment was done, someone else had coordinated it, someone else had talked on the phone with Don Rafael and watched the trucks go out and paid the workers and maybe flirted with Yenifer whose jaw he kissed, feeling her lips against his jaw, her quick voice in his ear telling him this was it, that Orejas was alone.

26.

THE PLAN WAS TO HIT. It was against el Club Campestre's unwritten rules for a man and a woman to play singles against each other. But once they broke a sweat, Jay knew it would turn into a match. He had acted on a rumor that Graciela played competitively as a teenager and told her she would be his guest. He made her run back and forth, his usual tactic, but she did not tire. She surprised him by cutting off the angles, hitting wrong-footed half-volleys and changing the spin. He found himself backpedaling to the baseline and falling down. She served to whatever line he was leaning away from. Midway through the set, she tapped into his paranoia, jamming him with shots that hooked into his body.

"Your backhand doesn't spin," she said. "Your grip is too tight."

After losing the first set, he felt like she had taken a pin and shoved it into an air-filled part of his body. He broke her serve on the first game of the second set, hitting low, flat shots to her forehand, but she adjusted and beat him again. It was good to lose. He always beat Rafael who was the better player but bad at winning. When they sat on the bench afterward, exposed to the eyes that saw the gringo bananero with Luis Alberto's ex-lover raised from the dead, he bragged about his Obregón Barracuda and wondered if she would like to see it.

"Tonight?" she said.

*

She sat with a glass of wine on Jay's new couch. Moles stood out on her neck like little islands. She wore an open-neck white blouse, and she had a leech-like clump of skin at the top of her chest and a long purple peninsula of scar on her shoulder. She spoke in a quiet, overly deliberate way, in contrast with Jay, who blurted what was at the front of his mind. Her lips were stuck together in disgust, as Jay explained how the life of a banana worker could be improved without much investment, just a few comforts, a break in the static of history. She slipped off her shoes and put her bare feet underneath her on the couch.

"You will never please the workers," she said slowly.

She walked across his living room, looking at the Barracuda, the Caballero drawing, and the new works: an Enrique Grau drawing, a Wilfredo Lam print, and a map-like blotch and scribble from David Siqueiros. She seemed tired, blue bags under her eyes and a sag to her shoulders, as she fell back into the couch heavily. She set her feet on his lap. They were red with swollen toes, maybe sore from small shoes. He carefully put his hand on her calf. She watched it but did not ask him to remove it.

He said Rafael was in Montería for another meeting with the paramilitaries. A dream come true, she said, for those men to sit at a table with a Restrepo, no matter how much they hated the oligarchy of Medellín, all of them, the guerillas and the paramilitaries, the left and right the same thing, they all just wanted to be like the rich and sit with the Restrepos and Gavirias and Echevarrías.

"It turns out one of our managers was a guerrilla," Jay said. "All these years. His name is Samuel Yuletis, but the people call him Orejas because he has big ears, both physically and, well, he's a traitor. None of it matters. These guerrillas are switching armbands every day, they just betray their compañeros like nothing and take a salary from the paramilitaries."

"It's always been like this," she said.

"The bananas are not important," Jay said. "They are to me and you, but to the people there, the ones we don't really know and never see, it's just land. We don't have a choice."

"There's a key difference," she said.

"What's that?"

"The men in Córdoba want all the land for themselves. The guerrillas don't."

*

Their friendship would have to be quiet, she said, and it was just a friendship. No lunches together, no kissing in Jay's office. All business at work. She had no patience for office affairs or gossip, so in meetings he should look at her like she was one more sales manager and never champion her ideas or contradict them. She did not want to be seen at his apartment building either. He could visit her when she invited him.

She had a medium-sized apartment in Laureles, a newer building, her walls mint-green with factory-made landscape paintings that gave Jay a headache to look at. Her furniture backbreakingly simple gray couches wrapped in fake leather, a white-tiled floor, a ceramic plug-in fountain with a turtle spouting water in the kitchen. He hated the fountain and unplugged it when she wasn't looking. The floor was a minefield of dirty clothes and shoes on their sides. Wrinkled outfits lay like bodies under the bed or hung from doors, as if she took off socks and bras and blouses and tossed them wherever she was standing. In her bed, Jay would feel a poke in his back and find a teaspoon or cookie crumbs or popcorn. The sink towered with dishes, and she ate like an American, cooking with a microwave or just eating out of a can of cold beans. In the bathroom was always a blue bucket of bleach where she dropped her white underwear. A maid cleaned on Mondays, but in a matter of hours the apartment returned to entropy.

He asked her about the scars on her chest and shoulder. She said Luis Alberto Echevarría hired a sicario to kill her. She was driving through la Sabaneta, she said, looking at a pharmacy where she received shots for birth control, and the killer emptied a clip of bullets into her car. In her shock she swerved and ran him over. He did not die, but because he had failed, doors opened.

"Ernesto," Jay said. "I've never loved him."

"You think you understand," she said. "The planters are not cleaning up Urabá for just the bananas."

"Bananas are almost worthless," Jay said, though he didn't believe it.

"It's where they grow," she said, "and they are not at all worthless. You're missing the point."

"You survived," he said. "I think I would like to be almost killed."

"Don't be stupid," she said.

They had sex with a lamp on beside her bed. The way she was in bed contradicted her harsh persona at work. She loosened up and laughed as they figured each other out. She told him where to touch her and she said she wanted more when they were done. How much did she want? He felt like he was chasing her around the world, as she grabbed his hair and twisted it into her mouth, and after they had made love again, she told him to sleep in the guest bedroom. She was not right in the head at night, she said.

"What will people say?" he said.

"What people?" she said. "Who's caring about us?"

27.

No one was innocent. The guerrillas blended into the plain faces of campesinos in the village. If Orejas looked hard, he saw it in their teeth, the way they kept their tongues hidden, the way they sent messages with their fingers. He glimpsed the other ones, the ones you could see, crawling around the ridges of the mountains, the flash of red in their bandanas, the squeak of rubber boots in the mud. He saw one crawl under the robe of a nun in the village's church, thinking he would grab onto her legs and hide. He could not. The nun would be expelled. Someone handed Orejas a can of black spray paint and told him to tag *ACCU* onto the outer wall of the billiard hall, but afraid he would spell it wrong, he handed the bottle to another.

Orejas beheld men in the sight of his rifle, following them behind rocks and trees, up the dirt trails until they were out of range. Far behind him, a campesino was shot off his horse, and Comandante Borrego rode it across the main plaza, warning the people of the new order. A brief silence. The village was not pretty. A dirty black river ran through its center, and in the cantina were men so drunk they did not fear death.

Orejas splashed gasoline onto the thatched roof of the building where campesinos weighed corn and plantains for the wholesaler. It lit like dried-out paper, the walls collapsing and the fire leaping down the block of houses. A woman dove into a burning house and emerged with a green bird in a cage. She ran for the river, but the bird was already on fire and the cage was melting in her hands.

Orejas loaded beer from the cantina into a truck. It was cold, but not that cold. He passed around bottles and drank one. He talked to the pharmacist and his wife and warned them not to sell medicine to the enemy.

*

In those first weeks, the paramilitaries advanced west from Montería, where they were safe, to Arboletes, then along the coast, confronting ragtag bands of guerrillas and cleansing the little towns near Necoclí, where Orejas found his farm gutted and spraypainted, the beds ripped apart, his cattle dead, and the plantains overgrown. Gloria and his sons were staying with her brother in Medellín. He had not seen her since that last morning when he went to work at Finca la Bella.

Orejas awoke cranky in afternoons in strange beds, a fly buzzing over him, sometimes a paid woman beside him, a TV babbling out the news. He would reach out for his machete and his Banana Bolívar uniform and instead find a rifle, and he located himself in his new life and felt a mixture of longing for the world of the plantations and regret for having spent most his life on them. Rafael Restrepo's voice still lived in his head, and Orejas spoke with him periodically to give advice on the bananas.

Orejas watched over Yenifer from a distance, asking his snitches how she was and where she was and if she needed anything. Each time there was a killing at the plantations, he readied himself for hers. He met her one night on the beach in Necoclí. She said she had what everyone wanted—the numbers, not just of shipments but all the profits at every level of the banana economy. She kissed his cheek like he was the same man. She said Rafael Restrepo called her at the office in Carepa fifteen times a day and the exports had gone up. She could feel it, she said, the ground shifting beneath her and everyone in the zone, that the guerrillas were crazy, suspecting everyone of disloyalty, and the workers had begun to hate them. There was a million-peso bounty on Orejas's head, and this made him paranoid in the dark, like his assassin was that palm tree on the beach, that upside-down chair. Being hated was not how he had anticipated it. The people did not have his full story, and he did not have the words to give it to them. He dug his boot into the wet sand of the beach, and a smell of dead fish seeped up from it. He said guerrillas had tied one of his old neighbors to a tree and bludgeoned his head with rifle butts until there was nothing there.

She put her feet in the water and walked up to her knees so he could barely see her in the dark. Just her voice and some light from the shore reflected off her eyes. She was splashing around like a child. She wanted to learn to swim, she said. "I have dreams where I drown in el Río Zungo."

"Gloria swims," he said. "She can teach you."

"Does she like Medellín?"

"No, she's a country girl."

He said he had bought Hotel Simón del Mar at a discount. Did she know it? There was no pool, but maybe down the road he would build one on the roof. No views of the ocean. Only fifteen small rooms on two stories, stuffy, odd-shaped, and the mattresses were old and would need to be replaced. But it was one block from the beach.

"You can hear the waves," he said. He wanted her to manage it, make it like the hotels in the book she used to love when they were children.

"Do you still have that book?" he said.

"You're like the butcher," she said.

He wiped sand from his pants, walked out to the edge of where the waves broke. He was not the butcher. It was almost normal, like they were standing there as children again, but when he put his arm around her shoulder, it was a mistake. She turned and said, "I think I would like Medellín."

"It's not for you," he said.

"You don't know everything."

28.

EMBARCADERO ZUNGO LOOKED LIKE A PITCHFORK from the air, three brown prongs that were the canal split into channels and at the center a cement slab, a rectangular island, where every day thousands of banana boxes were packed into the white containers and hauled downstream to the ocean. There were eight docks for the banana trucks to drop their loads, a metal roof so the fruit wouldn't cook, stacks of containers with the words Hamburg and MAERSK, streetlamps for night-loading, and cranes that swung the containers out over the canal onto barges.

At the hottest part of the day, Yenifer stood next to the canal, looking at Big Fernando's body floating. A dozen vultures looped through the sky, perched on containers and the roof of the inspector's office, keeping their eyes on the braceros who refused to work until the police came and removed the bodies. The other was Andrés Portillo, the foreman, who lay with a hole in his head at the first dock. A long line of trucks had formed at the gates, the drivers leaning against the front bumpers and shielding their eyes from the sun. The phone rang in the inspector's office, and she could hear the voice of an angry plantation manager worried about the delay.

Yenifer's white Banana Bolívar truck idled in the sun. She wore a white collared shirt with a little green banana on her right breast, and she was here to undo the logjam. There was no shade at this hour, except for the awning of the aluminum huts where the customs inspectors checked in the barges and processed the paperwork. Every so often they tore open a box to make sure it contained bananas.

She heard Rafael Restrepo's mad voice in her ear telling her to bribe whom she needed to bribe, that the paramilitaries would be here shortly to help. She carried a small tarp from the truck and covered the body of Andés Portillo at the first dock, flattening it with her foot, dropping a piece of wood at the corner to tamp it down. The wood slipped from her fingers and a splinter drove into her thumb, deep, and when she tried to pry it out with her teeth, it broke off. "Mierda," she said, walking back to her truck and looking for tweezers that were not there.

Her brothers had once worked here and got out during the surplus. One of them ran drugs across the plains in Bajirá. The other drove a taxi in Barranquilla. "You can come back," she told them on the phone, but they didn't believe her.

A silver Toyota pickup pulled up, two men sitting in the back with rifles, two in the cab. In the driver's seat, a man with his arm hanging out motioned with a finger for her to come. He had a mouth that looked like a pit in the earth, half his teeth gone, the others crooked. He wore a yellow Polo with a blue horse on his breast, while the other men wore green military shirts. Sunglasses masked his eyes. She had never seen him, and she wondered if this was Borrego, Orejas's comandante. She walked over, and he said, "I need a list of all the men here."

Yenifer said this was not her crew. No idea who was who. She felt wobbly on her feet, the heat rising off the canal, the glares of the two paramilitaries with the rifles pointed near her head. She had eaten only a cookie for breakfast. Her stomach was in knots. She smelled beer on the breath of the men in the truck. She touched the hot door and stared into a mirror of her body trembling in the black sunglasses. She looked tiny, bright and flickering with the canal passing right through the sides of her head.

"Tell the men to line up," he said. "Yenifer Contreras. Orejas said we can count on you."

"With all respect, I can't give orders here," she said.

Yenifer walked over to the braceros whose faces seemed drained of blood, jaws tight, eyes checking the empty barge, the open backs of the box trucks like they might hide somewhere, but the whole embarcadero was trapped by chain-link fence with three lines of barbed wire across the top, the sun high, and they had a good idea why Portillo was lying dead under a tarp, why Big Fernando, tattooed, monumental, a respected capataz, was falling to pieces in the water. Yenifer told them she was not with the men in the silver Toyota. She was here to see the shipment go out for Banana Bolívar. But the men in the silver Toyota wanted to know who was who.

"Who are they?" a bracero asked.

"Paracos," another said quietly. "We have to go."

Yenifer walked back to her truck, a thing to save her life, perhaps, and she took out some papers from the glove compartment, faking she had work, as Orejas always said—pretend you're more important than you are. Where was he now? She bit at the sliver in her thumb, driving it in deeper.

The braceros filed past the Toyota, where the driver checked his list and asked them where they were from and what union and who was their family. The sun beat down on the dark gravel. A bargeman sat in a gap of shade and lit a cigarette. She felt like everyone was watching her, but maybe this was not true. They took one man and sat him down in the back of the pickup truck, and then waved at Yenifer to come over. The other braceros stood in line, facing the canal. They looked away from the selected man, a near dwarf with dark curly hair, older than the others, hunched over, a drastic curve in his spine, his face in a grimace with tight lips.

The man who must be Borrego turned to the line of braceros and said, "A camellar. Go work. The police are not coming."

The braceros walked to the loading dock, clumsy, though these were not clumsy men. One of them had a look of agony, glancing over his shoulder at the man in the back of the pickup.

*

In the inspector's office, Yenifer called Rafael Restrepo and heard her sharp voice tell him that the shipment was moving again. He told her which containers to watch, that she was to stay put until she saw them on the barge and the barge unmoored and heading down the canal. As he spoke, she heard the braceros breathing and grunting as they lifted the boxes, their boots scuffing the cement, the creak of the containers as they opened the heavy doors. They must be hot inside, she thought, the men entering and exiting like ants through a hole. Their arms flexed in their T-shirts. Her own shirt was soaked with sweat. She hung up the phone and walked out into the sun. Someone pushed her, just a hand stabbing into her ribs—"Cuidado!" he said.

Two of the frontloaders were broken, so today the braceros used their backs and arms. They grabbed cardboard boxes from the first truck and stacked them seven boxes high on a crate with steel wheels. One man stood in the truck and handed down the boxes while another received and used the momentum of the box to swing it to the two men doing the stacking on the crate. A fifth man wheeled the crate to the correct container, each with a specific color for its destination.

The clock was ticking faster, she thought. Every day. More trucks rolled in. A gunshot sounded up the road and she and the men paused for a full three seconds and looked toward it. A few drew the sign of the cross on their chests. She walked back to her white truck, covered her face, and wept.

*

The long aluminum barge with a wooden deck and torn-open rubber tires nailed to its sides rode low in the river, its driver guiding it slowly out into the current, seeing the bow of another barge a few hundred meters to the north and sliding into an inlet to idle until it passed, waving at the driver, a friend. Something smelled awful in the white containers or in the canal, the vultures looping from one bank to another, and for a second the bargeman feared the banana boxes were packed with dead people. He felt bad for the braceros, having to carry on like nothing happened.

At the mouth of the canal, he steered the barge north along the shore, where he stopped for another customs inspection, two men with clipboards and a police officer with a dog boarding to check the seals on the containers and to sniff the cargo. The dogs were a fraud, the bargeman thought, untrained and stupid. As he steered his load across the gulf, waves slapped the sides, the wind throwing him off course, and with difficulty he moored it alongside a large white American ship with empty white containers he would take back to the embarcadero. The sailors shouted random Spanish words: "Hola," "Putas," "Cerveza, por favor," "Más cocaína!" They tied up to his barge and sent down the crane to lift the containers onto the deck. Up there the AC roared to life. When the barge was restacked with empty containers, the bargeman waved up at the sailors and returned south for another load.

That evening, the white ship weighed anchor and headed northeast through the brown, silty water of the gulf, yellowed at the mouth of el Río Atrato, whose delta stood out like a marshy shipwreck, where occasionally fast boats emerged with armed men en route to Panama. Past Boca Matuntugó, it was as if someone had drawn a line in the ocean, the water turned from brown to dark blue, the sailors checked the seals on the containers to be sure the temperature was dropping and gazed over the portside railings at the beach in Capurganá, huts on stilts, fishermen tossing nets over the gunwales of brightly painted boats, and said someday they would come back with their girlfriends.

*

They reached the port in New Orleans, the ship snaking up the Mississippi River, past the French Quarter, and under the high bridge to Algiers, sixty miles of port along the hump of concrete levee. Here cranes lifted off the containers and set them down onto the trailers of semis that were dispatched northward. One truck left town on I-59, northeast through Birmingham, Nashville, Louisville, and eventually it crossed the Ohio River to a refrigerated warehouse in Cincinnati. The bananas were still bright green inside, but if you looked closely, a trace of yellow had seeped into the green, and once this process started, once the bananas were exposed to the heat and light of the supermarket, they would mottle, then brown to black to garbage. The wholesaler checked off the numbers on his clipboard. He sent off the drivers, one of which bypassed downtown, the company's symbol emblazoned in blue and yellow on the side of the truck, a woman with fruit on her head. The truck backed into the loading dock, where a manager checked the columns of his clipboard and two young men in blue aprons stacked the boxes on dollies and hauled them out to the produce section, which looked like a sterilized diorama of a Latin American market.

Jay pushed his grocery cart up to the bananas, the greener the better, and he checked the stickers to see they had come from Colombia. He grabbed a bunch with four and then some vanilla ice cream from the frozen section, even if it was a cold night. He selected mostly junk food, in town for a couple days. Graciela had agreed to visit with him and meet the Cincinnati executives. She wandered through the aisles, bewildered by the variety of salad dressings, canned soups, sauces, a dozen mustards, breads, the bright white lights overhead making everything desirable. She wore a dark blue suit and a gold necklace that bounced on her scarred neck, and he felt her scars were a good thing in America. She said he was full of shit. She made him buy all the celebrity magazines whose covers carried photos of Tom Cruise and Mimi Rogers on the verge of divorce. The checkout clerk had one arm in a thick dirty cast, and she hummed along to the in-store music as she scanned the items. She looked up kindly when Jay spoke Spanish to Graciela.

At Jay's apartment, Graciela changed into a nightgown and opened two different bags of chips to watch his TV. She seemed paler in Ohio, the TV lighting up her face like she was made of wax. He liked the sound of her breathing, the heat in her skin, and all the other sounds she made as she walked around the apartment and touched his furniture, his pictures, as if measuring the size of the space to see if she fit in it. She seemed struck by how new things were. A young suburb. The massive shopping mall across the street. No drama in Cincinnati. She said safety was paranoia. Danger was, too, but she didn't know how he slept with this much silence. At dawn that morning, she had thought she was dead and in some afterlife when she awoke to the gurgles of his coffee maker, the smell of toast.

Soon after the movie started, she was sleeping on his beige leather couch, her head cocked to one side, Jay sipping a beer. Too much sugar at once—it did not taste good. His phone rang and it was Rafael. Graciela did not wake up. Rafael's voice sounded windy, like he was out at sea. He yelled over the line and said he had just traveled to see their land, was about to take off from Montería to Medellín. He had flown in his one-propeller Cessna that Jay vowed never to board. The good news was that their land was either covered in cows or bananas, and the surplus was ending. The bad news was that their friends in Córdoba wanted a meeting in person.

"In Medellín?" Jay asked.

"No," Rafael said. "Necoclí or Arboletes."

"Forget it," Jay said, touching Graciela's back and reconciling his friend's voice with the quiet of his apartment in suburban Cincinnati. "I don't have clearance for that trip. Not yet. What is it?"

"The early bird gets the worm," Rafael said in English. "We are that bird. These men want to shake your hand, brother. That's all."

When he hung up, Jay carried Graciela to his bedroom and buried her under the heavy down comforter. He dropped the thermostat to 63 degrees. "Hasta mañana," he said, but she was out. He walked in the dark to the guest bedroom and found himself reaching for the bed where it was not, smashing his knee into the mattress. It was cold with him alone on it. He lay awake for an hour and thought about Rafael flying over the Andes at night.

When he was drifting off to sleep, he had the sensation he was being driven across a flat valley where everyone stared at him. He crossed a rope bridge to a muddy path to the banks of Río León, stepping into a little boat with a motor on the stern, where Rafael was trying to tell him something, but he could not hear anything.

Someone was running a chainsaw. The motor erupted into flames. A woman was screaming for God to save her children who were being recruited for the war.

A VISIT

1994

29.

SWEAT ROLLED DOWN HIS SPINE as Jay squeezed out the narrow aisle of the thirty-seat plane with twin propellers. He thanked with too much vigor the young flight attendant who stared at him. A fumigation plane crossed right over the airport, its spray arcing out over the green banana fields. Jay stopped halfway between the stairs and the baggage claim to imagine the runway lengthened so jet planes could land, chartered from Miami, tourists and businessmen, a row of palm trees and international flags to welcome them. Maybe never. Maybe it would always be like this, makeshift, agro-industrial.

Outside the baggage claim, Jay ran his hands down his shirt and swung his little duffle bag over his shoulder. The taxi drivers surrounded him.

"Taxi, señor? A la órden."

"Señor Harrison?" said a man with huge ears, pink rims, wrinkles at his temples. Jay was surprised at how short Orejas was, his forearms thick and brown. He had the look of a man who was once handsome despite his huge ears, but his body seemed damaged, a double chin, a military buzz cut, scars on his chin and cheeks. A lady's man somehow. You just knew it with certain men. No eyes to know because he wore sunglasses. The sea of taxi drivers parted before them, and Jay could somehow feel everyone's heartbeats altered, the atmosphere thick with bad breath and sewage rising from a nearby grate, as Orejas led him to a silver Toyota Land Cruiser completely tinted, even the front windshield, engine running, and two guards.

"Don Rafael is at Finca Nueva Fortuna," Orejas said, taking off his glasses so Jay could see that his eyes were not dead but just regular eyes with brown irises, a little yellow in the whites, a friendly gaze. "He said to show you the other plantations, no?"

"If it's safe," Jay said. "Yes, yes, yes."

*

They crossed endless banana fields. Every so often workers appeared on the roads, detaching the supports for cables at road crossings, looking away from the SUV. They passed the gate to the Banana Bolívar office.

"Could you slow down?" Jay said, lowering his window.

A few white cement buildings, white trucks, a soccer field, a swimming pool. It looked inconsequential, like it would be swallowed up by the jungle tomorrow. Jay rolled down the window to taste the air and it tickled his nose. Craig Washburn would have him fired if he knew about the visit, but Craig Washburn was in Cincinnati, midmorning, sipping coffee from a foam cup in the break room, trying to choose a donut from a white box.

"Better raise the window," Orejas said.

Apartadó, the center of everything on the maps in Medellín, was in the motion of being built or unbuilt, its orange brick and cement buildings pasted together in random intervals, their unfinished upper stories poking into the sky with crooked rebar and elaborate homemade antennas, all in a web of sagging power lines. Here and there the reassuring glass façade of a bank or a pharmacy. None of the sidewalks connected—the pedestrians did not even use them, sticking to the streets. Motorcycles buzzed through it, barely avoiding the pedestrians, pausing at red lights but not stopping. Dusty rigs with black-tarped trailers loaded with banana boxes blocked traffic to make wide turns. People glanced without expression at the Land Cruiser, but it was mostly women in the streets, carrying shopping bags, one selling sausages and arepas off a smoking grill.

On the other side of Apartadó it was bananas again, green symmetrical fields of leafy plants six, eight, and fifteen feet high in the air. Orejas stopped at a vacant field with nothing but grass and a broken fence, and said, "This is yours."

Jay stepped out of the SUV and smelled the air—humid soil and waxy leaves baking, and he reached down through the fence for a pinch of dirt which he slipped into a Ziploc bag.

"That?" Orejas said.

"Soil is everything," Jay said.

The future was this vacant lot, as Jay saw it—four-story brick buildings, mini-balconies with wire clotheslines, home offices with computers and fax machines, the middle managers kicking a soccer ball in a green central park with gravel paths. A high steel fence with spikes because nowhere could you have wealth without gates and guards.

"Vamos," Orejas said.

They drove north on the road to the ocean, through villages— Río Grande, Currulao, El Tres—orange brick and muddy roads leading into slums and more plantations. Potential here. Jay saw asphalt shoveled out from big trucks, the houses painted white to reflect the sun, a new plaza with cafés, a school designed with large windows for ventilation, and why not another church?

"Where's the line?" Jay asked.

"What line, señor?"

"Between us and the guerrillas. Is it just access to the ocean? Rafael told me that anything south of Turbo was still hot."

"There's no line," Orejas said. "Everyone is blended together. This zone is complicated."

Orejas looked at the guards, and Jay suspected they were holding in smiles. He was the idiot of the car.

At Finca el Paraíso, Jay descended and stuck his long fingers into the soil, felt the moisture a few inches down and shoved some dirt into his bags. He saw the workers freeze at the sound of the SUV's tires. A tall manager emerged, shook hands with Jay, everyone sweating in the sun that was like a spotlight on a muddy, absurd stage, the whole thing rehearsed with everyone's smiles nowhere near sincere. The manager led Jay up a trail along a cable, showed him the age of some banana plants, and provided him with the sequence of the fields, the maturation and yields over the past year.

"Buen trabajo," Jay said.

Jay swayed like a buoy in the packing area while workers swarmed around him and cut bunches from stems and tossed them into the long rectangular tubs of moving water. He looked up at the high white canopy, the erased symbol of Banana Bolívar because this belonged to him and Rafael. The workers' eyes were on him. He imagined telepathy among the traitors who would love to tie him up, put him sideways on a horse and drag him into the sierra. Life, Jay wanted them to see, was this. It was discipline, it was cable to tub, tub to box, box to truck, and if they could just last a couple years without striking, they would be happy. He had a whole speech in his head, but in one look at a teenager with a rope tied to his waist, eight massive stems on the cable behind him, he realized that no one would hear him. Every man was in his place.

"Who's the owner over there?" Jay said, pointing across a drainage to a badly maintained field, the plants collapsed with black leaves.

"He lives in Bogotá," Orejas said. "They're running at half-production. No shipment today. You want a meeting with him?"

Jay held out his thick white business card, and Orejas flipped it into a breast pocket. He motioned at the manager with a pointed finger that seemed loaded with meaning. Jay imagined American tourists riding the cables into the fields to see where their bananas came from. There was no beach. It would have to be gated resorts, and those were in prettier places. Sweat dripped into his eyes and stung. He saw the land with such clarity that he would have liked to look away.

30.

THE MADAME KNOCKED AND said there were customers. She said, "Me hace el favor, Nanci? Porfa?"

Nanci said yes because she always said yes. She put on a purple skirt and a white crop top with pink stripes. She looked blind in her blue contacts, and the other women joked that she was in a trance, unless she was cutting hair or listening to a sad story.

The darkness of the brothel on such a bright day was pleasant. Nanci pegged the pale, ugly muchacho with the curly black hair bunched on the back of his neck as thoughtful and timid. She made small talk about Medellín, the price of rent, the dry sunny weather, what music was popular, what movies. She was known as la venezolana feliz, always laughing at her men's jokes, always keeping the girls' spirits up after long nights or dead nights or nights when the men were disrespectful or too drunk to finish. She was known as someone the women could talk to about their problems. She had a sound mind and would always offer two solutions, touching a woman's shoulders with either hand, like the options were inside your body. Her face was broad and crowded by her features, her eyelashes extended, her broken nose bigger than before, a Turkish nose, one man said, and she had no idea what he meant.

The older, darker one with weightlifter arms, a much better

face, almost pretty, asked if she could get them weed. She said she could not. Not here.

"The paramilitaries banned it?" the pale one said, truly ugly with pimples around his eyes and at the edges of his nostrils.

No one said anything critical about the paramilitaries, though the pretty one indicated with a shrug that a place without weed was a drag. He leaned into Petra who sat beside him, one hand on his beer to take a sip. He smelled her neck like she might not be clean, and Petra leaned back—she was, in Nanci's eyes, the prettiest of them all, the longest legs, always balanced, always in control of the men. "If you want to kiss me, I'll let you."

Nanci thought these two were nobodies, posers. They drank beer the madame had served two-for-one because it was a slow hour. There was an arrogance, a feigned ease and lilt to their voices that made Nanci suspect they worked with the guerrillas. The pale ugly muchacho said he sold insurance in Medellín, the pretty one was faking he did this, too, but she could see in his mashed and broken hands that he had grown up in the countryside.

"Can I have a sip?" Nanci said to the pale ugly one.

"Claro," he said.

She did not want to socialize. She knew there was something unexciting about her when the sun was out. When night fell, she was a top earner. She had the gift, the madame said. Yenifer said everyone on earth had a gift, obvious from the time you were born or hidden from you, and you had to find it. Nanci knew her gift was her vision for hair—she would open her own salon with her savings. Her savings were growing but she wanted to do it right, with steel scissors and good hair dryers, large mirrors, and sinks with cutout openings for necks. Yenifer paid her to keep track of who was who at la Picardía. What did the ladies know? Everything.

The pretty one was familiar. Nanci remembered him from a guerrilla camp in the sierra, where she had to disguise herself as a campesina in ratty jeans and T-shirt in case she and the others were stopped by the military. They had to service the entire camp, the comandantes first and last. This pretty one had fucked like a hysterical baby, trying to suck on her breasts and put her in impossible positions. He called her "mi gran amor," pretending they were on a date in the middle of a war.

The pale ugly one stood up and walked to the door, looked out at a car, and for a second Nanci worried he was leaving.

"Your car is safe," the madame said, waving him back to the ladies. "No one steals in this neighborhood."

Maybe these muchachos were not posing. They were into something today.

He sat back down and ran his hand along Nanci's leg. The beer made her hotter. A fan blew in the corner, but she was not close enough. She felt something was about to happen. Someone was about to walk in the door. The pale one stared at it. Now, she thought. Now. Nothing happened. Petra said she had AC in her room.

"Can we do it my way?" the pretty one was saying to Petra, a queen with her legs crossed, already sure of the things he would ask for, already bored with it.

"Of course," Petra said, taking his hand and leading him away.

"Are you visiting someone?" Nanci said when she was alone with this pale, ugly muchacho.

"We're going to Necoclí," he said breathlessly and seemed to regret it.

"I am, too," she said. "It's my birthday tomorrow."

"How old?" he said.

"I am not going to tell you."

Her mind was not in the conversation. She did not want to feel him touching her body, his cheek on her cheek or her breasts, though she knew it was inevitable. As soon as they started doing it, she would go to a purple room in her imagination. Close her eyes, and just breathe that purple air, a room freshened by plants and open windows. It was a clean room where you did not have to move around like a blind person and smash your foot on uneven cement. No, it was a purple room. Not in Colombia. Not in Venezuela. She could stay in the purple room as long as she needed. It was Easter, a money holiday, as the resurrection turned everyone on. It was also the purple month. In a few days, she would have her period, so she was impatient with everything, not just this muchacho but with the clothes on her body and the rasp of the leather heels on her ankles, the songs, the madame staring at her like she was being passive.

Why purple? the other girls asked. Nanci could not say. She did not like white rooms or brick or yellow walls. She hated the cracks of zinc roofs. She had given birth to her first son, a mistake, in a badly lit hospital up the street, the one all the girls said they were going to avoid and never did. Another woman next to her with a pink baby in her arms said, "Your first?"

"My last," Nanci said.

"Have at least two," the woman said. "One might get killed."

Yenifer stood there and told the woman to shut her mouth or lose her tongue. That was the sort of thing Yenifer could say and get away with. A way of sitting in a room the way few women could and making people speak carefully and check her for approval. Nanci's baby died anyway. A crib death. A short life. Fine. She had other plans. Yenifer cried a lot more than she did.

What kind of a world was it? A purple world. A world where she rubbed the sticky wood under the table and said, "Vamos?" as if this ugly muchacho was doing her a favor. He stood up because this was the game, and they were passing down the hallways, only she knew the turns, past empty rooms, the smell of bleach and perfume.

She took off his pants and dove into purple. Her breasts hurt and she held them while he moved her. When he reached for them she took his hands by the wrists and cupped them beneath her ass and smiled, thinking about the beach in Necoclí and wondering if Yenifer was there now.

31.

JAY GRIPPED THE GUNWALE as the bow bucked against the waves. Orejas slowed down, as if to steady the ink-dark blue image of the Gulf of Urabá. The boat turned up the mouth of a brown, dirty river, and on one side of the bank were men in camouflage with rifles and paramilitary armbands, who waved them through. Orejas gunned the motor against the current and jerked the bow toward a muddy bank. All in one motion they were moored. The guard in the bow grabbed Jay's hand to help him onto the ground, then tossed the anchor, a block of cement, up onto land.

It was a war zone, Jay knew, but light rain fell from the sky and coated his face, and the fields rolled out in a bright green, parts of them fenced in with barbed wire. Flat as a table. The river curved away from it, shaping a widening vision with multiple pens, a gang of pigs in one, chickens in another, and a slight rise where the white and black cows bent patiently over tufts of grass. Beyond were head-high brush trees that they would bulldoze to plant bananas in the coming weeks.

Graciela had told him to cancel the trip. She threw a potato and its peeler against the wall of her kitchen. "Don't trust Rafael," she said. "He is going to cheat you." She would hate all this. Too many bugs. Nowhere to swim. She was selling the thing she would never lay eyes on. Jay leaned down and scooped up a little clump of dirt, and Orejas told him to drop it.

"Pura mierda," he said. It was pig shit. The soil was over there.

The plantation house was not beautiful. He had not imagined a Virginia mansion with pillars and rocking chairs, but he had hoped for whitewashed walls, arched doorways, green trim, an adobe roof and a terrace where he might sit with his old friend at a table with cold beer and draw a map of their empire. Instead, it was raw cement with chipped orange paint, a broken, barred window at the center, metal doors locked up with chains. A guard, young, maybe eighteen, with a fake diamond earring, a white T-shirt, and blue jeans, was slouched with a rifle across his lap.

Rafael came around the side of the house, hugged Jay, shook hands with Orejas, led them to the front veranda with a little view of the ocean. They sat at a dirty white plastic table with a jug of dark yellow lemonade and blue cloth placemats. Two hammocks swayed in the breeze.

"Do we own all this?" Jay said.

"Thanks to this man," Rafael said, nodding toward Orejas, as the guard from the boat took position on a hump of earth where he could watch the ocean. "He's doing the real work."

A maid emerged from the house and poured the lemonade into plastic cups. Jay struggled to place Rafael here, in his muddy rubber boots and a straw hat, no reassuring art on the walls behind him. He wore a white, long-sleeved shirt with an open collar and faded blue jeans. He was unshaven and had grown fat, an extra chin hanging loosely on his neck, his chest and arms thin but with a hairy belly exposed at the hem of his shirt. His hands looked soft, gold-ringed, elegant. In them you could see he had never lifted a shovel or pounded posts into the earth to enclose cattle. *Our* cattle, Jay thought. He had never owned a cow until now. This was not his world.

"Are we in the final act of the play?" Jay said in English.

"What play?" Rafael said.

"Everyone is dancing circles around me," Jay said. "I would rather just see a normal day in the life."

"Only so much you can see," Rafael said. "The men here are showing you respect."

Orejas downed his lemonade and said they should get to business, that he had to pick up women for the party in Necoclí. The gringo should not be out here too long. Too many people had seen him at the airport and in Turbo. He could leave one of the guards with them.

"Not necessary," Rafael said. They would fly over Río Seco and Jaramillo, two villages south of Turbo where they were planning a mega plantation. They could not go by truck. There was unease in those villages. Jay looked toward the muddy runway to see a Cessna with a rusty propeller on its nose, a chipped blue stripe along it, the door open. A relic. He would have to fly in it.

Rafael opened a map. Jay felt a tingle in his throat like he was about to say something significant that would change the course of history. He saw himself with a bird's-eye view of the table, three serious men acquiring land. Unsure whether to be impressed or disdainful of this vision of himself: a man of power, or just another kind of tourist, playing at something he would never be.

"Finca las Aguas we'll call it," Rafael said. "Great access to water, but we'll need to improve the road to get there. Have you talked to the Messiah?"

"Not yet," Orejas said.

"I'll bring it up tonight."

"He expects it."

The hangup was that Río Seco and Jaramillo had been illegal settlements at their founding, land stolen by the guerrillas. The people were fighters. "Sí o no?" Rafael looked squarely at Orejas, turning to the maid and mouthing the word "ron" at her. She nodded and came back with a bottle.

Orejas touched the map and said, "We need a better reason to go in. The Messiah will think of one. Maybe a high cost."

"We can pay," Rafael said.

"No, not that," Orejas said. "It's political."

"We'll pay you with land," Rafael said. "You and him."

"Land is always good," Orejas said, "but I don't decide these things."

Jay feigned calm, his hands flat on his crossed legs, but inside he was seeing the worst of it, the houses burned, cement slabs ripped up out of their squares, angry men with sacks on their shoulders and stray dogs wondering what was happening. It was the cost of progress. Everyone knew it. It was like cleaning out the inside of a body so the limbs would grow. He did not smile. It was as if they were playing tennis, one of those evenings when Jay was serving well, both tracking the ball and hitting it clean, deep shots in a baseline game, Rafael with his spin, Jay with his power, a night where each man praised the other between shots, where they walked to the net and high-fived. Rafael's eyes said, you serve it straight and I'll finish it.

"Orejas," Rafael said. "There's no limit to our operation here."

"Zero," Jay said. "Zero limit."

Orejas stood up. It was time for each man to raise the little plastic cups of rum that Jay had poured overzealously. They toasted to the future. "He's going to want to meet the gringo," Orejas said.

"That's why I'm here," Jay said.

32.

MOST OF THE WOMEN were sleeping the siesta, though a few sat on straight-backed wooden chairs while their hair blew around from the overhead fans. Salsa played through giant speakers chained to the wall. A younger woman in red shorts and a white tank top was pushing a mop in between little wooden tables with stools. A fat banana manager sat in the corner, a woman listening to him as if he were interesting.

The madame greeted Orejas with false warmth. Deaf from years of loud music, she shouted everything: "Go wake them up!" This to the girl with the mop. "See who wants the money!"

"I need five," Orejas said. "Two nights in Necoclí, maybe three. I have to see them."

"What makes you think you know how to choose?" the madame said, kicking up one foot that seemed broken in half inside its high heel. "Are you going to tell me you want youth and no fallen tits? No one invites me to your parties. Coffee?"

"Por favor," Orejas said.

His eyes adjusted to the dim light, and for a second his head stopped aching. He saw flaws in the women who trickled in, barely dressed in skirts and blouses. They seemed sleepy without makeup. The madame explained the job, and a couple shook their heads, "Yo no," or "Qué mamera," but soon there were five volunteers,

Nanci among them, "la venezolana," the madame said, but Orejas knew better. He remembered her from the failed cantina, they
never mentioned it, and he knew she was a worker from beginning
to end. The madame said they needed another Black woman, so
someone went looking for one named Petra who was in the shower.

"Petra will have my job someday," the madame said.

Orejas sipped his coffee. The brothel did not fill him with
desire anymore. That muscle had atrophied. He wished he were
sleeping the siesta with Gloria, just the sound of the mosquitos
over the bed, the cows stomping around the pasture, his farm rebuilt at twice its size, and at a great discount he had bought a
neighbor's land. It needed new fences and drainages. After the siesta, he would go dig them. It was pleasureable on your own land,
to get dirty and hot and then go for a swim in the river.

"These are the ones," the madame said. "Don't doubt it."

"Fine," he said.

"Orejas," she said. "There were two muchachos here earlier.
They had a white sedan and there was something wrong with
them. One of the girls, Nanci, said they were going to Necoclí."

"I'll look into it," he said. "Gracias."

*

Their little suitcases and duffel bags filled the back of the Land
Cruiser. Petra, in a blonde wig, sat up front and the other four
piled into the back. One farted and everyone laughed. They were
jolly because they were going to make money and nervous because
they were crossing lines to party with men who could get them in
trouble in Apartadó. They passed the clothing shops, and Petra
pointed at the big-titted Black mannequins. She said it was all rags
from China, the labels false, that you could never buy good clothes

in Apartadó, how in two weeks she'd take her vacation to Medellín and get clothes for the year. The sidewalks were busy. They passed a priest in wire-rim glasses and a black T-shirt, a man as tall as the streetlamps.

"Padre Pérez," Petra said, holding up her pinky finger for the backseat and wiggling it.

"He's easy," said one in the backseat. "It's just crooked, and he smells like old bibles."

They hit the road to the ocean, exiting Apartadó, and Petra snatched off her blonde wig, rubbed her head with long fingers, her feet atop the glove compartment as she closed her eyes against so much daylight. She stretched her long arm out the window to catch a bit of rain that was falling right through the sunlight. "Can you turn up this song?"

It was new salsa from Cali. Petra sang and tilted her head back, and during the chorus, Nanci leaned forward and put one hand on Orejas's shoulder and the other on Petra's and rocked them a little.

Almost to Necoclí, the road was blocked with orange cones for a police checkpoint.

"Buenas tardes, oficial," Orejas said.

"Where are you heading?" asked the bull-necked policeman who was not from here.

"We're on vacation," said Petra, fitting the blonde wig back on her head and tucking the elastic behind her ears.

"It's illegal to transport prostitutes," the bull-necked policeman said. "This is not a sector of tolerance. It violates the code."

"Who said we are prostitutes?" Petra said. "We have boyfriends who are going to meet us at Hotel Toscano. What do you know, tombito?"

The bull-necked policeman stared at her, hearing the name of the hotel like a word he should remember for the day when he could afford women this beautiful, but he at least wanted a bite of whatever Orejas was earning, waiting for a ten-thousand-peso bill wrapped around his driver's license. The sun was hot, lifting humidity off the wet ground. Orejas had to get these women delivered and meet Don Rafael and the gringo at the runway. "Here you go, official, but it's not money you should take." He waved at the patrol, these scared teenagers with no idea who ran the zone, who gave them orders, but the bull-necked policeman seemed to realize his error and handed back the money.

33.

THE CESSNA SLAMMED INTO a wall of rough air. Rafael gunned the engine, the plane shaky in the wind.

"It's a beautiful machine," Rafael said, turning the wheel to lower Jay's side of the plane for a view of Río Seco, a three-street clump of houses, scraps of tin and glass, children running around a muddy field and women hanging wash from clotheslines.

They flew north. The rivers fanned out at their mouths with gray, polluted water curling into the gulf. Jay shut his eyes when the plane dropped into pockets of air. They were rising higher and heading straight out into the gulf, high enough that the air felt cool, his ears popping. He feared Rafael was going to drop his body out the side door or take them too low to the sea. Rafael patted his knee and talked about his love for this zone in between countries, looking northward, all the blues below, all the blues changing, lightening as the water was cleaner, all the blues in the universe down there. It was nice to leave the browns and yellows, though the whole Caribbean was a gutter, even the blue parts.

"A fucking gutter," Rafael said. "Only the surface is blue."

"We're low on gas," Jay said.

"Don't worry—I have life jackets," Rafael said, smiling.

Rafael made a sharp turn to the east. The land appeared as a thin green line that gradually thickened into a peninsula. They passed over Necoclí's port, a small hospital with a red cross on the roof, the brick buildings on a spiderweb of dirt roads. A gust of wind jerked them sideways. Rafael lifted them up above the trees. A group of farmers herded cows to one side of the field. Jay tightened his seatbelt and noticed Rafael was not wearing one. They circled once more for the final approach, and Rafael lowered the wheel so that in a second they were bouncing over the grass, the trees blurring in the windows, the shriek of the brakes, the insects crazed in their disrupted orbits. Jay swallowed bile rising up his throat.

Orejas waited on the side of the runway next to the Land Cruiser, as if he had stepped right out of a pore in the land, approaching the plane to help Jay onto the ground.

34.

OREJAS ORDERED HIS CREW to walk every street in Necoclí, and he covered the blocks adjacent to Hotel Toscano and the oceanfront. He materialized in doorways and patios before anyone had seen him, as if stepping out from an aisle in the grocery store or the mirrors in the barber shop. "Buenas tardes," Orejas said, watching his voice rip through people's bodies like voltage. The grocer knocked over a bin of red mangos when he saw him and said, "Buenas, Orejas, a la órden."

The barber offered to empty a chair if Orejas needed a trim. Orejas looked for a particular type of face, long hair, a gaze that was hard to describe but that belonged to guerrillas, anyone walking stiffly or avoiding his eyes. Everyone despised him on this street. He did not see the white sedan. The problem was the Easter holiday. There were a lot of unfamiliar faces here for vacation, even with the paramilitaries in town. People set their fear aside for a day to swim in the ocean.

The waves carried forth a few bodies of swimmers whom Orejas beckoned to shore just to look at them—a man in a red speedo, sagged low on his pelvis, an old lady with a wailing child hanging from her arms. It was a transgression to be alive. To be on holiday. Orejas wanted them to know it. He was here to forgive them.

Some women in a cantina asked if he needed them at the hotel. He looked at their sunken eyes, the wrinkles in their legs, the cheap makeup caked onto their cheeks and foreheads, gleaming in the single bulb hanging down at the center of the room. "Maybe later tonight, mis amores. Have you seen a white sedan?" The women pretended to think, staring at their bare knees in their shiny skirts, their feet locked into high heels, and said, "Nada. No, señor."

Everyone said: "Nada, Orejas, todo normal."

Orejas checked the cars by the hotel, telling the owners to pop the trunks and hoods and using a flashlight to look underneath them. None of the cars were white. He told his men to check any new car. He rounded the block a second time so the people would see him everywhere. He memorized people's faces and recited their names. He walked halfway up the block to the police station, nodding to one of the young officers who stood before the orange sawhorses that restricted passage here. Orejas glanced at the poorly drawn marlin on the white façade of his hotel, Yenifer somewhere inside it, either opening a room for a guest or doing the numbers behind the front desk. Orejas said, "Doña Yenifer, look at you," and decided it was a waste of time to check this block. The police could handle at least one piece of the town. He would walk this circuit in an hour. But for now he wanted to sit at Hotel Toscano and take off his shoes like the others, to dip his feet into the pool and drink a whiskey.

He circled back to the beach, the sun now set. A speedboat with two large motors passed the point, almost levitating above the water. The driver was his brother-in-law in a neon green tank top, who waved, twirled one finger to signal his route. This made Orejas want to go home to his farm. Gloria was probably swinging right now in her hammock on the cement terrace, watching for him even if she knew he wasn't coming. Fish on the stove. His sons were kicking a new soccer ball in the space between the rows of plantains and the packing area. Now was the best time to play, with the light fading and the heat lifting. His son Francisco had a gift for moving laterally, dancing over the ball and positioning his body so he could pass or run. He was quicker than other kids. He might have a gift. Orejas would build them a goal and paint it white. He could see Gloria now, standing up and calling them in. I'm in control, he wanted to tell her, but he was not so sure.

35.

RAFAEL SIPPED FROM A GLASS of whiskey on ice, sucking in his belly as the prostitutes passed him on their way to a pool shaped like a kidney bean. The terrace was fresh–sanded-down cement, blue tiles, plastic chairs, the hotel colonial with a mustard-yellow trim that to someone's eyes seemed like gold. It was a cheap illusion. Irritating vallenatos played from the bar. He was in no position to request Mozart. A prostitute tried to catch his eye, then discarded him before he could discard her. A hair-thin fishbone stayed lodged in his throat from lunch.

"Not too bad for a meeting," Jay said, his legs long and weirdly patchy with blond lustrous hair that was worn away on his shins from tight business socks. His two earrings looked ridiculous. The sky darkened, and the terrace filled with men who had been soldiers or were still soldiers in the new era. Cheap tattoos on biceps and necks. Bad teeth. Buzzed hair.

"If night falls, we're not going to wait," Rafael said in English. "He's late."

"Look up," Jay said.

On the roof perched men with rifles, one waving a hand at Rafael.

"You might want to swim now," Rafael said. "Once the dogs get in, it will be a sewer."

The prostitutes did not pay much attention as Jay slid into the water and swam the length of the pool in just a few strokes. The water was tepid, and he dove under and grabbed onto a plastic nozzle so he would not float to the top. Underwater, he could not hear the vallenato or the shouts of the men arriving. His mood had gone from carefree to jittery. It was time to go home. He imagined them lost in the night sky, flying circles over the mountains, trying to locate Medellín.

When he surfaced there were a couple men in the pool with cropped black hair, bottles of beer in their hands. They were dancing, their shoulders swishing little waves. One of the prostitutes, a tall woman with yellow hair, jumped down to swim. Along one edge of the terrace a monkey with pink hands swung off a clothesline to reach for raw meat on a grill. The cook snapped tongs at it and it ran up onto the wall. The monkey looked right at Jay. It reminded him of Craig Washburn. The sort of monkey that would neatly fold the newspaper after reading it.

"Whiskey!" one of the men in the pool shouted.

"Do you want a kiss, gringo?" said a prostitute with false blue eyes, flat blonde hair, and a crooked nose. She wore a white bikini with purple dots and her body had a healthy thickness. She was missing a lower tooth.

"No, gracias," he said.

*

Night fell, but still they waited. Rafael glared at the party in a trance, while Jay looked back at the door every so often. They were in the dirty part of the Caribbean, a place for Colombian tourists while the Americans and Europeans flocked to the blue waters of Cartagena. One should find beauty everywhere, Jay thought, his hair already dry from the swim. He had put on jeans to protect himself from the mosquitoes. All the wet bodies moved around him in a roiling mass. The live accordion player and the whiskey were loosening parts of his brain in a way that was not pleasant. The pool was too crowded, too splashy. A comandante ordered some of the pool partiers to go to the bar. He stopped by to shake Jay's hand and said he ran el Bloque Bananero. His name was Borrego. "Thank you for your support," he said. The eyes of the men shined too much in the dark. The women removed their tops. Orejas emerged out of the bacchanalia and sang a song beside the accordion player, his eyes wide open, and it seemed strange for such a quiet man to be this loud, his right hand marking the chorus in the air. Afterward, he pulled up a white plastic chair, reaching for the bottle of whiskey.

"Is this a good brand?" Orejas said.

"The best," Jay said. "You have a great voice."

"Gracias."

Rafael said it was time to go, but when they stood, a man in a red long-sleeve shirt approached the table, a white hook of a scar on his forehead. He was the sort of man Jay might pass on the street in Medellín and not look twice, a shopkeeper or a cattle trader, but the accordion player stopped, and there was silence on the terrace. Even the monkey paid attention.

"Comandante!" Orejas said.

Everyone went still out of respect. Jay shook hands with the Messiah, the leader of the paramilitaries, the savior of Urabá. At that moment Jay felt like he was joining two countries, two business conglomerates, two old buddies who had been walking toward each other for years and did not know it, the hand surprisingly smooth, gripping Jay's hand but seeming to grip his entire body and to lift him up beneath the canvas umbrella.

"Thank you for inviting me," Jay said. "It's productive land with happy people, despite their troubles." He bungled his Spanish because he was nervous. He could feel the charge and aura of this man whose bodyguards stood close at the table. No one looked at him.

"Right, yes, productive land," the Messiah said in a shrill, grinding voice, "but Colombia has wasted its potential. It has access to two oceans. What other country has that?"

Jay sipped whiskey because he thought it was a rhetorical question, but then the Messiah looked impatient, so Jay said, "No country ever."

"Your country, gringo."

Everyone laughed. Jay felt Rafael's hand under the table, a quick squeeze of his knee to say that there was no need to speak. Just listen.

"It's rare that I enjoy a party," the Messiah said. "I am always on the move. I have a beautiful wife, and sometimes I don't share her bed for months." He launched into a monologue with repeated words like "subversives" and "irregular war" and "new order" and "clean." Jay should witness the people applauding in the streets when the paramilitaries took over a town and cleaned it. Women had named their children after him. Victims of the subversives threw themselves at his feet. Businesses were opening in the zones they controlled. You could stand at Embarcadero Zungo and see the proud faces of the braceros because these were new men under a new order. The Messiah grew up on cold land, Amalfi, a tiny town in Antioquia where it was not easy to find books, and his father drove him and his brothers too hard. They milked cows on their knees at dawn. Amalfi was a place to labor and die without ever learning anything new. If he could, he would stop the war tomorrow and return to the university, to live in a boarding house in Medellín, to drink coffee and discuss Aristotle. Had Jay read Aristotle?

"Many years ago," Jay said.

After his brother was murdered by guerrillas, the Messiah said, not far from here, he had to prove himself as a leader of men. They attacked a group of sixty guerrillas in San Pedro. A suicide mission. The Messiah was ambushed on the road before he and his men arrived. He jumped over a barbed wire fence and caught his scrotum on a barb, all while they were shooting at him. He crawled into the exposed roots of a tree and waited to bleed out. He spent a night covered in mud. Gunfire flashed above him and saplings and grass split and burned under the bullets. It was not so easy to die.

But when he died it wouldn't matter. They would hide his body in a remote pasture in Córdoba. People would say he was still alive. There would be no more camouflage. No Bloque Bananero. He would exist in every drop of water and the bread people ate.

He wants our terror, Jay thought, for us to suffer the night like him. He was late on purpose. He's not crazy, like Craig Washburn or the others in Cincinnati would think. He has a vision.

No one had his legs crossed but Jay, the glass in his hand sweating, dripping from his wrist to his elbow and onto his chest and pants. The monkey, positioned on a ledge, was eating a sausage.

"Excuse me, comandante, but can we discuss business?" Rafael said. "Unfortunately we have a meeting in Medellín and must fly back tonight."

"The hotel is safe, safer than the sky," the Messiah said, "but you do what you want. Tell me something. There are three hundred and eighty-four banana plantations right now in Urabá. Why one more at the size you're proposing? I've always raised cattle. Can you believe that a banana is more valuable?"

"It depends who holds the banana," Rafael said.

The man named Borrego approached the table, saluted the Messiah, and snatched bottles of whiskey from the crate, filling the women's glasses, and then dove into the shallow pool, came up with blood on his forehead, screamed with humor, and no one told him to quiet down. The accordion player had changed songs, but it was all the same song, Jay thought, especially if it was vallenato. The Messiah did not want to talk business. He wanted to make them wait and fly back to Medellín and stare at their phones, and maybe a month would pass, and all the cleaning would happen, wherever the Messiah wanted, and the planters would foot the bill. Let's go, Rafael's eyes said. This is pointless.

"No one here works for free," the Messiah said to Jay. "We have to finance our army. Every muchacho you see is with us because he grew up poor. He would rather be reading Aristotle or studying biology. The planters have too much power. The zone where you want land is not good for us. Not yet."

"Our eyes are open," Jay said. "Or closed. Whatever you prefer, comandante."

"Do you like music?"

"Very much," Jay said.

"I don't trust anyone who dislikes music. Could you sing us a song from your country?"

"Better not," Jay said. "My voice is ridiculous."

"Maybe you recite a poem for us instead? Whitman? Eliot? My men would love it."

"I apologize, comandante. Not without the book in hand."

"Do you know Antonio Machado?"

"Of course. I lived in Spain."

The Messiah snapped his fingers, stood, and the band fell silent. He recited the famous poem, "Caminante, no hay camino," which Jay had once memorized, like all children, in a classroom in Madrid, and while there it was a call to existential freedom, here, he realized, it was for war. Barely pausing, the Messiah launched into another Machado poem about a man walking a dusty trail up some mountain and looking out to see el Río Duero, crossing the dry land in Castilla. When he shouted, "O, tierra triste y noble," Rafael looked sick to his stomach. The beauty of that dry valley in Spain was the beauty of this tropical land, the Messiah concluded, and Jay heard waves thunk against the shore. Men applauded and said, "¡Qué chimba" and "¡Qué maravilla!" The accordionist ignited with a vigorous squeeze and the singer blasted out a voice that sounded ancient.

Rafael stood and held out his hand. "Thank you, comandante, for the hospitality, but it's time—"

A thunderclap exploded overhead. There was a scream on the street, and something tore apart the umbrella over the table. An ambush, Jay thought, as something whipped him forward onto the pool deck, throwing him near the grill, where he rolled into the water and grabbed the nozzle to hold himself under.

He heard a second boom on the street, as he came up for air, his ears all static and ringing. He saw his quiet office in Cincinnati, a little swatch of the Ohio River, a color photo of a plantation in Guatemala on the wall with little perfect bunches of cavendish bananas, and Craig Washburn was in the threshold of the door, saying, "You are a fool."

36.

OREJAS SCANNED THE STREET with his rifle at his shoulder. The white sedan he had not found lay flipped against the barbershop. A couple dying men inside. He found his Land Cruiser parked up against the grocery store, the windshield shattered. Blood dripped down the side of his head. He told his men to stop every bus heading south and north and ask the drivers who was who. Likely the bombers had a second car or motorcycle.

He picked up a bolt off the ground. A dirty bomb, a gas cylinder or C-4. There were bolts and nails and other scraps of metal. He cleared out the broken windshield of his Land Cruiser and drove, circling outward from Hotel Toscano, looking for faces and vehicles. He passed a bar at the beach where a few drunk men lay in the sand. Salsa burst from a cantina as someone ran out, and then its doors closed. The streets were empty.

Wind blew against Orejas's face, bits of glass sliding along the dashboard. Little bluish splinters of it stuck to his arms. He was at fault. He could flee, cease to be Orejas and follow the nearly washed-out gravel road back to his house, grab Gloria by the arm, pick up his two sleeping boys, and put them all in the Land Cruiser. He saw boxes of plantains on the scales that they would not ship. He had the keys to the boats in the port. He could lay his boys on a bed of life jackets in the stern. He could sit his wife beside him and tell her to watch the land and the islands. She had eyes for distance.

He would fuel up and buy water in Acandí, and they would follow the coast until it was time to turn north to Mexico. In San Andrés they would fuel up again. Providencia, Jamaica to the east, travel through the night and fuel up again for a final stretch. No one would expect him to be in the middle of the Caribbean with his family. He could store a couple rifles in the bow. The sun would rise and he would cover his boys in the life jackets and tell them to appreciate the beauty of the wide-open gulf. Northwest to Vera-cruz where Orejas had a contact. He would beach the boat outside the city and avoid the Coast Guard. Within a few days he would find a job.

Orejas drove past the orange sawhorses and up the one block he had not thoroughly checked before the party. He asked one of the policemen if he had seen a white sedan, and he said yes, parked right by his hotel.

"Open the door," Orejas said, tapping with the butt of his pis-tol on the red metal door of Hotel de Simón. "Open, Yeni. I know you're here." She didn't answer, so he raised up his rifle, opened the lock with his own key and entered, pointing his barrel at the desk where Yenifer was eating a hamburger.

"Don't lie to me," Orejas said. "Where are they?"

"Who?" she said.

"A white sedan," he said. "Two muchachos. Are they here?"

She said not now. An ugly muchacho and another one had gone out an hour ago. She assumed they came for the holiday. One asked her if she knew where they could find marijuana, and she said she had no idea. They paid cash and signed the registry, and she wrote down their ID numbers. They said they wanted the second floor for privacy.

"What room?"

She led Orejas upstairs without breathing, the taste of burnt hamburger and raw onion rising in her throat. She opened the door to the room, and a guest peeked out from across the hallway and closed his door.

Orejas upended the garbage can, leaned over the bed with the imprints of bodies and sniffed the fabric, which seemed insane to Yenifer as she hovered in the doorway, scanning with her own eyes for any clue, but they both knew they would find nothing. He grabbed a plastic bag with dirty clothes inside.

"Come with me and talk to the Messiah," he said.

Right then the lights went out in the room and through the window she saw it was the whole town. She waited for the flash of his rifle or a blade to her throat, and she gripped the edge of the door. Her old friend, Orejas.

"Light a candle," he said.

"In the office," she said.

She found matches in a desk drawer with candles that she would hand out to the guests. The match snapped to life, and they were orange people in the glow of the tiny flame. His eyes shone like two deformed moons in his face. His finger snaked in and out from his mouth to his nose, nervous, waiting for her to guide him. He rested his hand on her bony shoulder and asked why in the world he would kill her. She was family, wasn't she?

He felt the puckered cut on the side of his head, a hunk of glass in it. He said he feared his brain was leaking down the side of his face and down his collar. She was reaching for a towel under the desk and passing it to him. He mentioned his plan to disappear to Mexico with his family. She shook her head like it was a fantasy.

"Your life is here," she said.

"Forgive me," Orejas said. "The Messiah doesn't know you, but I'm going to make it clear. Let's go, Yeni. No pasa nada."

37.

A DETACHED ARM FLOATED at one end of the pool. Jay tried to stay underwater. The topless women had run for the rooms. An ambulance siren beat a track up the block. He was careful not to plant his feet on the bottom because they were full of glass.

He was waiting for strong hands to force him to the surface, for Rafael to say, "Let's hunker down in a room." It was quiet underwater except for a zet-zet-zet ringing in his ears. He looked over the lip of cement to where the tables had shattered, the glass sparkling in the terrace lights, and he saw two men carrying Rafael's body on a stretcher toward the exit. He seemed dead, but Jay could hear his voice telling them not to take him to the hospital. The right thing would be to help his friend. He grabbed the plastic nozzle and dunked back underwater.

*

The youth pulled Jay from the pool and threw him over his shoulder like he was an especially long farm animal, his fingers scratching Jay's legs, and the youth grunted under the weight, "Un tronco, qué gringo pesado," heaving him up the stairs to the second story and along a railing to a room, kicking the door somehow without dropping Jay and saying, "¡Putas de mierda, abran!" The door opened and two women in swimsuits grabbed Jay's legs while the youth clutched his shoulders.

"Cuídenlo al gringo," the youth said. "No salgan para nada."

Jay lay face down on the bed while the Black woman with blonde straight hair plucked glass from his feet and tried to clean them with a wet towel. The other with false blue eyes was singing to herself a song with a song with a refrain that was "Me dejaste, mi amor, por qué, por qué?"—bouncing her hips on the bed and drinking straight from a bottle of Chivas Regal.

"I don't know if I can get the smaller pieces," the Black woman said.

"He's fine," the other said, unknotting her hair, a blonde that was almost white, a fluorescent color of candy, letting it fall over her back. She tipped the whiskey bottle into her mouth and held it above her the way a football player might do it at a party. "He's a sweetheart. Do you have money, gringo?"

"Are we safe?" Jay said. The room spun like a merry-go-round, his skin stank with a burned chemical smell. He did not hear gunshots or sirens. He heard only the booming voice of the Messiah and the screech of the monkey in his cage.

"I am Petra," said the Black woman taking care of him. "Ella es Nanci."

"You're going to die if you drink like that," Jay said. "It's meant to be sipped."

"I've never felt this good," Nanci said.

"Es una guerra muy cansona, gringo," Petra said, pressing the towel into Jay's feet that were now free of glass but flowing with more blood. She said they were used to it. There was no gunfight tonight. Only a bomb. A guerrilla maneuver that was definitely bad for business. Wasn't it a pretty hotel? Like in the movies! New rooms with real mattresses and clean bathrooms.

"I am a military objective for the guerrillas," Jay said. "I should be hiding."

"We are not guerrillas, gringo, not even close," Nanci said. "These men are going to find the bombers."

Jay asked Petra if she minded if he took off his jeans. They were soaking wet and uncomfortable.

"You're going to mess up my work," she said, having wrapped his feet in white towels. Her face seemed shaped around a proud thing, her eyes large with it, her lips pulled back in a permanent smile. She peeled the blonde wig off her head and tossed it onto the other bed.

"We've seen what you got," Nanci said. "We're not afraid of it."

Petra expertly unbuttoned his jeans and wrenched them off, along with his underwear, which he tried to keep in place.

"I don't want sex," Jay said.

"Not even a blowjob?" Petra said.

"No, gracias. Could you help me sit up?"

"What are you, a homosexual?" Nanci said. "If she doesn't fuck you, are you still going to pay us?"

"We have all night to do whatever you want," Petra said.

The lights went out everywhere. Nanci pulled back the curtains to look out and said it was the whole town. The whole ocean.

"We're fucked," Jay said.

"Tranquilo, gringo," Nanci said. "No one is going to touch you. The Messiah is right down there in the office and that man won't die tonight. This is the safest spot in town right now."

Petra lit a cigarette, which provided some light, and there was a half moon above the ocean, and gradually their eyes adjusted to the dark so they could see each other. Jay covered himself in a sheet. Nanci sang badly—"Por qué, mi amor, por qué?"—and Petra shut her up. She washed out three glasses with hand soap in the bathroom and poured whiskey into them. "Fiestita," she said, setting Jay's glass on his chest, but he didn't drink. Time passed with only their breathing and the sound of cars on the block, the sound of a man barking orders at the pool. Jay could feel the hotel emptied out and wondered if Rafael was alive. He could see him fallen from his chair, thrown not toward the grill where Jay had landed but in the other direction.

"There was an arm in the pool," Jay said. "From the shoulder down."

"Qué asco," Petra said. "Don't talk about it. We're trying to relax."

"The gringo saw something," Nanci said. "Let him talk. I saw more than that. The guy I was dancing with fell on top of me and he was gone. My ass hurts."

"I need to contact someone," Jay said. "I should call Medellín."

"Tranquilo," Petra said. "Let the Messiah solve the problems."

"Are you two from here?" Jay said.

"She is," Petra said. "I'm from Buenaventura."

"Why are *you* here?" Nanci said, putting her hand on his bare stomach, but he removed it firmly and she laughed at him. "Are you a narco?"

"I work in the bananas," Jay said.

"Of course, same thing," Nanci said, running her fingers through his wet hair, combing it to one side. "Gringo, tell me something. What does a whore make in the United States? Per fuck?"

"Maybe two hundred dollars?" Jay said.

"Mierda," Nanci said. "What's that in pesos?"

"Eight hundred thousand," Petra said, "more or less."

"We're wasting our time here," Nanci said.

"She's a hard worker," Petra said. "We could do twenty men a night, each. How much would that be?"

"A lot," Jay said.

Nanci lay down beside Jay, whistled, swung her arm around his neck, and put the glass of whiskey to his lips, and said, "Marry me, gringo. I'll only charge you one hundred each time."

"The room is turning," Jay said.

"It always is," Nanci said. "This is the circle room. It never stops moving. Are we going to sleep or are we going to party? My friend works for you, I think. Yenifer Contreras. Do you know her?"

"No," Jay said.

"She's the one," Nanci said. "She's the one to promote because she knows everything."

"That's good," Jay said, "I will look for her."

"Look, gringo," Nanci said. "Trust me. She'll tell you the truth about your plantations. How much does a hairdresser make in the United States?"

"She cuts hair," Petra said.

"Thirty, maybe sixty dollars a cut," Jay said.

"Ave María," Nanci said. "Marry me, please. I'll cut your hair for free."

Nanci went to the window for air and leaned out for the slight breeze. She drank from the glass Petra had cleaned and lit a cigarette.

"She has a lot to give," Petra said. "People think our lives are over because of our work. Our lives are just beginning."

*

"How do you know Orejas?" Nanci said, lying down next to him again and resting her head against his chest.

"He used to work for Banana Bolívar," Jay said.

She said she knew Orejas before he was anyone. A banana

worker. She had not liked him then and did not much now. He and Yenifer Contreras were "like this," her fingers curled together. But he had never hurt her, and that was rare. Most men had tried to hurt her. He chose her for the parties. Prettier girls were out there, but Nanci was worth every peso. Orejas had humiliated all the people who used to look down at him. Wasn't that everyone's dream?

"If I weren't so drunk," she said, "I'd be timid with you."

Petra's breathing deepened on the other bed, fast asleep. Nanci called him her "marido," fiddled with her swimsuit that squeaked against her skin, something uneven about the room. She talked in elliptical shapes, a little hard to follow, about her life, a bakery, the drudgery of these parties and long nights, a purple room she escaped to, men confessing their sins to her and wanting her in tiring ways. She said Yenifer was right here in Necoclí, running a hotel. They could sneak out and see her, let her try this whiskey.

"Mi amor," Nanci said. "I drank too much."

Nanci dozed off. Jay knew he had no chance at sleep. Her legs against his were boiling hot, and he was sweating into the itchy sheets. A humid breeze puffed up the curtains. He thought of his bags of dirt forgotten in the Cessna. He saw all his land rolling by him in a green strip, Rafael patting the rump of a fat cow, a servant setting down fried snapper and coconut rice, Jay spilling his lemonade onto the map and angering Rafael who blamed it on the servant, Graciela awake in bed, waiting to hear his key in the door. Everyone was elsewhere, Rafael probably hooked up to a bag of blood in the hospital, a subpar doctor stitching him closed, or perhaps they realized they had a Restrepo on their hands and were already flying him to Medellín. What about me? Jay thought. This would be his last night in Urabá. He would never come back, not even when there was peace.

"Are you asleep?" Jay said.

He felt lonely, just like on summer nights in Ohio, the TV on with no sound, everything futile, and he was always looking in the wrong direction.

38.

IN THE LAND CRUISER with no windshield, the insects pricked Orejas's face like pebbles. One of his headlights was busted, but the other one guided him. He could have driven these roads in the dark. Every curve and dip and bridge were in his mind's eye.

At a packing area in el Mellito, bananas everywhere, the two muchachos were tied to posts like human-sized dolls, their heads removed, their limbs folded together in what had once been pain.

"You were supposed to wait," Orejas said.

"Cantaron," said one of his men. "They confessed."

He doubted it. They looked like banana workers, not bombers. He stood in the single headlight of his Land Cruiser. Someone handed him a bottle of Chivas Regal.

"Sigue la rumba," they said, and bantered about how each had experienced the bomb, some of them launched through the air, others fucking in hotel rooms.

One of the men passed Orejas a plastic bag with mushrooms, dried up, coin-sized, and slapped his shoulder. They tasted dirty and fell to pieces in the back of his mouth. He washed them down with whiskey. Later, they would drop him in another country, not unlike Mexico, where all the voices were distant, where touching a street dog would cause the fleas to jump individually into the air.

"Hang them up in Necoclí," Orejas said. "Then go find more. The Messiah wants bodies."

"What about the heads?" one of the men said.

"Put them back on," Orejas said.

He had left Yenifer with her knees together in the office at Hotel Toscano. Her hair straight above her head in a messy ponytail. A candle lighting up her eyes in a way that reminded him of a birthday. The Messiah asked what she knew. She spoke as Orejas had told her to speak, making promises she would have to keep about Banana Bolívar.

The Messiah asked her for names and she gave them. Take it easy, Orejas wanted to tell her. Everything you say will be confirmed. You can't take it back.

*

Necoclí seemed suspended in the air by the power lines, so many, so thin, woven together, filled with light. Little houses seemed open to Orejas as he drove past them. He could walk into any house to have a sip of water or lie down in bed with a man's wife. Borrego had been gravely injured by the bomb. There was a gate for Orejas to walk through and become the comandante of el Bloque Bananero that was just one front in the larger movement. They wanted the whole country—the oil wells and gold mines, the drug routes that began as far south as Putumayo and spread north in hundreds of forking lines. His place was here. The newly titled land. The port with its influx of manufactured automobiles and TVs, its outflux of raw things. He would police it.

Orejas stopped at the beach and walked down to the water. He saw fluorescent blues and reds in the sand and sky. He wondered how it was that most days there was no color, just the dull green of pasture and bananas, the white and beige of the houses, doors to be opened, men to be questioned. Every door he entered he had to close. It was as boring as his early days with the guerrillas, but now he was getting somewhere. He leaned into the sand and kissed it.

*

At Hotel Toscano, the Messiah called Orejas and said Yenifer had been sent back to her hotel. Don Rafael was dead in the hospital. A lucky woman and an unlucky man. They needed to get the gringo out. He called the gringo "el paquete" and said the safest way to get him out was by boat to Panama at dawn. Orejas would take him. The Messiah had switched his red party shirt to a camouflage uniform with sleeves rolled up. His lips looked like dry worms. His hands seemed to float above him and his voice echoed all around Orejas, who struggled to hold it together. He felt the power of one man's will like an electric surge radiating light into the room. His guards stood in the doorway and against the wall. One said it was time for the Messiah to get out of sight to a camp somewhere in the jungle.

The Messiah said, "Worry about the gringo. Tell him he can call us directly. Give him your cell number."

Orejas told him the names extracted from the two muchachos who had participated in the bombing. He decided they were guilty. There was no room for uncertainty in this world.

39.

Jay was sweating in the stuffy room when light cut through the window. Nanci had moved to the other bed. He looked at her in the gray light, her feet askew with purple nails on bent toes. Her face seemed thoughtful, like she was answering a hard question in her sleep. He was tempted to look out the window but he did not want to put any weight on his feet. Petra lay beside her, the blonde wig hung from the neck of the whiskey bottle. His sheets were damp and grimy with sand.

He put on his underwear and jeans, everything still wet. Orejas stood beside him and said they had to go immediately. The police were here to investigate the attack. The women had to leave, too. Orejas crossed the room like a swimmer, cutting through the air with his hands before him.

"Vamos, chicas, vamos," Orejas said, grabbing Nanci by the skull, squeezing it until her eyes opened. He said, "Wake up your friend."

"Are we getting paid?" were Nanci's first words.

"I have your money," Orejas said.

*

The sea seemed to Jay as flat as western Ohio. He dipped his fingers into the water and smelled the intense salt, rubbing a little into his neck. The bodyguards unmoored the boat and tossed ropes onto the bow. A seagull landed on the stern and stared at them all.

Rafael was dead, Orejas said. He said it like one would announce the probability of heavy rain in the afternoon, just a minor setback in a voyage. A shard of metal had cut Rafael's neck and he bled out en route to the hospital. Jay had to pry these details out of Orejas. The boat felt more solid now. Jay touched the ropes, the shaft of a harpoon, and he felt these objects were proof that the world persisted and that the death of a Restrepo was no different than the death of a soldier last night. He was surprised by how little he felt. He shut his eyes to say a quick prayer. He asked for Rafael's soul to be delivered safely, but he was interrupted by the jerk of the boat, the revving of the motors.

He looked ahead at the flat ocean, but through it he saw the deeds for land and a stack of contracts in Rafael's office. He saw wooden stakes marking the corners of their land, his land, and the others from here to Medellín who at the first sight of blood would begin testing the fences. He saw the clay courts at el Club Campestre and the wooden bench in the steam room where the planters would gossip.

They were at sea and the motors made talking impossible. Outwardly, he wanted to seem calm, his knees spread apart, his hands on his knees as he faced the bow, looking right over the shoulder of the bodyguard who happened to be the same youth who had carried him to the room.

"Una mierda," Jay said in his toughest voice, but no one reacted. Urabá was just a thin green line in the distance. Panama was out there at the end of the blue horizon.

As they crossed the center of the calm gulf, Orejas smiled at him. He raised the throttle so high that the wind seemed to rip out Jay's eyebrows and hair, it might tear his clothes from his body, his eyeballs dry and his stomach fluttering as if his body were left behind him, and he signaled for him to slow it down a little. He saw green, rocky islands to the east, and what was probably Triganá, then Capurganá and Acandí, white-sand beaches, wooden huts with hammocks, places for tourists, Orejas said, as if reading his mind. "Guerrillas control it. For now."

Jay assumed it was a drug boat. There was rope attached to the seat, and Rafael had told him that the drug runners tied themselves down to not fall out. Slowing down was not an option.

"Rafael was a good person," Jay yelled over the roar of the motors, and Orejas shrugged.

The ocean turned bluer as they exited the gulf. They crossed the invisible line for Panama. Their bodies vibrated with the motors. El Darién, all mountain, rose up green and dense over the horizon. He knew migrants and drug mules got lost on those routes. The sea was better. They passed villages on islands, disconnected from the rest of the country by the jungle, nothing but boats and landing strips. The water very blue now, smashing against the cliffs of the little islands where no one lived.

*

"Everything is about to happen," Orejas said, slowing down so they could hear one another. He glanced over his shoulder at a fishing vessel, probably out for tuna, to the east. He said the whole Caribbean would belong to the Messiah in a year. Follow the coast all the way to Santa Marta and la Guajira and draw a line to Mexico, and Jay would find a man like him. He could count on it. Everything was "a la órden." Everyone on this boat was loyal because they wanted business, and the difference between a friend and enemy, unfortunately, was sometimes money. "The death of Rafael is convenient for you. Excuse me for saying it."

I may have to see a shrink, Jay thought. He would sit in the
aquarium on Monday and tell a frightening story to the executives
who had not seen their plantations in many years, if ever, and they
would call him "un atrevido," stupid for nothing. Urabá was still
and always a war zone. At the dock in Colón, he would ask Orejas
to wait while he went to a cash machine and took out the maximum
amount with two cards. He would give him a tip for getting him
out of Necoclí and he would tell him that they were partners now,
that if Orejas saw to Jay's interests, he would make him a rich man.

"Estamos en contacto," he would say. "Gracias, hermano."

"A la órden," Orejas would say.

But in reality none of these things happened. They passed the
San Blas Islands late in the afternoon. Tourists lay intoxicated on
hammocks and on lounge chairs, little kids selling coconut water
and coconut candy, a man with a foam cooler of beer, and Orejas
said they could not enter Colón directly. Too many eyes there. He
would drop him right onto the beach of a resort and no one would
ask questions because he was a white man, and Jay said, how can
I pay you back? Orejas said the bananas would pay for everything.

It was paradise here, cleaner than Colombia, Jay thought, the
people more relaxed, the water as blue as blue crayons. The bodyguard helped him over the bow onto the sand, the motors up so
they wouldn't run aground, and Orejas waved and looked away
like Jay was no greater than a box of merchandise being set on
foreign soil.

THE BANANA WARS

1995

40.

WHAT YENIFER REMEMBERED about that night, a payday at Banana Bolívar, was how she had been in a good mood. She was walking home from the corner store with a bottle of Coke, a bag of plantains to fry, and saw the three pairs of headlights widening on the dirt road. She hated el Aracatazo, the cantina between her and her house, its music starting early afternoon and storming the whole neighborhood, wedging into the cracks in the walls, saturating her sheets, the refrains of vallenato and salsa trapped in her skull, and while everyone had a right to their music, she could not relax or sleep, even when she stuffed her ears with toilet paper.

From the patio of el Aracatazo, a drunk drove a finger into his mouth like that finger was her body and said, "I could fatten that butt for you, mamita," and one of the banana workers who knew her grabbed the man's shoulders and anchored him to a chair, whispered something in his ear, probably telling him Yenifer Contreras was a friend of Orejas—she was not just any woman on the street.

She accelerated her pace and in a second was inside her house, sliding the bolt on her metal door, and by the time the trucks arrived at the cantina and the shooting started, she was already under the bed and forgot why she had been out in the first place. When it stopped, she noticed the bottle of Coke on the floor, the bag of plantains, and then something more upsetting, a muddy print on the clean cement floor of her living room.

Her motorcycle was parked in its spot. A sharp taste of bleach in the air. Her little TV was unplugged, the screen cracked. A woman was screaming from el Aracatazo and the trucks rattled her house as they passed on their way out. Yenifer opened the door to her back patio, pushed her motorcycle under the clothesline and into a gap in the banana field. She had never walked it, but the fields were all the same, the cable would lead to a packing area and a road. She fell into a furrow, her motorcycle tipping onto her, and for a second she was hurt.

Sirens approached from Carepa. Don't be naïve, Orejas had said. Your neighbors are all guerrillas. Beyond the dark, men were screaming along with the women, saying who was dead and who was still living, calling on God for help, and she got to her feet and pushed up a trail into the darkness lit only by the grease of the banana cable and a glimmer on the leaves of the plants.

41.

RAFAEL'S FUNERAL, WELL ATTENDED by banana men and politicians, felt like a business conference, lots of handshakes and whispered humor. The tributes were delivered with a business rhetoric, as if they were standing before investors, each man repositioning himself to take advantage of the opening. Jay sat in a pew by Ernesto Echevarría, who said, "Todo avanza, todo avanza, everyone has their moment." The governor of Antioquia, a thin, small man with a cold, tough-man voice–the future president, some whispered–spoke at the altar and called not for an end to the war but an intensification of it.

Jay cried a little but for who knew what reasons, riding in an SUV with Graciela, who looked away. "You and Rafael were not that close," she said. Outside was the center of Medellín, old men buying lottery tickets, young women standing in front of a giant underwear emporium with pink bras and leopard panties, a man with a megaphone shouting, "Barato, barato, barato," and in Jay's eyes it all looked revelatory.

Jay hired lawyers in Bogotá to examine the paperwork. Rafael's children had returned from their schools in the United States and seemed disappointed with the size of their patrimony. They wanted nothing to do with Urabá, which was in the papers almost daily and would soon become international news.

"When do we sell our share?" said Rafael's son, an effete young man with black-framed glasses, nervous lips he bit into while speaking. He insisted on English with Jay. He was afraid of Medellín and whatever his father had been a part of. He went everywhere with a bodyguard who looked like a campesino in a suit and was more paranoid than him. Rafael's daughter, a teenager, sat silently in the electric chair with no straps in Rafael's apartment, narrow-faced with a pinpoint nose, her hands balled into fists.

"Like, why were you there?" she said in English.

*

It took months to sort out the contracts. At first, he would stop by Rafael's old apartment and drink coffee with the maid, who knew that any day they would sell the apartment and put her on the street. She asked strange questions about Jay's European ancestors and his education, and he realized she was drinking through the liquor cabinet, filling the scotch bottles with chicken broth and the vodka bottles with water. He hoped she had stolen enough objects to sell and survive in her world. There were gaps in the walls where the paintings had hung, everything at auction in New York.

At Banana Bolívar, they replaced Rafael with Graciela, the first woman to sit at the table in the aquarium at the banana corporation. It was not a good time to be CEO. The massacres were bad news, and Graciela was at the head of it. In meetings, she stood with a slight lean forward, as if on a ledge. She did what the others did. She said "positives" and "negatives." The murder of a guerrilla was a "positive," while that of a Banana Bolívar manager or worker was a "negative." Occasionally, Jay would repeat something she said aloud so that the banana men would hear it, but her voice had a sharp, unapologetic bite, and like the Messiah, she displayed her ruthlessness in her first month on the job by firing a number of accountants and auditing the office in Urabá.

The massacres were terrible for production. On days when a plantation was attacked, work stopped and shipments were canceled. Even workers nowhere near the violence had to travel the same roads, and when they saw the trucks with armed men or simply smelled it in the air, they turned around and went home. Strikes happened weekly. Protect us, the workers demanded, and the planters were not receptive because who had ever protected them when their plantations were on fire?

Any day, Orejas was going to clear Río Seco and Jaramillo, where Jay would open a plantation. No Restrepo to back him. No Banana Bolívar to hide behind. The wheels were turning. He just had to step aside and root for his army.

42.

THEY WERE THERE BEFORE anyone heard them. Orejas's crew muscled house to house, kicking open doors and walking through the open ones, stepping around children and finding men in chairs eating breakfast or crouched on the floor with their boots half on. They ordered everyone to the village school. They grabbed people by the necks and hair and dragged them out onto the street.

Orejas knew Río Seco well. His mother had lived here during a brief split with his father, and Orejas had visited her and played soccer with the children who made fun of his ears. The village school was a cement rectangle with holes for windows with no glass, a puddle at the center of the room. All open land around them, the houses were crowded together, made of cheap orange bricks, mostly unpainted, though here and there were splotches of color. The residents were banana workers, all members of the union allied with the guerrillas.

Not until he arrived did he realize he did not want to be here, but there was no question of going backward. He had swallowed mushrooms an hour ago with a slug of aguardiente, so the village was imploding with disrupted molecules. It was fragile. A poke of his finger would knock it down. The houses floated on mud. A brown pig with fan-sized ears was tied to a post at the side of a house, and she was watching him, daring him to be alive. Five nipples stuck out like pegs on her belly. She nibbled on a bit of grass growing at the edge of the street, and the green of it was intensified by the rain to an emerald craze. He saw all of it burning. He saw the people gagging on smoke. He saw them face down in puddles of excrement.

"Vean, vean," said Orejas, a new white gold chain glinting across his neck, his brown ears huge in the sun. He announced himself as the paramilitary comandante of el Bloque Bananero, leading the offensive against the guerrillas of Urabá. He said this to groggy faces, glazed by the shock of the two silver Toyota Tacomas, by men with bandoliers of bullets across their chests and assault rifles in black-gloved hands. Orejas pronounced the names off a list and no one stepped forward. He said they would murder the babies first if the people did not collaborate. The wanted ones emerged from the crowd. Orejas's men bound their wrists with yellow banana rope and crouched them against the wall of the school.

He heard them breathing. He heard a child ask his mother what they were doing. He wanted to answer the child: "We are cleaning out the bad ones, so you can live." He heard a bird flap down from the roof of a house, but it was not a vulture. It was just a white bird with a damaged beak. A baby cried and its mother nearly suffocated it with her breast. She was breastfeeding at a massacre. He could hear the milk being sucked into the baby's throat and he could taste it sweet. The white bird was doing flips over the road.

"Vean, vean," Orejas said. He told them to watch what happened to guerrilla collaborators and politicians of la Unión Patriótica. He listed the names of the banana plantations where they worked, Finca la Primavera, Finca Currulao, Finca la Fortuna, Finca Pa' qué Más. His voice amazed him. He felt as if it was made of light. His mouth an intense flood lamp even brighter than the morning sky, and the light bounced off the metal roofs and up into the skin of the people and lit them up near to burning.

"We give you twenty-four hours to leave," Orejas said. "Your village belongs to las Autodefensas de Colombia."

Orejas flipped over Jorge Montoya Borjas, a known political leader who was tied up against the wall of the school. He pulled up his chin and with a machete cut off his head and set it beside his wife, Teresa Quintana Rodríguez, whose wrists were also tied. The crowd seemed to sway and look through him to some other place he would also like to see. "Vean, vean," Orejas said. He wiped his hands clean on his thighs.

The whole point was to have an audience. The Messiah had ordered him to generate terror. Orejas wanted his face imprinted like a golden figure in the backs of their eyes and for it to be in every landscape and every room they looked at from then on, especially when they closed their eyes at night to sleep. A light that would change them.

The paramilitaries beheaded all six men and Teresa Quintana Rodríguez. When the heads were free, they lined them up, and Orejas repeated, "Vean, vean! Two days!"

Orejas saw houses that would fall. A new road ran right through them. The people filled canvas sacks and did not look back. A packing area right there where the school had been. No one was learning in that school anyway. Orejas imagined the white bird teaching the children. A column of words on the board. The children being saved now from a dream.

All this happened in an instant. He was already elsewhere at some plantation, counting money on a table and setting it aside for specific people. He raised his rifle, sighted the pig that lay low, snout in the air, its body plastered with dust and mud. He squeezed the trigger and nothing happened at first. There was some delay between the jerk of his finger and the noise and then the sight of blood fountaining up from the pig's neck and then the steady waste of it. He told one of his men to put the pig in his Tacoma.

*

As they drove away, Orejas saw it all dissolve into the dust and heat. The man beside him wore a filthy white shirt that looked like a bloody animal tied to his chest.

"Take it off," Orejas said.

The road was a mess, too narrow for the trucks, as porous as a sponge with all its potholes and puddles. At a rise, he saw the ocean and el Río Zungo and a coastal line that went straight to the embarcadero. He braked and said, "This is the piece I want for myself. Mi botín de guerra. What do you think?"

"Está bueno," the man said, shirtless, drinking from a bottle of aguardiente.

Orejas saw the bananas poking up from the earth, just a single curled leaf and then the stalk and another leaf, this sickly plant you had to douse with a dozen chemicals so it would not die from the sigatoka plague or el moco. It seemed humble, no better than these villages, no better than him, but it multiplied into millions, if you knew what you were doing. He would call the gringo Jay in Medellín and tell him that it was done. No Restrepo involved.

"We saved those people's lives," Orejas said. "Ya lo van a saber."

*

Later that day, he pulled up to his mother's house in the silver Tacoma. Green paint was flaking on the stucco and gold triangles and gold-trimmed windows shone bright in the sun. He leaned back to look up at the antenna on the second story and was pleased to see it also reflecting light. He had bathed at his hotel in Necoclí, wore a clean white Polo, and he felt the clarity and ill humor he always felt descending from his flight with the mushrooms. He carried two thick pork chops rolled up in newspaper, firm of flesh, and he wanted his mother to cook them while he lay in a hammock on the roof terrace, staring at a patch of green ocean. He would sit in the dark because the lamp attracted bugs in the evening. He could already see love in her bloodshot eyes, her body heavy in a blue cotton dress.

"I brought it for you," he said.

She slapped him, the heel of her palm connecting with his chin, and he dropped the meat. It rolled free from the newspaper, the pink flesh and white fat cloaked in dust. She tried to slap him again, as if to wake him up, out here in public where people crossed the street to get out of his way. He grabbed his mother's wrist, squeezing it to let her know she was done, and held the dirty package up to her and pressed it against her stomach, grown fat from all the good food and easy days.

43.

At Finca Los Kunas, guerrillas selected eighteen workers and shot them on the soccer field. It was payback for Río Seco and el Aracatazo. Yenifer hung up the phone at the Banana Bolívar office. No one was answering in Medellín. Early still, she made coffee in the office kitchen and typed a report on the electric typewriter, trying not to look at her fingers, making calculations in her head about August rainfall. When she called again, someone picked up and said they had sent her the numbers in a fax, and she said the fax was not in the tray. "Send it again," she said, and by then her manager was there and said, "Stay off the road to Carepa." He locked the door to the office and the security guard stood at the gate with a shotgun, but what happened was already over. "No one goes anywhere," her manager said.

She drank water in the little kitchen and stared out the little window. The world was on pause. No traffic on the road. No birds in the almond tree. The gravel in the parking area seemed to sparkle in the morning sun, and she heard it talking, these voices in the pebbles shifting from the heat, like the whole landscape would explode and speak. But nothing happened. It was always elsewhere. Orejas would call her any minute to see if she was OK, and she would tell him not to call here, but he would call anyway. She called Finca la Bella, and Daniel Giraldo Fonseca said the shipment was postponed. No workers today. Also, her cousin was among the dead at Finca Los Kunas. He had danced with her once at a party. She waited for the song to end and he pulled her underwear up her back and said he loved her. "Te estoy queriendo un tantico, prima." There was something wrong with his mouth that tightened into a kiss she walked away from. Daniel said he needed a payment for Orejas that day, and she said she would wait and bring it in the afternoon when things were quieter.

44.

ON A SATURDAY in September of 1995, someone shot the butcher outside Tierra Santa in Apartadó. He had a bag full of blouses. A rumor Yenifer paid Orejas to have him killed. Nanci said this while they were standing in the water in Necoclí. Yenifer had just learned to dive underwater and swim a few strokes. Nanci said, "Let's not think of it," and they ordered fried bocachico with coconut rice at the little restaurant, but it was full of paramilitaries who stared at Nanci, asking how much, so they went back to the hotel to eat. They listened to the radio and a guest from Montería hung around the front desk telling them about all the movies he saw in Bogotá. A movie a day. Sometimes two. There were theaters every few blocks and it was not expensive.

Later, Nanci thanked God the butcher was dead, and asked, "Are you going to get your land back?"

"He has brothers."

"So do you. Yeni, don't pretend you are not dangerous."

45.

"WE HAVE NO CHOICE," Jay said, sitting before a small audience of executives in Cincinnati. It was late on a Wednesday, a blue March dusk. Ties off. Jackets hung on the backs of chairs. No lawyers here. Somewhere a clock ticked. This had happened before. An operation grew so violent, the company too deeply involved, and they had to sell, wash their hands. Jay was fatter than before. A gut not big enough to rest a fruit bowl on, but enough that when he sat down he could feel it folding over his belt. Graciela did not mind, but Jay was embarrassed to see himself in the mirror.

"What's in it for this so-called messiah?" Craig Washburn said.

"He stands in a toll booth," Jay said. "Turbo is what everyone wants, Craig, that and the ocean. And you know what they say there? No hay dios ni ley en Turbo."

They stared at him in disbelief.

"Enough Spanish," Craig Washburn said.

Jay simplified the war into a dichotomy of civilized and primitive. The Messiah was pro-civilization—production was rising and the bananas crossed the ocean. Urabá was close to the Messiah's heart. He often showed up at farms and stores to drink coffee and shake hands with the people. Urabá was also a test. If they defeated the guerrillas in a stronghold, they could go anywhere and do the same. That's why Rafael Restrepo had risked a visit to Urabá and died. It was just too soon.

"He sounds a little scary to me," Craig Washburn said, "but maybe that's a good thing."

"He's saying what no one else is willing to say," Jay said, remembering the Machado poem, footprints in the dirt, a paramilitary getting head on the other end of the pool, right before the bomb. Nanci telling him they should walk through the night to meet Yenifer Contreras. The voices in the dark. The waves on the shore. He was very alive at that moment, in that room. "There are peace marches in Bogotá, Craig. The pope blesses the negotiators. The presidential candidates wear white shirts and promise it all. The Messiah has given up on these political solutions. They've been doing this for forty years. It's war now. Peace later."

"What do they want?" Craig said.

"Who?" Jay said.

"All of these bandits."

"They want what you want, Craig. A house and a garden."

"Jesus," Craig said.

Jay made sure to lean back far in his chair when he spoke at these meetings. He swung one leg over the other to pose confidence. Later, against Craig Washburn, he played tennis like a madman and pumped his fist after winners. Craig was not happy with the extra topspin on Jay's forehand or the way his serve cut sideways into the deuce serving box. Craig stopped chasing the more difficult balls and he changed the score to lose faster, to be done with Jay. They talked weather and women. Craig said Jay should conduct his own cleansing in the office, shred documents, even the seemingly innocuous ones, make certain phone calls from random places.

"Maybe it's best not to understand," Jay said. "We are being extorted by paramilitaries, Craig. That's our story."

"It's a good story," Craig said.

46.

AT DAWN, ONLY A WEEK after the massacre in Río Seco, thirteen guerrillas wearing police uniforms stopped a caravan of banana buses on the road to the ocean. They boarded the first bus and ordered the driver to take them to an intersection known as el Hoyo.

Near the back of the first bus sat Nanci, a new secretary at Finca Rancho Amelia. Everyone called her la venezolana, as a funny, annoying way of reminding her of her time at la Picardía. She looked healthier, happy to sleep through the nights and to work during the hot days. Many of the workers considered her a friend, especially when she handed out the paychecks and joked with them kindly about their bad haircuts and asked about their wives. She answered the phones and did basic paperwork on shipment days. Though she spent the day in a chair, she rode the bus like everyone else, and said "Buenos días" to everyone when she got on and "Buenas noches" when she got off. It was known that she was close to Yenifer Contreras, who was now a manager at Banana Bolívar and rumored to be a paramilitary.

The guerrillas' mouths and noses were covered with red and black bandanas, just their eyes checking the faces, their breath billowing in the cloth.

"Don't cry," a guerrilla said to a man who was weeping in the front row. "Sea macho."

A guerrilla stood next to Nanci and his stench was nauseating, the reek of sulfur in the earth, sweat, a rotten egg odor. Nanci recognized his droopy black eyes. He had been a regular in her room in la Picardía.

Next to Nanci sat Mykal, her boyfriend, whose praying was freestyle, a sweeping love for every man and woman, and a confession, conjuring up all his sins, how he used to steal food from his younger brothers, how he once pushed down a girl and kissed her. Nanci took his hand and whispered some of her own sins, thinking God was worth calling in such times. The other passengers were looking at one another in numb silence.

Her life seemed too meager. All she owned was a one-room house in the poorest neighborhood in Apartadó, a TV, a decent bed, and worn-out clothing. Not much for a life of work. Not enough. Yenifer had told her the real money was coming now. An expansion of plantations and the whole Gulf of Urabá as a waystation for the drugs shipped north, all this money that would spill over to the people of the zone. What makes you think they will win? Nanci had asked. I've talked to the Messiah, Yenifer said.

Everything had been a dead end. After the bombing at Hotel Toscano, she had woken up in a room next to Petra and the gringo who never paid. She had looked at the empty bottle of whiskey and she crawled into the bathroom, overtaken by the worst feeling of her life. No one was there to drive them back to Apartadó. A few days later, the guerrillas entered la Picardía and killed the madame. They searched all the rooms and stole the women's money. They told them that if they did not quit, they knew what was next. Nanci was sick of sex. She was sick of dressing and undressing, of the music blasting at all hours in the bar, of the purple room. Yenifer offered her a job in the bananas. She told her it would be a severe pay cut—after a year, she could work her way up to something better. Anything is better, Nanci said. The plantations are a bloodbath, Yenifer said. Nanci insisted that of all the plantations, they would not attack hers. If they did, they would not kill a woman, especially one who had given them so much pleasure. Yenifer stared at her because she was wrong.

What Nanci did not expect was to fall in love with a worker who lived with his mother in Barrio Obrero. She had never been adored. She had never had a man look at her like she was more than her body. A man who did not drink because of some problem with his esophagus, who saved his money and planned to open a hardware store. He smelled good, like fruit drying in the sun. He did not give orders or expect her to ask his permission on how to spend her hours or her money.

"Mykal," she said. "Te quiero."

He was praying too loudly. He grabbed her leg and told her to pray with him, "Que Jesús te proteja, que te lleve al cielo, que el señor te guie, que tu alma sea pura, Jesús will protect you, he will carry you to heaven, the holy spirit will guide you, your soul will be pure."

"Bajénse!" the guerrillas yelled as the bus stopped at el Hoyo, just a crossroads with an old gravel pit turned into a pond.

She followed Mykal up the aisle. More workers were crying now, looking out the windows at the guerrillas in police uniforms. She put her hand on Mykal's shoulder and squeezed it hard as they stepped down onto the road. A warm breeze lifted her hair. A mist of rain made everything glisten, the trees, the fence posts, the metal of a sign, and she heard birds calling to one another, announcing something to the landscape.

"En el piso, todos," the guerrillas said, and Nanci lay down on her stomach beside Mykal on the road. A guerrilla tied her wrists with yellow nylon banana string. It surprised her how strong it was, how thin, how it hurt her. Mykal was still praying in a big voice. He turned his head to the guerrillas and said, "Jesus loves you like his own children." A guerrilla leaned over and shot him in the head.

She heard the feet beside her body and a guerrilla asking if they were killing women too. Someone answered that everyone was already dead. She felt a hot barrel against her neck, then her shoulder. An act of mercy, the bullet exploding through her body.

"Be dead," the man said.

When it was finished, the guerrillas walked the line. Nanci was awake. She heard the thwack of machetes. She heard one very close and realized it was her own neck, her own head being cleaved from her body. She fell unconscious. She walked across a purple corridor into a room, also purple but enlivened with potted baby ceiba trees. Purple grass to sit on. She wondered if she was in heaven.

When she awoke, she felt her legs burning. She did not know it then, but she had been on fire. "This one's alive," a man said. "Check that other one. She's breathing!" She heard the quiet snapping noise of fire and smelled plastic and oil burning. Not long after, she heard tires on gravel and the sound of car doors opening.

Yenifer was standing there, a hand on her stomach, yelling at the paramedics to deal with Nanci first, to stop her bleeding, and get her onto a stretcher. When they did, she forced her way inside the ambulance and said Nanci was her sister. In her delirium, Nanci wondered if this was the night that her father had thrown her out and punched her in the mouth in front of her sisters like she was a man and told her to never come back. Yenifer was finally opening the door to the bakery.

At the hospital, Nanci heard that another man had survived, but not Mykal. She felt Yenifer's hand on her forearm, the prickle of her calluses, her stubby nails, and heard the sound of her skin chafing, and she told her to stop, to not touch her.

"We'll go to the movies," Yenifer said, leaving her hand there because it was possible Nanci could not speak yet. She was saying things in her head. What movie? she asked but could not say, and Yenifer was talking about the size of an actor on the big screen, the darkness of a theater, the devotion of the viewers in their seats. Like a church, she said, but more fun.

47.

OREJAS ORDERED A KID to watch Yenifer's motorcycle, and they rode in his truck through Barrio Obrero and across the banana fields to Río Seco. He was not right in the head. He spoke in a childish voice about his new bird collection and how he was going to build a room for them at his new house in Triganá. He had a little pool. Round, he said, taking his hands off the wheel to make a circle. A round pool, he repeated. A house like the capos. A garden full of flowers, and birds she had never seen. She crossed her legs and lifted the seatbelt that stuck to her chest.

In Río Seco, all the houses were hollow. They peeked into them, but the people had hauled away their beds, their furniture, even the toilets had been yanked out. Nothing but bare walls. She imagined the new packing area and banana trucks and workers sitting in the shade of the awnings. The sky opened up for a minute with a blue gash. She felt tall. She could hear the water being sucked up from the earth to wash the bananas.

Orejas said the gringo wanted her to manage it. Would she? A cell phone rang, and one of his bodyguards said there was a meeting with the mayor in Chigorodó. Her gums hurt and she tasted blood. "Am I bleeding?" she said, opening her mouth, and he got close to her and said she was not.

48.

Yenifer lit the flame on her stove. She boiled two beef bones for a broth and sliced up carrots and yucca and splashed them into the pot. She chopped a pile of cilantro and quartered a lime.

"Eat, mi amor, or you're never going to feel better," Yenifer said.

"Maybe if I could taste it," Nanci said.

She was sitting in a plastic chair in Yenifer's house in Carepa, the walls painted a new silver gray, the window an open hole with four bars across it. She had a bandage over one eye, her shoulder a raw purple knot as it healed. She seemed there and not there. She was already in Medellín, Yenifer thought, angry and ungrateful for the generosity showered upon her. Maybe we held on too long, Yenifer thought. Maybe that's what friendship was, holding on too long and then knowing it was over but holding on anyway and arriving at a sad night with nothing to say.

"Where did you get the money?" Nanci said.

"Don't ask dumb things, mi amor."

Yenifer said she had ridden that morning in a boat to Finca las Aguas where all the new bananas were dying and the workers did not care. She did not care either, but she hated riding in the boat, fearing that at any moment they would tie an anchor to her ankle and drop her into the gulf. The gringo did not care because he just inherited what Don Rafael had started, and surely his managers on the ground in Urabá were lying to him. The money was good regardless. Everyone was like fish biting at the same food, but by the end the bulk of it went to the big fish far away in their glass buildings. Some nights Finca las Aguas was full of blue barrels packed tight with stamped black packages. The fast boats landed and departed, like phantoms, the drivers nameless and faceless, grown men with no hair or teenagers with baby faces and hard eyes. Occasionally the police stopped by and investigated their own footprints in the sand, but it was just a packing area, the cooling tubs full of green bunches like everywhere else.

"I can't love that gringo," Nanci said. "Petra fixed his feet and I consoled him, but he didn't pay us. Does he know about the barrels?"

"He looks away."

"It's bad to see the barrels."

"I've seen worse. So have you. Nothing changed in this world when you found God with Mykal."

Nanci picked up a pair of scissors and began cutting an old shirt into little squares, doing it badly because she could not see straight.

"Why are you doing that?" Yenifer asked.

"I'm making a blanket for Medellín."

"We can buy you one."

Nanci looked confused, like you could stay at any friend's house with scissors and an old shirt and cut it into rags and call it something better.

A truck, parked across the street, blasted trumpets and keyboard and fake love, bad Panamanian salsa for the whole neighborhood. A drunk yelled for people to get out of their beds and dance. "Who can dance?" he yelled. A dog barked. If anyone knocked on the door, Yenifer would raise the pistol from behind the garbage in the kitchen. She listened while the pot boiled. Nanci looked so unhappy, peeling back her eye bandage and gazing at her as if she were too honest of a mirror, not smiling to reassure her but just coldly matching her gaze. Yenifer reached out to touch her face, though Nanci leaned away from her.

"Just tell me what to do," Nanci said, because she had said yes to Medellín but no to going there alone. She already missed the heat and the ocean. What she least wanted was a solitary life in a cold place with no friends.

"You are not done with your life," Yenifer said.

Nanci had lost her beauty, everyone said, but Yenifer didn't think it was gone. If she slept more, the dark bags would disappear from under her eyes and her face would brighten with color. The doctor said she would never regain her full vision, but Yeni believed the doctors were guessers and had taken her to see a healer in Necoclí, who rubbed her temples with stinky oils and minerals and said she should bathe in the ocean daily.

"Tell me more about Medellín, Yeni."

Yenifer said the best part was the worst part. No one knew you there. The people sized you up in a glance based on your clothes and your haircut, and they discarded you if you were not wealthy. It was friendly enough, but the people were selfish and spoke like they already knew everything, especially the men. But the women were awful. No butts or lips, no heat in their eyes. They walked around like they were supermodels when they were ordinary.

"I'll hate it then," Nanci said. "Orejas is leaving for el Cauca."

"I know. You don't have to tell me."

"Is that why we're leaving? We can't live without him?"

Urabá was in his blood, Yenifer said. He'd never leave for good. He had a new house in Triganá, a blue pool next to the ocean. Why swim in a pool with the ocean right there? He was high all day, Gloria fat and pregnant beside the pool, his sons crying too much, as if everyone knew that the planters would get rid of him at some point. He had buried money for her, not in the ground but in the little businesses and farms he had bought. He said the paramilitaries, just like the guerrillas, were going to negotiate peace with the government.

Yenifer tasted a piece of yucca that was soft and starchy in her mouth. The broth needed salt, but it was ready. She sprinkled the cilantro into two bowls, squeezed the lime quarters, and spooned servings. Nanci stood up from the stool and walked right into the wall. Yenifer had some doubts about her navigating a large city.

"Sit," she said. "You have to eat, niña."

"When do you leave?"

"In the morning. The apartments are ready. There's money in the smaller caleta in the back. You'll know it's time for you to go because I'm going to call. I'm sorry, but you'll have to take the bus."

"When you see the gringo, tell him he owes me money."

"Forget it."

"I offered to marry him."

Yenifer smiled and poked her in the side with the handle of her spoon. "True love?"

"You have no idea what they charge for a haircut in his country."

*

At the movies, Yenifer read the subtitles of an American thriller with a handsome detective and a killer who left clues all over a bathroom made of marble. If the killer were Colombian, she thought, he would pay the detective to go away. She sat alone at the back of an old theater on Calle 15, dust in the tunnel of light from the projector, and she was afraid someone would catch her and ask why she was not working. Ninety minutes belonged to her in that dark. Only one other moviegoer in the front row who, washed over with light, slept. She wondered if her own body might appear on the screen, her shoes yanked from her feet and a stab wound in her neck, or might she be the handsome detective checking for hair in a sink and dusting fingerprints off a doorknob, her smug voice mumbling into the dark room.

The gringo was waiting. She walked through the center of Medellín and was amazed by the speed of it. Taxis turned sharply into alleys, up ramps onto the high roads, stopping suddenly for people with upraised arms. She felt the eyes of the clerks in the doorways of their stores, a bookseller unkind when she said she was just browsing and not buying. She wore her best clothes, a white polyester blouse, scratchy on every inch of her back, white with patterns of orange and red lips, a fine thing for Apartadó, but in Medellín there were women in dresses that clung to their hips in solid greens and blues and there were men in wool suits with beautiful red ties. Her shoes did not fit. Her heels blistered as she walked up a hill into el Poblado with its new glass towers and green parks with bamboo woods and flowerbeds and benches where young people smoked cigarettes and talked about God knew what. It was a dream, she thought. Beneath the glass façades was everything no one wanted to see. It was the vultures who ate Big Fernando's eyes in the banana canal. It was Nanci with her magnifying glass trying to read a fashion magazine. It was giant tanks of gasoline on Finca las Aguas for the fast boats. It was Orejas's mother in a three-story house in a slum. It was Hugo's bakery turned into an office for a human rights agency that purported to save lives but did nothing but write down what happened around them.

A security guard checked her with his eyes, determining if she was a servant or an intruder—with one call to the police he could ship her back to her place.

*

At Banana Bolívar, the gringo seemed friendly, handing her the envelope with money for Orejas that she put into her purse. His hands were everywhere, moving his pens and papers around the desk, pointing at a chart, and he asked her about the weather, what it felt like on the ground, what people were saying about him. He smelled sweet and fruity, like he was made of candy. No one looked at her in the office. Men sat in cubicles and passed by the glass wall with their heads down. But the gringo was a starer. He eyed her legs in her skirt. He looked at her misfit shoes, her dry heels, a little cut on her knee. He offered her coffee. She said no. A woman in a blue smock stepped through the door with a tray of little chocolate cookies and two cups. He filled her cup with milk and two spoonfuls of sugar. Usually it was in and out. Usually he did not want her here.

"Finca las Aguas is a disaster," the gringo said, looking through her head at the wall behind her, and she looked over her shoulder to see a giant map of something she did not recognize at first. It was the gulf of Urabá, a red circle around Turbo, and she saw for the first time the place where she was from in perfect order. "It's not your fault. We can't get that road to stop flooding. We'll need a bridge. There's no budget to undertake a project like that. So we'll send the boats on shipment days and we'll fumigate. Is the soil still good? I remain optimistic. Are you?"

She said the soil was fine. Optimism? Maybe it was time for that, she said. The guerrillas were mostly dead or hidden in the sierra, just a few campesinos having their meetings late at night. The Messiah sat in Plaza Martina in plain sight and drank coffee with his men and no one was going to say anything to him now. No more bombs. No more bodies hanging from the cables at the plantations. Let the gringo think it was over. A quiet in his office. A place to concentrate. She imagined Nanci in bed with him at the no longer new Hotel Toscano, and she wondered if that ever happened. He seemed too smart to put himself in that kind of danger. He took a phone call and said he would be there in five minutes, and the setting sun lit up the pens on his desk.

"And Orejas?" he said. "Will we survive without him?"

"Everything is organized, señor."

"Good, Yenifer, good. Thank you for making this trip. Everything is complicated for us right now. We have to use cash, and it's going to be cash next year until we don't have to pay anyone. Is someone trying to buy Finca las Aguas? I heard a rumor. I'm sure you would know. The Messiah?"

"He has his own land in the south."

"Should I sell it all or is it too early?"

"How can I know, señor?"

"You are my eyes there. Believe it or not, there's a lot of uncertainty here. It looks elegant at the office, but we're always a step away from crisis."

"I deserve a raise, señor." She paused and met his blue eyes. "I'm risking a lot being here every two weeks."

"Give me a number," the gringo said. "Let's agree today."

*

She took a taxi from el Poblado to Avenida Ayacucho. Rain poured down on the center of the city, the sewers bubbled up with water, the traffic jammed, and people ran with their coats over their heads or waited in the eaves of the businesses. She was dry. She rubbed at her arms and reached her fingers down the neck of her blouse and scraped at her back. It was time, she thought.

Something about the gringo's look let her hear the ticking of a watch that someone held over her head, and her time was up, maybe tomorrow or at the end of the year, but when it was actually up, she would be dead.

She shoved her key into the bolt lock of the first apartment. A neighbor's TV echoed with laughter down the hall. A door opened for a second and then slammed shut. It was not elegant, as the gringo would say. Fourth floor, no elevator, the smell of dog piss in the stairwell. She caught her breath in the kitchen, put her head under the faucet and drank water that tasted like nothing. No electricity yet, so she sat in the dark on the hardwood floor. All around her the city hummed and grinded with voices in the rain. There was a blanket in the closet. A pillow too. She counted the money in the dark, just the light of a streetlamp, and she was a kid again, trying to read a book, only now it was numbers on bills, and Orejas waiting for her already in Turbo, and if she didn't show up tomorrow, he would know why, and no one would ever tie an anchor to her foot or tell her to walk into the jungle. She was the detective, a step ahead. She took off the itchy blouse, her bra, her heels, and she walked the length of the apartment, into the bedrooms, the bathroom, back to the kitchen, the main room, as if memorizing the walls in the dark, and then she lit the gas water heater and turned the shower faucet and waited for it to heat up. Tomorrow she would fly to Bogotá and that was where they would not find her.

49.

Maybe the cleansing was over. Weeks passed where Jay had nothing to report to Cincinnati but the yields of the plantations.

"No killings this week," he said, knowing that the word alone put Craig Washburn on edge. Only the usual mayhem—a body not belonging to Banana Bolívar found slung over a fence in Nueva Colonia, or an angry wife in a packing area, attacking her husband with a carving knife for not coming home after a payday.

The Messiah had drawn a curtain around Urabá to make it a zone of silence. The journalists reported what they were told or found themselves without a job or dead in a ravine. Local businesses tithed like Mormons. No one ever robbed a banana shipment. The trucks went straight to the port. The barges crossed the gulf. The human rights organizations published reports about a new morality, a ban on homosexuality, women deprived of rights, forced recruitment of teenagers, and total impunity, the paramilitaries in every neighborhood watching, but no one read these reports except people in Bogotá and foreign countries. Jay did not read them, but handed them to an assistant and said, "Find the other side of the story."

Graciela moved in with Jay and redecorated his apartment with a theme of water—a blue sofa, blue walls, her fountain placed in the entryway to clash with the Obregón barracuda. They took a vacation to Madrid to see his mother. She lived in a working-class neighborhood with gray Franco-era buildings that seemed like factories, old ladies staring out tiny windows and hanging laundry, smoking black tobacco and spitting into the street. He was not close with his mother and they did not fake it. She had no interest in fruit exportation. She and Graciela took a quick sniff of each other's cheeks on the welcome kiss, and that was it—they wanted nothing to do with each other.

After a few dinners, a visit to el Prado where the only thing that bored Graciela more than Goya was Velázquez, the visit was complete. They would rather be working. These were wasted days. Madrid had once been a swamp. They drained it and built a cathedral with a great plaza. Then the high-rises and freeways and a subway system. A muddy plateau where nothing grew, where there was no great river for commerce. Too hot in the summer. Freezing in the winter. "I miss Medellín," Graciela said. They took a train to Sevilla and Córdoba to see the Muslim architecture but found themselves in a horde of tour guides learning to give tours, so they decided to fly back ahead of schedule. The one highlight, Graciela and Jay agreed, was that history was nothing more than a pillar of cement, a bronze plaque on a forgotten corner of a city.

*

In Medellín, Yenifer Contreras did not show up to receive her salary plus the per-box payment that was dropped off every fifteen days in Turbo. Jay called the office in Carepa to investigate and learned that the manager, Daniel Giraldo Fonseca, had fired her for missing work three days straight.

"You can't fire her," Jay said.

But they could not find her either. Daniel sent someone to her house in Carepa. It was vacant with holes in the ground behind it, and according to one neighbor it had been sold to a family up the road.

"Holes?" Jay said.

"Something strange," Daniel said. "The neighbors thought she was hiding caletas. It's foolish."

"Keep her on the payroll."

"Fine."

"What's the gossip?"

"Someone saw her get on a bus to Montería with a woman who used to be a prostitute in Apartadó. That's it. The rest is too crazy to tell you."

"And Orejas?"

"Should we talk like this on the phone?"

"Just say it, Daniel."

"I keep my head down, jefe. I come to work and I go home and sleep. I love my family. Every day I go straight. I don't want to know about Orejas who left for el Cauca but is also seen here, like he's everywhere. We make payments to el Guapo, or that's what we call him. His name is—"

"Just make the payments, Daniel."

Graciela did not seem worried about any of it. She had only seen Yenifer across the office, noticed her blouse with the painted lips all over it, the shoes that did not fit, and she saw herself in her. She saw smarts and a strong will. Not everyone died in a conflict. Some people got away. On the surface, Jay accepted this as normal in a world of insanity, but inside he was beginning to have doubts. It was a country where everything was temporary, the hinges loose, the sky about to fall. As soon as he put his feet up on his desk and relaxed for a minute, the phone rang with some emergency. His knuckles were swollen from cracking them. His feet sweated in his new socks. His bones ached in his legs from too much coffee and not enough water. His hair seemed to be growing faster than normal and his face was aging, graying, his eyes sinking beneath the rim of his forehead. He took antidepressants to dull the edge and to even out his mood swings. He slept more, but he did not smile as much and the employees noticed this, asked him if he was well. He noticed a corner cigarette seller marking a notepad every time Jay arrived, and he began to vary his routine, to be completely unpredictable, and this was not easy—he had always loved the smooth timing of his life.

Yenifer's disappearance had planted a sliver of doubt in his brain; it came as a whisper in his ear while he waited in line at the pharmacy or leaned into the urinal at work. "What is it?" he asked her.

At the tennis courts at el Club Campestre, Graciela played terribly, and Jay crushed her without pity, hitting the ball at her feet as hard as he could, serving into her backhand that was misfiring, and doing the thing that most infuriated her, which was to give her advice on her mechanics. They sat in silence after the first set. She moaned a little, stretching her right arm across her chest. She was soaked in sweat and said she wanted to buy an apartment in Santa Marta. A vacation condo with two bedrooms and a view of the ocean. A new building in Rodadero owned by a friend. Jay imagined making love to her on a sandy bed, the boom of stereos everywhere, a little private pool on the side, the smell of chlorine and sunscreen.

"Why not Cartagena?" he said.

*

"We may have to start calling you el capo," Ernesto said. He sat down next to Jay in the steam room at el Club Campestre and brushed his shoulder against Jay's and spread his legs to lean on his elbows. His body glowed with paleness and the red fire of his hairy chest. "You are not a typical gringo, except you like money."

"Excuse me?"

"You have your hands in a lot of pots," Ernesto said. "Banana Bolívar is posting record profits. I wonder when the gringos are going to leave."

Jay felt like he was back at the pool in Necoclí, that he would be asked to recite a poem he could not remember and that at any moment a bomb would explode in the locker room and it would be his blood on the white tiles and new green carpet and giant mirrors where all the oligarchs posed with their penises semi-erect from shower touching and doused their necks with cologne and rubbed gel into their perfect hair. No other gringos were here. Jay was the exception, el berraco, Ernesto said, and somehow Ernesto was always here when Jay was.

"Urabá is the future," Jay said. "We're outproducing Guatemala and Honduras combined."

"Urabá es un mierdero," Ernesto said. "Always will be, hermano."

Another man entered, muscular and tan, a white towel on his waist. He paused for a moment, greeting Ernesto who nodded at him as a way of saying he could stay but not too long. Jay and Ernesto made small talk about Urabá, the increased shipping costs as oil prices rose, the upcoming elections in the key municipalities, knowing that the Messiah had chosen candidates aligned with the planters. The man sensed he was in the middle of something and walked out.

"Es un maricón," Ernesto said. "Also a lawyer."

"Him?"

"He was looking at you."

"I doubt it."

"He finds gringos who think they are straight and he seduces them."

"Disgusting," Jay said.

"He's married, too. Poor woman."

Jay stood, holding out a sweaty hand that Ernesto did not take. The heat felt good in his bones. His body seemed to relax for a minute. He flexed his toes against the rubbery mat. Ernesto told him to sit a minute. He listed Jay's accomplishments with the new Finca las Aguas that was finally shipping its worth. He questioned Jay's contributions to the banana corporation, his commitment to the other goals of infrastructure. The gringos only fixed their own pathways to the sea, but what about the others? The region was advancing too slowly. The tax revenue, once the politicians had siphoned half of it for themselves, would be used to invest in social causes. Graciela was a success at the company, no? She was lucky to have found a good man.

"Hatred is hereditary, no?" Ernesto said. "It's like a necklace your mother gives you for your birthday."

"I hate no one," Jay said.

"Hard to believe, but you gringos are smilers who hire others to walk through shit. In January, we might suffer a drought. All the rivers will dry up. The wind will knock down our plants and we'll be begging Bogotá for subsidies. Or maybe we'll have steady rain all year, no dry season at all. Europe doubles its banana orders. Our governor is elected president and Bogotá is no longer out of reach. Can you imagine? No one knows. I have investors who will buy everything for a good number. You've done a lot to help us. It's time to let us run it."

"Banana Bolívar is not for sale."

"I'm not talking about that."

"My own holdings are flourishing."

"Are they?"

Ernesto looked like an active volcano, his chest bifurcated by rivers of sweat that flowed into and out of his creased skin and onto the tiled seat where it touched Jay's sweat. I must be losing it, Jay thought, breathing deeply from the steamy air, and he imagined the lawyer locking the door, Jay suffering a slow death of suffocation. He felt a fresh, burning sweat stream down his spine and into the towel around his waist. He ran a hand through his soaked hair and sniffed the minty shampoo scent on his fingers.

"You deserve a payday. Men will bow to you. They will write down what you say."

Jay teetered so noticeably that Ernesto reached out with one hand to touch his hip and steady him. A charge surged through the man's fingers and up into Jay's armpits.

"Graciela is waiting for me," Jay said. "I'll think about it."

"You should take the offer."

"You haven't given me a number."

"It's your number. Then mine. Then yours. No?"

*

"He's testing you," Graciela said.

They were speaking through the wall. Or really through the doorway and across the hall, a space of only thirty feet, but safe enough for Graciela who could not do the necessary things in her mind to sleep in a bed with Jay, especially that banana bed with its jagged pieces of steel at the head. Jay was holding a book about the gold rush in South America, stretching his arms over him, trying to fully inhabit a pleasant night, post-exercise, his legs leaden and warm under the blankets. He wanted the appearance of his life to be true. The phone was ringing in the living room, but they both ignored it. It was after midnight.

"He decided you grew too much," Graciela said. "He wants to rename the whole state Echevarría and put his name on a skyscraper in Apartadó."

The phone rang again, and Jay heard Craig Washburn's voice on the answering machine.

"Don't pick up," Graciela said.

Jay knew what it was about, that they wanted him to fly to Cincinnati. The lawyers freaking out. Terrorism was the new word. Banana Bolívar was financing it, both directly and indirectly. He had already acted out the full conversation, the lies he would tell the lawyers who gave sound but impossible advice, trapped, as they were, in the immaculate reality of Ohio.

"When the paramilitaries are gone," she said, "there's going to be a moment where everyone tries to get back what they lost. There are going to be a lot of armed men, unemployed. Maybe in five years, maybe less. Ernesto sees this. Did you hear about the land he bought along el Atrato? He's not just thinking bananas. He's thinking African palm and shipping."

"Will they ever be gone?"

"Maybe not."

Her voice faded at the end, like she was already sleeping, saying things she had said the night before and the night before that. There were a half-dozen official titles for every plot of land, Jay thought. The backbone of society is counterfeit paper. Not enough for everyone to own. The Messiah had cows on new land all over Urabá, and even near the airport in Carepa. Money in flesh and blood. A cow eating and expanding like a stock option.

"It's like the Bible," Jay said. "Old Testament."

There was no moral high ground, Jay would say to Craig tomorrow. Going rogue, Craig would say. Yes, Jay said. They could say no to the paramilitaries but they were still saying yes. The paramilitaries were not just poor muchachos playing in their camouflage—they were dangerous because men in camouflage were always dangerous. They were good people, Jay thought, those boys at the party in Necoclí, dancing and listening to the Messiah's poem, and that nice monkey who probably knew there was a bomb before everyone else. Good muchachos. Good mico.

"Do you want me to visit you?" Jay asked.

A silence. She did this—she went through the steps of the winding tunnel of her consciousness and found sleep.

"And do what?" she said.

"Make love. We sell everything tomorrow. Invest in the American stock market. Stare at the numbers in my pajamas each morning and make trades. Talk your ear off about the news."

"No," she said. "Don't think it."

He would buy her the apartment in Rodadero. Not far from the sierra where he could go fishing. Pristine rivers and fat trees and paramilitaries guarding those towns. He would drive past the windowless white banana estates with peeling paint, swimming pools full of weeds, so much heat, dry, bad heat, the bananas stunted, ripped out by the wind, these dusty towns—Fundación, Tucurinca, Aracataca, la Ciénaga. All so he could return to the ocean, Rodadero, Graciela on the balcony with a glass of rum for him, a view of the Caribbean in all its splendor. Not a gutter, as Rafael said, but a great body of water for those who loved it.

No foreigner had ever lasted in Urabá. Graciela was saying don't sell to say sell. Because he was a man and stubborn. You'll be rich, Jay thought, but money was a letdown. Everyone had it. Even the stupidest people on earth, in Ohio and Saudi Arabia and Paris and Bogotá. They inherited it or made one good move. It was nothing. It was numbers on paper. It was compound interest until they dug a hole for him in Cincinnati. He should have children to inherit it, but Graciela was the only woman he had ever met who said no chance.

Patrimony. The single pursuit of all great men was to have eternal names, for your descendents to hang a picture of you in a room where no one entered. A myth. El gringo bananero.

He sat up. He touched the jagged pieces of his bed. If he walked down the hall to tell her what he had decided, she would scream. To sell was to die, he realized. That's why everyone hung on too long.

"Come," she said.

"Me?"

"I can feel your electricity. Come, mi amor."

THE FUTURE
2001

50.

WHAT SONG HAD THE WORKERS been singing before the guerrillas boarded the bus to take them to their deaths in el Hoyo? Nanci would wonder about this, suffering from certain gaps in her memory, as she shampooed hair and massaged necks. She would hear a word of it in the pop music she played on the salon stereo.

This was years later in Medellín. She wore bottle-thick glasses and held her brown eyes just inches from people's hair in order to see what she was doing. Gradually she learned to feel the hair between her fingers, to use other senses to know it. She answered the phones, scheduled appointments, rented chairs to the hairdressers, and handled all the money. Nothing fancy, but the salon was on a respectable street at the edge of el Poblado. Medellín was friendlier than expected. When she took the wrong bus, people would help her find the right one. If she was short a few pesos at the corner grocery, the owner would wave it off. She inspired sympathy in people. The scars on her pretty face. Her bad vision. Even when Nanci did not follow a customer's instructions, the woman would look up in the mirror and say it was fine. Nanci had a softer way of talking now, an attention to each word she used, though she was impatient with conversation. Everyone was saying the same things about the price of food and the ridiculous president in his white peace outfit giving the country away to the guerrillas.

Occasionally, men walked into the salon. They looked around at the four red vinyl chairs and the hairdressers, three women and one gay man they sometimes avoided. If someone was on break or sick, Nanci would work a chair. It was on one of these days when the gringo walked by and glanced in and seemed not to recognize her, but passed again a few minutes later and opened the door.

He looked nothing like he had that night in Hotel Toscano when his body was pale and bloody in a wet T-shirt and jeans. He was sharp in an orange and blue striped shirt with a blue tie, blue suit pants, brown shoes. His cologne smelled like mangos. His eyes were very light blue, and they matched his pants and tie. He looked unsure of the salon, the red chairs, the pop music, and the smell of hairspray. He was clearly above the usual clientele.

"A la órden," Nanci said.

"A slight trim around the ears and neck," the gringo said. "Nada más."

He sat in the red chair and she pinned a black sheet around his neck. She stood behind him and touched his neck and hair. As soon as a stranger sat in your chair, you could touch his hair and move his head in a way you never could in the world. No, he did not recognize her. Her hair was no longer blonde. Her eyes were not blue. She had gained some weight, not a belly or big legs, just a thickness throughout, her face rounder—healthier, Yenifer said, and more beautiful—but she knew Yenifer was wrong.

The other hairdressers seemed self-conscious, saying polite things to their customers they would not usually say. As Nanci sprayed water at his head and combed his hair, he seemed to lean into her body with his elbows, a tall gringo, his limbs everywhere for her to get around as she grabbed her comb and scissors. They made small talk. He said he was going on vacation to Santa Marta tomorrow.

"Qué delicia," she said. "I miss the beach."

"I know you," he said when the chair next to him had emptied. Their eyes met in the mirror. "Necoclí. I am Jay. You are the whiskey lover."

Nanci kept cutting his hair quietly. She hoped the gringo would not say anything about her time as a prostitute.

"Back when I was growing and shipping bananas," he said louder, as if to answer a question she had not asked. "Your friend, the Black woman who helped me with my feet?"

"Still in Apartadó."

"She's doing well then," the gringo said.

"Yes," Nanci said. "Very well."

"And you?"

"I am the manager here."

She trimmed around his ears and shortened the hair on his forehead, even if he did not ask for it. She took out the straight-edge razor to clean his neck and get close to his ears. Whenever she did this for a man's haircut she felt more blind, like she might press the edge of the blade into the windpipe and draw a speck of blood. They sensed her energy, they shifted. She would touch their heads and tell them to be still. Just a few seconds. With the gringo she pressed harder. She wanted him to feel the blade scraping. She would not rub his neck with aftershave. She would not praise his hair, though it was thick and blond.

She paused to take money from the two customers who were done. The hairdressers stepped out to smoke in the back alley. She was alone with the gringo.

"Do you hear from Yenifer Contreras?" he asked, as she sprayed his hair with more water and held her eyes close to it to see how even it was, using her fingers to measure. To an outsider it might look as if she were kissing his head.

"What makes you think I know her still?" she said.

"I have infinite respect for her. She disappeared."

"Don't worry," Nanci said. "She's alive."

She unpinned the sheet and grabbed the horsehair brush and swept it across his neck, flicking away bits of hair on his collar. She waited for him to stand up and pay her.

When he did, she watched him walk through the door and tug on his earrings, as if she might have stolen one. He was so confident. He looked both ways at the street crossing and turned uphill. She hated him for his bearing, like she was here just to give him answers, and yet she also wanted his approval. She wanted him to come back and shake her hand for surviving the massacre at el Hoyo.

*

Occasionally, Yenifer would visit to see how the business was going and to check the numbers and make suggestions about hanging glossy pictures of well-coiffed white people in the windows. She never stayed more than a couple nights in the apartment Nanci and another woman rented from her. She would cook a sancocho from a hen and vegetables and buy a bottle of aguardiente. Her hair was short like a man's, a dark copper color; there were lines around her eyes, and rarely a smile. She talked about the movies in Bogotá, some so peculiar she wondered if the directors understood the story. She pushed Nanci to see a movie with her in Medellín, but Nanci said there was no point—the screen would be a blur.

"I can tell you what's there. You can listen."

"I have enough noise," Nanci said.

Yenifer said that Orejas had flown up from el Cauca to Neco-clí, thinking he would be celebrated. He had gone for a swim with the Messiah, who said if he didn't surrender, the army would kill him. "Now he's one of them," she said.

"A snitch," Nanci said. "He always was."

They had put him before a judge, Yenifer said. He thought a Colombian courtroom was a place for redemption. It was not. When he started naming names, they sent him away to the United States for drug trafficking. That was the warning. Sit in a cell and be mute. Gloria had lost the farm and the house in Trigraná, lived in Medellín somewhere, staying with her father, studying to be a lawyer. She would come out ahead.

"Is he still your friend?" Nanci said, clearing their plates and pouring more aguardiente.

"Who knows?" she said. He had been loyal to her. He never wanted to work, but then when he did, he was good at everything he touched. "He's the reason we're here," Yenifer said. "Friend or not friend isn't even the right question."

"They'll kill him," Nanci said.

"He won't talk anymore," Yenifer said. "He's the quiet one."

*

Every day, Nanci put the salon's earnings into a zippered pouch and a security guard from the building would walk her to the bank. If it was a good day, she would take a taxi rather than a bus to get home to the old apartment on Avenida Ayacucho. She drank coffee and chatted with her roommate, who did nails for rich ladies in their homes. Nanci would hold a jeweler's loupe to the newspaper to read every word of it, including the advertisements and classified section. She listened to salsa on the radio and sometimes danced by herself with the door closed. No men visited. As her vision worsened, her hearing seemed more acute, and she struggled to sleep at night. Cars accelerated and braked at all hours on Avenida Ayacucho. A drunk yelled at another drunk. When she heard gunshots, she would take her blankets and sleep under the bed or lie on the floor of the bathroom.

Like her dead boyfriend Mykal, she found comfort in religion. A hairdresser at the salon took her to a new church where the pastor saw the scars on her face, shades lighter than her other skin, and he hugged her. On Sunday mornings she zoned out during sermons, just waiting for the chance to sing with everyone. Light entered through a rear window, a woman howled that the spirit was in the room. Nanci felt it, she felt released from the rope on her wrists, from all the men who had fucked her, from all the shitty dreams she would never realize. At that moment the world was a place not of good, but of light and spirit, and if you looked hard enough, you could see an underlying harmony. You just had to be crazy to see it.

ACKNOWLEDGMENTS

I AM GRATEFUL TO the people who supported this book: Enilda Ji-
ménez Pineda, Raúl Spj, Leonardo Rodríguez Sirtori, Shaka, Elu-
bina Jiménez Pineda, Neli Jiménez Pineda, Albeiro Jiménez Pineda,
John Jairo, Kiko, Alberto Salcedo Ramos, María Korol, Jen Beagin,
Alberto Gullaba, Izzy Prcic, Michelle Latiolais, Amanda Urban,
Michelle Dotter, Mike Levine, Ellie Davis, Willie Tolliver, Char-
lotte Artese, Christine Cozzens, Nicole Stamant, Jamie Stamant,
Waqas Khwaja, Bobby Meyer-Lee, and Kamilah Aisha Moon.

Certain books were especially important to make this one:
Clara Inés García's *Urabá: región, actores y conflicto, 1960-1990*,
Morales Fernández's and Beatriz Natalia's *Entraron a la casa*, Ro-
berto Bolaño's *2666*, Toni Morrison's *A Mercy*, John Keene's *Coun-
ternarratives*, Caryl Phillips's *Crossing the River*, Fernanda Melchor's
Temporada de huracanes and *Aquí no es Miami*, Pilar Quintana's *La
perra* and *Los abismos*, Gabriel García Marquéz's *La hojarasca* and
La mala hora.